Praise for *Carrots and Jaffas*

'A tale of abduction and heartbreak at its most immediate level of involvement, *Carrots and Jaffas* is also an engaging study of individual identity and its sources. Boldly plotted, diligently crafted, Howard Goldenberg's story of identical twins, violently parted at the age of ten, reveals the hunger that dwells in all of us to stand distinct in the gaze of God. The book goes further still, for when the maelstrom of the abduction has passed, we are left to ponder the mystery of belonging, and the role of love as the great agent of our survival.'

Robert Hillman

'With his customary gusto, Howard Goldenberg continues his investigation into what it means to be born into the unique and ancient landscape of Australia when your spiritual tradition – in his case, Orthodox Judaism – comes from somewhere else.'

Martin Flanagan

'Goldenberg's story is operatic in tone and scope. A kidnapped twin boy is but one victim as vexed issues confronting reconciliation with indigenous Australia unfold. The heart of this high octane tale, for all its puckish humour, is impelled by great moral seriousness: one cognisant that the entitlement to the fuzzy choral warmth of "calling Australia home"' demands sacrifice.'

Rod Moss

'There was so much I liked about *Carrots and Jaffas*, so much that made me think afresh. A gesture of healing of that great and terrible national wound of the stolen generation from an entirely fresh perspective, Goldenberg's novel brims with insight and wisdom.'

Simon Cleary

'Howard Goldenberg's *Carrots and Jaffas* is a story of mothers cheated of their young. It is a sensitively crafted tale of twin boys wrenched apart and the mothers who care for them. This tale of cultures meeting and merging brings to life the northern Flinders Ranges – its characters, its landscape and its traditions.'

Kristin Weidenbach

CARROTS AND JAFFAS

A NOVEL

Howard Goldenberg

HYBRID
PUBLISHERS

Published by Hybrid Publishers

Melbourne Victoria Australia

©Howard Goldenberg 2014

This publication is copyright. Apart from any use
as permitted under the Copyright Act 1968, no part may be reproduced
by any process without prior written permission from the publisher.
Requests and inquiries concerning reproduction should be addressed to
the Publisher, Hybrid Publishers,
PO Box 52, Ormond 3204.

First published 2014

National Library of Australia Cataloguing-in-Publication entry
Author: Goldenberg, Howard.
Title: Carrots and Jaffas / Howard Goldenberg.

ISBN: 9781925000122 (paperback)

Subjects: Twins – Fiction.
                  Kidnapping – Australia – Fiction.

Dewey Number: A823.4

Cover design: Gittus Graphics ©
Cover painting by Craig Penny ©
Typeset in Minion Pro 11.8/16
Printed by Ink Asia

For Miles and Toby

Author's Disavowal

With two exceptions, nobody you know, living or dead, appears in this work; the characters are otherwise entirely imaginary. The exceptions are Talcum Malcolm, derived from 'Talc Alf', sculptor, philosopher and amateur etymologist of Lyndhurst, South Australia; and Sahara, the whippet-Staffordshire terrier cross who belonged to my late brother Dennis. Although I have tried, I have fallen short of creating on the page the true aggressiveness and malice of this real-life bitch. Sahara menaced everyone she met but she adored Dennis, whose charity exceeded even Sahara's malignity.

Nature …
Why hast thou made us but in halves –
Co-relatives? This makes us slaves …
What Cosmic jest or Anarch blunder
The human integral clove asunder
And shied the fractions through life's gate?

From 'After the Pleasure Party: Lines Traced Under an
Image of Amor Threatening', by Herman Melville

My mother groaned, my father wept,
Into the dangerous world I leapt …

From 'Infant Sorrow', *Songs of Experience,* by William Blake

'Are the twins identical, Peter?'
'One is, Rabbi, one isn't.'

Snatches of conversation overheard at a double *bris* ceremony

My heart and my mind, my bones and flesh and all the organs of my
body are bound together with the cords of the stories I was told.

From *The Honey Thief,* by Najaf Mazari and Robert Hillman

Part 1

Ⅱ

1. Golem

A tall thin man in his thirties sat in a small Japanese car. He crushed two small white tablets, carefully opened a carton of chocolate milk and mixed the powdered tablets into the drink. He closed the carton and secured it with a thick red rubber band.

Two heavy blankets rested on the back seat.

His hands shook as he got out. He opened the back doors and located the child-proof locking devices. He set them on 'lock'. He tested the locks on both sides. Neither opened. He pressed a button on the console that disabled the rear window switches. Then he sat in the back and tried to operate the windows. Neither budged.

The man stepped from the car slapping his pockets. Everything was there: his smokes, his lighter, wallet, cash. He checked again. He carried no credit cards: *No bloody bank would issue a card to an ex-con. Anyway, too easy to trace.*

The tank was full and he had two jerry cans of spare fuel in the boot. He wouldn't need to fill up until Mildura, which would be late at night. From there he'd get to Burra in the early hours. He'd fill up again, buy bread from the bakery. No more stops until Copley. Then he'd take the back road to Greta's shack, near the settlement.

His hands trembled as he checked his pockets again – wallet, keys, smokes, lighter – all there, all right. The man stood for a moment, made to walk to the kerb, stopped, rechecked the windows and the doors. They remained childproof.

The old girl will be glad to see me again. It'll be good to see her. And the family. It's been a long time. That old lady loves kids. She'll welcome these two, she'll take them in, same as everyone else's.

That old lady never says no. She never stops thinking about her own boys, stolen from her. She torments herself thinking about them, two little fellas without a mother's care. Greta raised her other two boys, then she mothered most of her kids' little ones, lots of great nephews and nieces too.

I've seen it: she never says no. She'll take these two, no problem.

I'll spend a week with that old lady, I'll see the happiness in the old girl's face. That will make up for anything – anything the white-fella people back in Melbourne might be feeling. I'll drive back, bring the car to Mum, give her a kiss, tell her I've got my head right.

It'll be dark soon. Those two kids will be playing in their front yard. This is the right time.

II

The man drove the car around the corner, slowing as he passed the house. Now he saw them. They were kicking a soccer ball. It was always soccer; Australian footy wasn't good enough for their mother, some sort of foreigner. Fifteen metres further on he parked. He unfolded his thin frame and stepped away from the car. The man opened the near-side back door and waited. He chewed at his fingernails as he watched in the gloom.

He didn't have to wait long. One of the two boys kicked the ball out of the yard onto the quiet street. Both of them chased it, pushing and pulling each other as they raced to take possession.

He stepped onto the roadway, scooped up the ball and strode towards his car. He threw the ball onto the back seat.

The boys ran towards him, shouting indignantly. He stood and waited by the back of the car. They ran past the man to the open door. One grabbed the ball, and they made to run home, but the man blocked their way. He grabbed the wrist of the first boy and secured a grip on the collar of the other's shirt. With sudden violence, he dragged the two to the car, throwing the first boy into the interior. The second boy pulled away, wrenching his shirt free.

He ran a few steps towards the house. Abruptly, the child stopped, screamed one word – once, twice.

The screaming boy's hands tore at his hair.

He turned and looked to the car's interior, his body taut, stretched between escape and rescue. The man slammed the car door shut and advanced a pace towards the escapee. He closed on the boy, his face empty. He said nothing, moving implacably closer. The child's face worked in rage and terror; his legs were stone. The man was almost upon him. The child turned again and ran for home.

From the gateway came that same word, an obscure cry: 'Jaffas!'

The man hesitated a moment. The boy's cry tore the air. The man threw his head back. He hurried to the car and drove away.

2. How to Make Babies

Carrots and Jaffas were in their first year of school when they asked Bernard how they were made. Bernard explained, 'I fertilised one of Mami's eggs and you grew inside her.'

The next morning Carrots was late to breakfast. He appeared eventually with bits of straw hanging from him and an egg, warm from the chook house, in his hands. 'Papi, if you fertilise this, Mami can make us another baby.'

Bernard elaborated: this was the wrong egg in the wrong place. Further, he was unable make a child alone. Two were needed for this very particular tango. What's more, it was a private matter, too private to describe.

Their father a disappointment, the boys approached their mother. Luisa replied, 'Your father knew me. He came in unto me and behold, two were in my womb.'

'How did Papi come in unto you?'

Luisa told them.

Her response confirmed the improbable information they had from a classmate. The boys digested Luisa's answer, but they were no wiser about themselves.

Meanwhile, Bernard mused. He read a textbook of embryology; he considered the intricate chain of events that led to the birth of a human. The arithmetic staggered him: so many sperm cells, such extravagance, such wastage – all for a singleton child.

And his own boys, twins. Their existence a fluke.

Bernard contemplated the fleshly acts of babymaking; he could see the biology as comedy. Those facts were straightforward. It was the meaning, the *twinness* of the boys, for which straightforward biology was inadequate. *What does it mean to be a twin? Identical? What will I say when they ask me? Now the boys are asking and I'm no wiser than the day Dr Griblet announced, 'It's twins.'*

II

The newspapers were full of a story about the conjoined twins whom surgeons hoped to separate. The Australian government had flown the mother and her unborn twins to Melbourne from a poorer country, to give them a better chance. Any chance. A nation of foster-parents held its breath while the babies were delivered by the most intricate caesarean section. Alive.

Soon after, in an epic of fraught surgery, surgeons dissected brain from brain, allocating, calculating greatest good against least harm. Two separate humans, little girls, emerged.

A nation prayed. The babies held on to life.

Avid for insight, Bernard followed the bulletins on line. Of the two, one was left with some deficiency, some damage that interfered with her learning.

While in their mother's womb, those twins – identical girls – were joined at the back of their heads; during their gestation they never 'saw' each other, they never sensed each other except perhaps as an organ attached from the rear, less realised than the umbilical cord and the placenta, attached at the front. Between those two, sensations of an intimate other were not experienced, twin consciousness never developed. Whatever sensations those twins experienced were those of solitary persons.

After the successful separation of the sisters, their carers created frequent opportunities for them to see each other, face to face. Sister gazed upon sister. Both individuals – the 'quicker' baby and the 'slower' one – reacted alike: as to any other non-twin.

II

When Carrots and Jaffas are ready, I'll tell them: 'One plus one make one. As a general rule. But there are exceptions, such as you two: when one pregnancy tears itself apart it creates two identical individuals; one becomes two. Bernard ruminates further: *Each is a fragment, the human satellite of the other. What follows?*

He chases his thoughts in circles. He ponders questions of integrity versus incompleteness. He realises he has nothing clear or useful to tell his children. *I suppose life will bring answers in good time.*

3. Bernard and Luisa

Bernard tells anyone who asks, 'I work with computers at The Grand.' In fact, Bernard heads the team of technicians who maintain the hotel's ever-ramifying nervous system.

He accepted this job although his Doctorate in Information Technology over-qualified him for the position. He chose it because he enjoyed the hotel's people – its guests and its staff in all their stations – more than the academic life, which had mutated, becoming corporate and impersonal. *A great hotel is a world,* he decided, *a university is a ghost town.*

Bernard selects the hotel's hardware and develops much of

its software, installing and maintaining it. Although he has his minions, he delights in responding to the minor emergencies and glitches that occur with the high-tech security locks and the electronic safes in guest bedrooms.

Bernard's pager beeps: *Room 1418. Domestic locked in room. Lock malfunction.*

He is friendly with the domestics, who come mostly from the Philippines, Vietnam and China. He pictures an anxious young woman, having limited English, struggling with the obdurate lock, perhaps weeping, probably frantic.

Bernard grabs his toolkit and hurries to room 1418 to work on the lock. In no time the door falls open. He walks into the room, announcing himself breezily, 'It's me, Bernard, come to rescue a maiden in distress.'

He stops short. This is a maiden he's never met. She doesn't look Asian – she is taller than the other girls – and she is not in distress. The young woman sits decorously on the bed, reading. The room has been made up.

The first thing the young woman notices is the surprised look on the man's face. He is tall with a mop of light brown hair and a cropped fair beard. And a boy's grin. She sees a patch of pink scalp high on his left temple where the hair does not grow. Naked skin, like a baby's.

She rises, offers her hand. 'I am Luisa. Peace be unto you.' The handshake is firm. Bernard cannot identify her accent.

'G'day, Luisa. I'm Bernard. Glad to know you.'

The young woman's olive skin reddens beneath her dark fringe. Indignant, confused, she frowns and withdraws her hand. 'You cannot *know* me, sir. We are not married.'

It's Bernard's turn to be confused. Somehow he has offended this young woman, something he said. An awkward silence.

He tries again, a neutral remark: 'What's that book you've got there, Luisa?'

The young woman looks down at the red-covered volume in

her hand. Her face relaxes. 'I read the Good Book, Mister Bernard.'

'Really? Why?' The words tumble from Bernard. He stands, mouth open, waiting for the frown.

Luisa is smiling. 'From this Good Book I learn Good English. Do you know, I find it in every bedroom, this book of the Gideon people? After I have cleaned a bedroom, I read. One room clean, one chapter.'

Bernard looks mystified. He cannot think what to say to this serious young woman. He would like to continue the conversation. Suddenly he does not trust his own English.

'Behold, Mister Bernard, the chapter I read today is from Leviticus.' The young woman holds open her good book and points to a passage of priestly sacrifices.

Bernard, a sceptic, wants to say, *Are you really reading Leviticus? Not much narrative.* He examines the text briefly and nods politely.

Standing in the doorway, he is stranded, his tools in his hands. He takes in this exotic person. What was her response to his greeting? Something about marriage?

He tries again, a fresh start: 'Your accent, I can't place it. Where were you born, Luisa?'

'I was begat in Buenos Aires, in Argentina. My parents were in like manner also begat in the land of my birth, but in Cordoba, in the village of Capilla del Monte.'

Bernard, all ears, is bemused. She seems happy to talk personal history and geography.

The woman smiles. 'And you, Mister Bernard, where were you begat? What is your homeland and who are your people?'

'Eh? I'm a local. My people? Well, Mum is a local ... all of us, all locals, all Aussies born and bred.'

'And your father and your mother, is there peace unto them?'

'Er, yeah. Well, not exactly. My mother's good as gold. My father, well, you could say there is peace unto him.' Bernard checks his watch: 'Look Luisa, it's just about smoko. You want a coffee? We can go next door. There's a little coffee joint where we can talk a bit.'

'Thank you, Mister Bernard. For you will be smoko; for me will be *desayuno*.[*] I will take a coffee and I will break bread.'

Bernard stands aside from the door, allowing Luisa to pass. She limps slightly. He glimpses a scar running transversely behind her right knee.

In the coffee lounge, Luisa orders orange juice, a croissant and a long macchiato. The milk barely stains the black liquid.

Bernard is intrigued. He looks down at his cappuccino and his Mars Bar, and observes, 'That's a man-strength coffee, Luisa.'

'It is like unto *caffe cortado*. All *Portenos* drink this.'

Bernard watches Luisa attack her breakfast with gusto. As he watches, a flake of croissant settles on Luisa's upper lip. Bernard wants to touch it away. Instead he places his palms firmly down on his chair and sits resolutely on his hands.

Luisa takes a slug of her orange juice and looks up. 'Tell me, Mister Bernard, wherefore did you decide to become the keeper of the locks and the saviour of maidens?'

'Well, I didn't really set out to fix locks. At university I studied computer science. Before that, as a boy I fell in love with science … It was the study of the un-magic workings of the magic-seeming universe. In my last year at school I won a nation-wide essay competition. I wrote an essay titled "Theoretical Condensed Matter – the Properties of Nano-Diamonds". Nano-diamonds are unimaginably small, only one million atoms wide.' Bernard's face is suffused. *Oh shit. The nerd confesses.* His blushes deepen.

Luisa is touched. 'You fell in love with science and you remain faithful to your love.'

'Er, yeah. Anyway, I won a scholarship to study computer science at the University of Technology and here I am, the lock guy.' He laughs.

Luisa does not laugh. Love is a serious enterprise.

'How do you like The Grand, Luisa?'

'I like it very much. In every room I learn something.'

---

[*] breakfast

'Bible language.'

'Yes. Also I learn the ways of the sons of men. This one is so crazy for clean that he cleans before me; that one leaves in the toilet his shits; another one reads the Bible; a fourth reads a dirty magazine. Many commit adultery. I clean, always I learn and I enjoy. But not last week.'

'What happened last week?'

'I am responsible to clean all of the rooms of the fourteenth floor. I read the sign – Please Make up My Room – I knock, there is no answer, I unlock and enter and commence to clean. Suddenly a man comes from the bathroom and he does a dirty thing. This I do not tolerate. I take the phone and I call Security. I say, "I am Luisa. The guest in room 1404 has revealed unto me his nakedness." Then I leave.'

'Good on you, Luisa. What happened to that man?'

'Nothing. It is normal.'

'What do you mean, *normal*? Security always calls the coppers.'

'I do not know what is "coppers" …'

'Police.'

'Ahh, the police. Yes.' Luisa says no more. She addresses her cup, finishes off her macchiato and looks down. Her face shows indecision. She considers for a time, then looks up and faces Bernard.

Abruptly she rises and steps away from the table. She turns her back and lifts the hem of her uniform slightly. She looks over her shoulder to Bernard, points to the back of her right knee and says, 'You see this?' Luisa's face is not composed now. She corkscrews her spine and arm, daggering the air. 'That *escar*? For this I do not speak to police.'

Bernard blinks. His mouth opens, closes. He wants to ask, *What? Why?* Alarmed by Luisa's intensity, he's fearful he'll find wrong words. Words that will offend.

'Luisa, please come and sit down. Let me get you another coffee.'

Luisa sits. Bernard waits.

After a time, the woman looks at her watch, rises and produces a smile. 'Six days shalt thou labour. This maidservant whom you rescued must return to her labours. Thank you for *desayuno*.' Her cheerfulness jars. She pays and leaves. Her scent lingers: *Gardenia*?

Bernard stays and ponders. He thinks about the human brain, how it differs from the computers he works with, how its systems are non-linear, how the human has passions, power surges that start as a sudden fire and throw sparks of light for a brief time. Then persist, to smoulder unseen.

He thinks about the music of the young woman's voice, her quaint speech, studied and archaic. Her choice of words, often holy-ish, occasionally innocently coarse. He pictures the heavy plait of black hair and the olive skin of her long neck that runs matt and smooth to her hairline.

The young lady is not frivolous. She is a melody in a minor key: black hair, brown skin, the scarred and damaged leg, her skittish nervousness when he'd said *glad to know you*.

The melody of her name haunts Bernard. He repeats her name, LU-I-SA, a song in three bars. Bernard tries to recapture her scent.

A decision takes shape in his mind: he will spend more time on the fourteenth floor.

II

Bernard's beeper starts to play up. He receives a message: *Possible lock malfunction, Room 1414.* Bernard hurries to 1414. The lock works perfectly. He enters the room and finds it empty. A red volume of the Gideon Bible sits on the dresser. And Bernard detects that scent.

The next day another phantom message: same floor, same time of the morning, around smoko. Once again, the Bible. In the air a hint of gardenia.

The same again the following day.

At mid-morning on the fourth day, Bernard is waiting. When his beeper summons him to the fourteenth floor, he walks swiftly, away from the elevators, towards the hotel exit. He hurries to the coffee shop next door where the serious Bible scholar sits, enjoying an orange juice, a long macchiato and a croissant.

She laughs, a soft caramel gurgle: 'Will you take a coffee with me, Mister Bernard?'

Luisa wants to know all about Bernard's family. 'It is your father alone who has peace? Your mother not so?'

'Well, Dad is dead. Resting in peace, as they say. But Mum's okay.'

Luisa's hand covers her mouth, contrite. 'Forgive me, I never imagined …' She looks up at the man, anticipating his pain, marshalling her features for tenderness.

Bernard has not looked up. He sits with head bowed. The hairless patch is exposed, pink, with the vulnerability of a child.

Bernard says levelly: 'Dad went to Russia for the world chess championships when I was a little fella. He died there. The Embassy flew him home for burial. The Embassy doctor's certificate said *Natural Causes: food poisoning*. But Mum always said he was assassinated.'

A silence.

It is as if Luisa has not heard Bernard's final, astonishing word. Her voice is soft: 'And you were still a child.'

'Yeah, just started school.'

When Bernard finally looks up, the Bible scholar's face is averted a little. Her eyes glisten.

The next morning he receives no phantom call from the fourteenth floor. Bernard looks for Luisa in the coffee shop but she is not there. He corners one of the Filipinas who assures him Luisa clocked on with the rest of them in the morning.

Although Bernard itches to see Luisa, to comfort her, to assure her she did not cause him pain, he stays away from the fourteenth floor. *She looked more upset than I was. As if she took Dad's death personally.*

Bernard fears he'll crowd her. He doesn't want to scare her off, this brittle girl.

The next day all the locks at the Grand function properly. Bernard heads early to the coffee shop and takes a seat with a clear view of the entry. At smoko Luisa appears. She walks directly towards him, gives a diffident smile and, unexpectedly, extends her hand. Her grip and handshake are not diffident. Not aggressive either.

She speaks: 'Your father was a chess genius, Oceania Champion at twenty, International Grand Master at age twenty-five. He went to Russia to challenge the great Boris Spassky.' Luisa produces some sheets of A4 notepaper. With slow care she reads: 'Boris Vasilievich Spassky was thirty-five when John Wanklyn challenged him. Until Wanklyn, Spassky had been the youngest Grand Master in history.'

Bernard nods, smiling.

'Play commenced at midday. Wanklyn opened conventionally. Spassky went immediately onto the offensive. "For psychological reasons", the commentators said. This was the Cold War and chess was the battle front. *Pravda* called the match The Battle of Leningrad. The *Pravda* editorial read: "*Boris Spassky was born in Stalingrad, a city that has never fallen to the foreigner. Neither Napoleon and his French nor Hitler and his fascists ever took the city. We doubt that the Australian, John Wanklyn, will conquer where they failed.*"'

Bernard smiles widely.

Luisa goes on. 'Spassky did not learn his chess in that city. During the war he was safely in the mountains; he learned to play in the Urinals.'

'Don't we all,' murmurs Bernard, his smile huge now. Aloud he says, 'Urals.'

Luisa resumes her reading: '"Spassky's aggressive opening proved rash. Exposed, he left himself open to Wanklyn's novel counterattack – what the Australian called the Ferntree Gully Gambit."'

'We lived in Sassafras, in the Dandenongs. The local chess club was in Ferntree Gully. Dad used to take me there sometimes. He was teaching me chess. The Gully Gambit would have died with him, but the Aussie chess press observed and recorded it. It's a classic.'

Luisa is in no hurry to speak. She loves the strange music of Aussie place names: *Murrumbeena, Maralinga, Dundenungs* ...

She returns to her sheet: '"At twenty minutes before midnight, Spassky pleaded illness and was granted an adjournment. Wanklyn, fifteen years his junior and 40 kilograms lighter, appeared the picture of youthful good health. The match never resumed. Spassky took his place at noon the following day, apparently recovered from his indisposition. He looked confident. When the Australian failed to appear, officials entered his room where he was found, dead. The cause of death was said to be food poisoning. The Australian government officials in Russia did not dispute this determination. They were engaged in delicate trade talks at the time, a deal to sell Australian wheat. There was no autopsy. ASIO said a request for autopsy *would show an undiplomatic lack of trust in the Soviet authorities.*"'

Bernard recognises Luisa's A4 sheet. It is the Grand's notepaper with 'Google' conspicuous at the top. 'You were at the Business Centre during smoko yesterday?'

Luisa, uncertain, nods.

'Luisa, the Australian press said it was Phar Lap all over again.'

She looks mystified.

'Phar Lap was another Australian champion that died overseas under suspicious circumstances. Mum always believed the KGB killed Dad. All I knew was Mum was sad and I needed to look after her. So I did. I still do.' Bernard smiles wistfully.

In the silence that follows, he forgets he is a nerd.

Luisa does some mental arithmetic. If Bernard was just starting school when his father was twenty-five years old, he would have been born to very young parents. 'Your mother was very young when you were born?'

'Yeah, I suppose so.'

17

'Perhaps when your father died, she was still a child, needing someone to look after her. Did you decide you would minister unto her?'

'I suppose so.'

'The other Australian champion you spoke of, Far Lap: what sport did he play?'

'He was a champion but he wasn't a man. Phar Lap was a gelding.' Bernard explains the gelding of horses and the perfidy of American track officials and gamblers.

'Yes, in South America we know America.'

Bernard searches for the Gideon phraseology: 'What about your parents, Luisa? Is there peace unto them?'

'The same as your father, I think. I do not know.'

'You don't know?' It is Bernard's turn to be incredulous.

'They were "disappeared" during the time of the generals. Like many others. I was three years old. Baba, my greatmother, took me to the park. When we returned my parents were not there. None of us knows what happened to them. After that, Baba cared for me. She used to take me every day to the Plaza to sit down among the *Madres* of the Disappeared. We sat on the stones, outside *La Casa Rosada*.

'Baba is now very old, advanced in her days, but still she goes. Every day she sits with *Las Madres* and she waits for my parents. She does not forget them. I *hope* there is peace unto my parents.'

Bernard finds no words. His silence is comfort enough.

II

Bernard and Luisa meet every morning for coffee and *desayuno*. After work they walk along the river and picnic in the Royal Botanic Gardens. When the weather is unkind, they catch a movie or listen to live music or – once a week – they go somewhere quaint or elegant to dine. They take turns to choose, never repeating; they imagine trying every eatery in the entire city.

A month or so into these pleasant outings, an envelope appears on Bernard's desk. Square in shape, lilac in colour, unbusinesslike, it sits on his keyboard like a question mark. Curious, he picks it up. A hint of gardenia in his nostrils. Bernard, more than curious, hefts the envelope, feels its substance. Fast fingers break the seal and Bernard reads:

> La Señorita Luisa Morales
> Has pleasure in inviting
> El Señor Bernard Wanklyn
> To Mate.

Bernard reads the address – a flat in Burwood – and the date: next Sunday, at 3.00 pm.

Excited, nervous, suddenly a shy adolescent, Bernard wonders, *what do you wear when a young lady invites you to mate? Do you bring flowers? Or send them the next day? And what about a condom?*

He dresses with careful casualness – good tired jeans, a fitted shirt, sneakers. Fifteen minutes before three Bernard finds himself outside the block of flats. Cream brick, they are genuine 1950s, the style and period of his mother's childhood. He parks, checks his watch and paces the street. *We lived in a neighbourhood like this. I suppose Luisa is just like Mum – both of them women living without a man, women establishing themselves in a modest independence.*

Bernard's reverie ends as a human arm slides inside his. Surprised, he looks around: it is Luisa, also early, also restless. From her window she sighted the pacing Bernard and decided not to wait. Her smooth arm rests inside Bernard's. The skin of his arm flames.

Inside Luisa's apartment – it is no longer a 'flat' for Bernard; too individual, too distinctive – a vase of poppies on the small kitchen table, framed photographs of an aged lady (*her grandmother, Baba?*) and a younger one with a cloud of curly hair (*her mother?*), create an atmosphere of refined refuge from the world of a menial at the Grand.

Luisa boils the kettle, places some pastries on the table, pours boiling water into a tall, stainless steel vessel with a strangely sinuous shape. 'Now we wait for the *yerba mate*. It is a ceremony.'

Foreign words in a foreign accent, Bernard supposes them to be Spanish. He doesn't quite know what is going on, beyond evident preparation for afternoon tea. But Luisa sets no cups at the table. Now she lifts the curved steel jug and Bernard notices a hollow wooden tube emerging from its neck. Luisa places this before Bernard and, beaming like one introducing a prized friend, says, '*Mate*.' She pronounces it 'mutt-ay'.

'Please, Bernard, take first.'

'What?'

Luisa indicates the wooden drinking tube.

'You mean, drink?'

Luisa nods, still beaming: 'Please.'

Bernard applies his mouth to the tube. Hot liquid enters his mouth. He swallows, coughs a little, tries very hard to suppress his cough, inhales some of the fluid as a result. He coughs more now, a small storm of insubordinate explosions that he tries to suppress with reciprocal violence. His eyes run, his nose fills, his face reddens.

He looks up, sees Luisa laughing quietly. She enquires, her voice kind, 'You do not like *yerba mate*?'

In fact it is not the taste – a vegetal flavour, an experience like drinking strong black tea for the first time – but the astringency that provoked Bernard's first deep indrawing of breath.

'No, no. I like it, honestly.' Bernard draws heroically on the tube.

Now Luisa laughs aloud, a merry sound. And Bernard relaxes. 'What is this stuff, Luisa? I mean, what's in it?'

Luisa takes a small package from the kitchen bench and passes it to Bernard. It is surprisingly light. He peers inside the open pack – dull green chaffy stuff. He sniffs – a mild herbal aroma. On the packaging Bernard makes out *Argentina*. On the obverse, *Yerba Mate*.

'Luisa, what do you call this?'

'*Mate*.'

'Ah, mutt-ay. I see: you spell it like "mate", but that's not how you say it.' Bernard nods his head, nods again. 'This is the first time anyone invited me to *Mate*. Thank you.'

The two spend a relaxed hour in Luisa's kitchen. Afterwards they walk in the sunshine. Bernard takes his leave of Luisa at her front door, turning to go. 'See you tomorrow, Luisa,' he calls.

She pulls on his sleeve, he turns, and she surprises his lips with a fleeting kiss. 'I see you tomorrow, Bernard.'

Bernard walks to his car. Groping in his trouser pocket for the car keys, his fingers encounter a small thin rubbery package. He laughs as he drives away.

II

Two months into their movable feasting, Bernard surprises Luisa. 'Go home and dress up. I'm taking you somewhere grand.' Luisa complies.

Bernard calls for her and drives to their unnamed destination. Luisa notices his fitted black shirt. He smells of aftershave, an unexpected grooming aid on her bearded friend.

Bernard will recall that Luisa looks lovely tonight, but he will be unable to describe her garments, only the flowing of diaphanous fabrics with the movement of her slim frame. And her hair, dressed in an elaborate weave and worn high, exposing her long neck; the slow curve of skin and sinew sing to him like a poem.

Bernard drives. He brings the car to a stop. Luisa recognises their workplace and wonders what is happening. He parks and hands the keys to the valet, walks around to Luisa's door, helps her from the car and takes her arm. He guides her to the elevators, where he presses a button that he conceals with his body. When the lift comes to a stop, Bernard once again takes Luisa's arm. He guides her to *La Grande,* where the maître d' greets them and seats them by a window.

The city stretches out beneath them. They can see the Botanic Gardens, floodlit seagulls circling the Arts Centre spire, the striking facets and angles of Federation Square. The river is a darkening serpent, St Kilda Road a bright ribbon, the Cricket Ground an emerald.

'This *is* grand, Mister Bernard.'

Bernard recognises the mock formality of 'Mister', Luisa's reference to their first encounter, her signal – *look how far we have come*. It is her gesture too towards a large question: *How much further will we go?*

Before their meal they drink cocktails. Later, Bernard orders wine. They consume the bottle together. And liqueurs with their coffee. At the end of a languid liquid evening, Bernard declares, 'I'm not fit to drive and you don't have a licence. We'll have to improvise.'

Bernard escorts Luisa to a guest room on the fourteenth floor, a suite. They enter. Luisa closes the door. She says, 'Let us not disturb two beds. We must think of the poor chamber maid. Perhaps we will share.'

Bernard is agreeable.

Afterwards, Luisa sighs with pleasure. She lies still for a time. She notices the small hairless spot in Bernard's scalp glowing bright pink in the light of the bedside lamp.

'Is that your Ferntree Gully Gambit, Mister Bernard?'

4. Gravid

Luisa's breasts are tender. She examines them, intrigued to find the aureole of pigmented skin around her nipples has darkened. She notices small lumplets, mere puckers, little gathers in the skin, forming a circular pattern around the nipples. Every so often she's giddy. She feels odd, with moments of nausea. She awakens from sleep during the night; she needs to pee.

Her body is a nest of portents. Luisa waits and hopes.

When her period is late, she feels excited, exalted. For years she has wondered and worried for her fertility. Now she senses prophecy fulfilled in her own body. She has a knowing, an unshakeable sense of rightness, a conviction of pregnancy as destiny.

Hints of destiny were revealed to her in her teens at Capilla del Monte. Lost on a hilltop, lost in her own self, Luisa stumbled upon a site at the summit, a place forbidden to men by ancient custom, reserved for women who would congregate there for fertility rites.

She had come with her grandmother to her parents' birthplace at a time of crisis in her life. Distracted, she thrashed her body, seeking calm through physical exertion. Day after day she strode the high hills of Capilla.

On this particular mountain peak, Luisa stumbled upon a tight ring of tall pines. She made her way between them and entered. At the centre of a dished circle of grasses she found a scattering of scorched stones, ruins of some ancient structure. A place of fire.

She stood still and listened. The cry and song of the high winds, so loud on the slopes, was hushed here. Luisa felt the shiver of arriving somewhere new and feeling she belonged. She listened to the silence as if for a message. Alone in the hushed place, she squatted and waited, expectant.

Beneath her and above, space, immense and giddying, stretched away with the fall and fold of the hills and the vast canopy of sky. The stones, scorched and weather-scoured, spoke of endless time. She lay on her back upon the earth and watched the wheeling clouds. They swung across the sky, dragging Luisa's gaze, fracturing, scattering shafts of sunlight. Blaze followed shadow, light chased shade, the play of the heavens lifted Luisa from herself.

Now the sun, intense, entire, broke free of cloud. In its fullness the sun shone on Luisa. She saw it as if for the first time, golden.

No, not gold, not merely yellow, nor yet red: the sun was fire and the fire penetrated the girl and took possession of her. Luisa knew she was called.

She felt dizzy, drunken, newborn into some extremity of being. She remained motionless, her spirits lighter than she remembered. Meaning was at her fingertips. Peace, long a stranger, might touch her.

Eventually, the light faded. The western sky blushed and bled. Shadows fell. Luisa shivered. Unwilling to leave, afraid to stay, she hurried down the mountain, chased by the unsettling dark. She wanted to cry but she couldn't run and weep at the same time.

She asked her grandmother, Baba, what she knew of the place within the trees. The old lady's face puckered in thought. She looked hard at her ward and said, 'In the old days, I mean before the conquistadors, tribal women gathered there for ceremonies. There are stories of young girls, virgins, who would climb up to that circle to dream their babies. There are other stories, stories of girls who had never known a man who came down and were with child.'

II

Bernard sips his coffee and watches Luisa at her *desayuno*. Something has changed: there is the orange juice and the croissant, but in the place of her masculine long macchiato she drinks a pallid green tea. Missing too is Luisa's gusto. She looks pale.

Bernard sneaks a look at Luisa's breasts. *They're bigger.* 'Luisa, you're not … we're not expecting?'

Luisa nods, uncertainly. *Will he flee?*

Bernard is on his feet, the table is upset, coffee, green tea, orange juice and tears anoint the news.

Bernard helps Luisa to move her possessions from her flat into his apartment in Brunswick. He hefts boxes, lugs them out to the borrowed ute. He forbids her to lift. Carefully, he wraps her few special things, the photographs, her Good Book, a minute bottle of gardenia scent.

Tentative, almost shy now, he sets these down in the bedroom – their bedroom. She affirms all with a smile that seems, to Bernard, to come to him from new depths. Finally, he sits Luisa down in the kitchen, unwraps her *yerba mate* makings and prepares a brew. 'El señor Bernard invites la señora to *mate*,' he says.

II

The bleeding starts insensibly during a Friday night. When Luisa awakens, her nightclothes are soaked through. Gouts of clotted blood bind hair to thigh to fabric.

Luisa cannot alert Bernard. He is presently attending the annual conference of the hotel chain's Directors of IT, in San Diego. She calls a cab. She tells the despatcher the matter is urgent, a matter of health. The driver will sound the car horn and will wait for Luisa to descend from the third floor.

Luisa jams a bath towel between her thighs and pulls on a tracksuit. Her baby is lost. She knows this. Bleeding like this – in the course of the short ride to Emergency, the bleeding soaks through her towel, through her clothing – no pregnancy can survive. *Can I bleed this flood and remain alive?* Next to the loss of her baby, the thought of her own death is weightless.

The cabbie sneaks a look over his shoulder and sees the mess in the back. He drives right up to the hospital and parks in the ambulance bay, leaps out and runs for help. Help is a young man with a wheelchair. As Luisa rises to her feet, a gush runs down her legs and into her shoes. She has no energy for shame, no mind even for the biblical expression for her plight. She is grief-blind, grief-numb.

In the hospital, the bleeding slows, eventually trickling to a stop. Kindly young doctors insert IV drips, take blood, prepare for a transfusion. Gentle nurses mop Luisa's stricken face, offer her tea and sympathy. Someone produces a bedpan and coaxes Luisa to pee. She is too sad to object.

The urine pregnancy test is positive.

'The test frequently remains positive for a day or two, especially if the miscarriage is an incomplete abortion.' The speaker is an older doctor, possibly male, the voice high-pitched and gentle. Luisa is not curious about gender, too apathetic to notice. Just another kind person in an unkind world.

'An ultrasound will tell us if the miscarriage is complete or not. If it's incomplete, you'll need a small operation, a clean out, so you'll be all okay inside. For next time.'

Next time. Luisa has no faith in a next time.

'We don't call the ultrasonographer to the hospital on weekends – unless it's an emergency … Once the bleeding stops – like yours has, Luisa – a miscarriage is not an emergency.' The doctor sounds apologetic, even embarrassed. Luisa will have to wait until Monday for her scan.

She lies in her bed. A stranger's blood runs through tubing into her body. Her racing heart slows and her blood pressure recovers. Her body is theoretically restored to health, but Luisa does not notice.

She does not notice that her breasts remain tender. She is unaware of her persisting urinary frequency. She is acutely aware of nausea; life itself nauseates her at present.

A familiar image forms. Luisa's eyes refuse to register. A voice at the bedside, intimate, insistent; bristles abrading her face softly, lips caressing her cheek. The voice, the familiar feel of another's tears where her own have dried. It is Bernard.

It is Monday. The scan shows a uterine cavity with its conceptus in place, entire. 'The bleeding came from elsewhere inside the uterus: a mural haematoma,' says the kindly voice. 'You thought you were miscarrying; we thought the same. We overlooked a single clue – you had no pain, your womb was not contracting, not working to expel your baby. You can go home, Luisa. Your pregnancy is intact. *Alive.*'

II

The obstetrician sits across the table from Luisa and Bernard. She opens her mouth and shows her teeth in a sort of smile. The teeth are alarmingly large. 'So you had a little bleed, dear?'

Little? Luisa shakes her head.

'No bleeding since you left hospital, dear?'

Another shake of Luisa's head.

'Lie down over here and we'll just do another scan and see how your baby looks now.'

Luisa obeys.

'There's a second heartbeat … must have been obscured by thrombus on the earlier scan …' Another display of teeth. 'Twins! Righto, Caesar! At thirty-eight weeks. The womb will be too dangerous after that.'

The doctor makes a note then looks up. She says again, 'Caesarean section. At thirty-eight weeks.'

The doctor calculates a date, books the operation and closes the file. 'Any questions?'

Luisa has many questions, but she is too fearful to ask.

Bernard searches his wife's face. Luisa will be floundering, wondering about dangers of the womb. Neither speaks.

The doctor pats Luisa's shoulder. She offers Bernard her large hand and shakes vigorously. Bernard wonders how that hand can negotiate the narrow passages of a woman's interior. The doctor faces the door. The hand waves them out.

II

Bernard searches the internet and finds an article on the obstetric management of multiple pregnancy. The authors are two teachers at Yale, Professors Nartik and Quim. The article begins with the maxim: 'Multiple pregnancy presents a multiplicity of multiplying risks.' It continues: 'C-section, properly timed, minimises those risks.'

The question is, when to deliver? Nartik and Quim declare that babies will achieve all the growth they are going to by thirty-eight weeks.

Bernard reads on. There are perils everywhere – prematurity, postmaturity, placental problems, dysmaturity – a horrifying condition of a baby mature by dates, born gaunt, sick, starved in utero – the photos of a newborn, shrivelled as with age, disturb Bernard's scientific detachment.

Then there are haemorrhage, polyhydramnios, toxaemia, eclamptic seizures, acute kidney failure – the list goes on, ending with stillbirth. In rare cases, twins are conjoined and undeliverable without surgery; sometimes the surgery to separate creates unthinkable results.

In other cases, a foetus shrivels away to a papery vestige, *foetus papyraceous,* a sibling destined for oblivion. Sometimes a shred or shade of unshaped memory haunts a surviving twin.

Hazards everywhere, endangering both mother and babies.

It doesn't bear thinking about. Bernard decides he'll keep his thinking to himself. He certainly won't share Nartik and Quim's list with Luisa. Thirty-eight weeks is the least dangerous time; he'll just focus Luisa on getting safely to thirty-eight weeks.

II

Luisa is pregnant. This is normal. But twins? Bernard needs to understand. The usual guides for expectant parents do not satisfy him. He likes hard science so he resorts to a text on embryology and another on obstetrics. These books explain *how* but they do not answer. Bernard, scientifically trained, is surprised to find himself seeking new perspectives, asking new questions – questions that touch on purpose. On meaning.

The scientist in Bernard has always rejected the teleological and the metaphysical. But now he seeks more than phenomena. He scans bibliographies. On multiple pregnancy, all point to one authority, the text by Nartik and Quim.

Bernard returns to the Yale masters. He borrows the massive volume, turns the heavy pages and pauses, uncharacteristically, at the Introduction. It is this passage that approaches Bernard's need. During the pregnancy and for long after, he returns to it often. The Introduction is authored not by those male doctors but by a poet, Drawoh Harpaz, herself a twin. She writes:

> *There was the Bang, then dispersal.*
> *Ever since, the universal*
> *Pull to unity.*
>
> *Living things take form, evolve, differentiate.*
> *Last on the scene, primates*
> *Multiply miserly*
> *And the singleton pregnancy is born –*
> *New in the profligate animal kingdom.*
>
> *Primates couple*
> *In a novel configuration: faces faced.*
> *Primates discover*
> *Uncover*
> *Sometimes love, a taste*
> *For intimacy.*
> *Sexual reproduction*
> *Penetrated now by the human.*
>
> *Of seven billion, two find each other,*
> *Fuse, become one.*
> *Of hundreds of millions of thrashing invaders,*
> *One sole sperm*
> *Arrives, spent, at the surface*
> *Of a single egg – itself one daughter of millions:*
> *Lonely egg,*
> *Rapunzel in her tower,*
> *Renounces all hostility,*
> *All power,*
> *Succours the sperm –*
> *As if it smelled destiny.*

One female, impregnated by one sole sperm,
Expects a singleton child.

Except one
Among the many
Departs
Under some unknown and irresistible
Influence, some atavism,
Reverts to the multiple,
Shears, halves, rends itself
Somehow
Into two individuals

The halves survive,
Connected in evanescent dependency
To the mother ...

5. Childbirths

With the operation date still two months away, Luisa awoke suddenly, as if someone had switched on a light. During the night she'd had some aching in her belly. The pains were bearable; they came and went.

It is only dolor de estomago.* *There is a time for everything under the sun. This too will pass.*

Luisa got up early – before the sun – and she did her housework. She leapt into the work; tasks she normally found stale were fresh this morning. She cleaned every surface in sight. She set about the laundry and when that was finished, she ironed. She ironed towels and tea-towels, jobs she normally left to Bernard. After a few hours her man found her in the laundry, pale and a little breathless.

'Luisa, what are you doing?'

---

* stomach ache

'Ironing.'

He looked at her, searching her face. 'No, I mean why are you doing what you are doing?'

'I like to iron occasionally …'

'Yes, but you're ironing my jocks! No one irons jocks. And no one gets up at 5 am to wash and iron. What's going on? Are you okay?'

'Yes, no, well, my stomach hurts. It is nothing …'

'Stomach pains! And you do realise you're bleeding, don't you?'

Luisa looked at him.

Bernard pointed to a trail of red leading from the bedroom to the laundry. Luisa looked at the red splotches. Bernard brought a chair. He took a towel and sat her down on it. He hurried to the bedroom for her baby bag. Then he called the hospital and spoke to the midwife. He nodded, listened a little and nodded again. 'We're on our way.'

He took the bag in one hand and, helping Luisa to her feet, guided her gently, urgently to the car.

With Luisa safely stowed between bedrails, the trolley took off, leaving Bernard in the hands of Reception, where Important Forms had to be signed and waivers avowed.

'Bernard!' Luisa's cry was lost as the trolley sped away.

A pain hit Luisa hard. Bernard and the car were left somewhere behind. She lay flat and breathed and tried not to writhe. She sweated with the effort.

The pain slipped away and Luisa noticed her surrounds. A world of ordinary things, ceilings, fluorescent lights and walls, white, all of them white like the orderly's scrubs.

Everything the same, everything fleeting.

Nothing was normal. Luisa knew the world was not the same, could never again be the same. She would give birth. Two babies would be born.

The trolley flew around corners, through an artificial world where every perspective was partial. Luisa whirled through this all-white northern hemisphere that had no south, of passages taken and passages passed, of corners and no floors.

She felt dizzy. It was too fast. She fought down a surge of vomit. The pain struck again. She felt a spasm in her rectum. She thought, *I'm going to vomit and make a shit and where is my man? How will he find me?*

Sudden relief as something gave way, and Luisa felt warmness and fluid around her lower body and between her thighs. *I have wet myself! Where is my man?*

Abruptly, they were in Delivery. Trolley man said: 'Got yer here safe and sound, missus, all in one piece. You'll be right now, missus.'

His face was lined. She could see his features now in the light; he looked like Uncle Umberto. She wanted to confess her disgraceful lack of control. 'I wet myself. I've made a mess. I'm sorry.'

'No you haven't, love. Your waters just broke.' A new voice, a woman's, came from somewhere beyond the large bulge of her tummy. The voice was close, somewhere between Luisa's legs. A nurse's face rose up into view above her belly, a smile, a gentle hand moved over her abdomen. The nurse said, 'You're going to have your baby tonight. What's your due date, love? Your little one feels a good size, about full term, I reckon …'

Luisa started to cry. She wanted to shout, 'It's not a baby, it's two, and they can't come today. It's too early!' But her words would not come. A pain shook her, sudden and massive. Someone put a mask over her face. 'Breathe up on this, love. Won't be too long now.'

Helpless, voiceless, hopeless, Luisa tossed her head from side to side. *No, no, no!*

She heard a man's voice, Bernard explaining, heard her name, her clinical facts – first pregnancy, not due for another eleven weeks, twins …

'Twins! At twenty-nine weeks!'

The nurse pulled a mobile phone from her gown. She spoke

urgently to a doctor. Luisa recognised the name of her obstetrician. 'Yes, Leonie, yes.' A pause, with the midwife nodding.

'Okay. Okay. We'll shoot her over to the Mater now. What about tocolysis?'

Tocolysis? What was that? Something medical, something vital? Lots of medical words were just jargonised Latin. Luisa searched for a Latin root: hopeless. She looked at the nurse, hoping for explanation.

The nurse was nodding, writing on the sleeve of her gown. 'Nifedipine, 20 mg stat. Repeat twice at twenty-minute intervals. Goodo, Leonie. We'll give her the first dose now and more in the ambulance as we whizz her over to the Mater.'

The nurse hurried over to a cupboard, groped in her gown for a key, returned with a glass of water and a tablet. 'Luisa, love, this is a tablet to slow down your labour. It's called Nifedipine. It might also lower your blood pressure. You might feel like vomiting. And one more thing: we're going to transfer you to the Mater. It's a much bigger hospital. They have Neonatal Intensive Care there. We don't look after really little babies here. The Mater is just the ticket for prems. Just swallow the tablet now and see if your contractions ease off a bit.'

The nurse made a couple more calls on her phone. Luisa heard 'ambulance' and 'orderly'. Then the nurse was explaining, apologising: 'I'm going to examine you internally, to find out how close you are to childbirth. If the internal is uncomfortable, breathe up again on the mask.'

A squirting, farting sound, the feel of cold antiseptic and a rubber glove, probing fingers, stretching here, pushing there. Gentle, firm, impersonal sensations, strangely un-intimate.

'Six centimetres. Head's well down, Luisa, it will be tonight. Your womb is working very efficiently ... *Where's that orderly?*'

'Here I am, Nursey. Don't have kittens.'

Uncle Umberto again: 'Lay flat, missus.'

Luisa lay flat and closed her eyes and thought about her babies, her boys. She knew their names, she had been talking to them for months. She whispered the names, their secret names, repeated them again and again, a prayer, an incantation, like her grand-mother's spell against *el mal de ojo*, the evil eye.

Thinking of her grandmother filled her with a longing she had never felt, not once, in the years of her Australian adventure. Tears gathered, swelled and tumbled over the threshold of her lids. She felt them run down her cheeks, tasted salt.

When she was small, it was Baba, her grandmother, who com-forted her. Luisa could not remember her mother: Mami was a photo. Unlike some other orphans, Luisa had not been adopted into an officer's household; she had Baba, who claimed her and kept her safe. Baba had wiped away her tears and mothered her.

The pain came again, a monster this time. The nurse took Luisa's hand. 'Don't cry, love. We'll look after you.' She held out a green plastic tubular gadget. 'Breathe on this, Luisa. You'll feel better.'

The motherly face, the voice, the gentle hand were full of kindness.

Luisa cried more.

She sucked on the green gadget. The pain lessened, she felt swoony, a little drunk. Nifedipine wasn't working. 'Tocolysis' was a medical word for failure.

Her babies would come tonight. She whispered the names again, breathing the sounds with intensity, over and over, slurring, weeping fierce love, whispering her ferocious determination to protect her babies.

In the ambulance, the medics took a long time making her safe. They propped up her back, they applied wide belts of stout web-bing across her upper torso and another across her lap, wherever that was. They offered cushions for her flanks. Luisa didn't want to be comfortable. She wanted her babies to be safe. But she said thank you after every kindness. She wouldn't be rude.

At last the medics were satisfied that Luisa was stowed safely.

The nurse steadied the short pole that supported her intravenous drip. Luisa swallowed another useless tocolysis tablet and suddenly they were moving.

She had heard of the Mater. It sounded Catholic, reassuring. She asked Uncle Umberto whether it was a Catholic hospital. 'Yep. Catholic hospital for wombs of all religions.'

That's right, thought Luisa, 'Catholic', *universal*.

Wherever the Mater was, it was a long way from the local hospital. Travelling in the ambulance was like a second trolley ride, but longer, and although it must have been faster, it felt slower: moving through space backwards, more hemispheric views, more corners felt before seen – too many – more nausea. More fear.

II

Dr Griblet materialised. Formless in her scrubs, her face and teeth obscured by a mask, the doctor spoke. 'You can have a spinal, if you like.' Luisa wanted to see her babies born, but she didn't want to feel someone cutting into her belly. She jumped at the doctor's offer. Then had second thoughts, but it was too late. Trembling in her inadequate gown in the cold operating theatre, she didn't know whether she was chilled or nervous.

She didn't have long to wait. The anaesthetist's name badge read *Brian*. He introduced a needle into the front of her left elbow as he spoke. 'Do you have any allergies to medications or to iodine, do you have a fever, do you suffer from asthma, have you any heart trouble, has the pregnancy been normal, have you ever had a reaction to an anaesthetic, do you mind if I put you out to it to spare you any pain?'

Luisa didn't know whether Brian knew she had twins inside her. It was important. After he had shot out his questions, she said, 'No. No, to all of those questions, including the one about a normal pregnancy …'

'Righto,' said Brian, turning away. 'Count backwards from ten.'

Luisa said: 'TWO! There are …'

'I said count from ten, not two. Start again.'

He began injecting as he spoke.

'There are two ...' muttered Luisa.

II

There were two paediatricians, two pairs of two nurses and two cots next to her. She looked down and saw two small faces, vernix-smattered, shrouded in flannel. The faces were fine-boned, impossibly small, not human in scale.

One of the nurses checked a thermometer and spoke to a paediatrician. Luisa heard *hypothermia*. She looked at the babies: *little pink rats*. Where was her husband? *A father of twins now.* She found him over against a far wall, gowned and masked and sanitised. They eyebrow-mimed *I love you! I love you too!* Tears fell from Bernard's masked face. More tears from Luisa.

In that couple moment, Luisa barely heard voices saying nursing words: 'Good Apgars.' 'No subcutaneous fat.' 'Hypothermia.'

Luisa floated. She looked around. Someone was missing. Who was it? Luisa, now a mother, needed her own mother, acutely. She saw the face of Mami, smiling as always, from beneath her cloud of hair. Mami was a photograph, a memory or a dream.

Luisa looked down again to see her babies. They had disappeared, into the dangerous world.

II

New sensations: a whitening glare penetrates
womb gloom. The wall in front suddenly riven ...
touch ... sound borne on air, raw and harsh ...
coldness – sudden, abrupt, undreamed.
Harsh voices, rapid sounds attack the ears.
A collapsing of the womb as our waters drain
away.
An acceleration of all sensation: events cascade.
Finally – unthinkably – we are torn apart.

Where is he, where am I?

Who is whom?
We were us. There is no other pronoun.
We are undone. Spirals unwound.
Divided. Halves, separated.
Alone!
This despair.

This new intimacy – with loss.

6. Intense Care

The last thing Dr Gabe had said to Luisa was, 'Your little fellas are perfect, they are doing fine.' *Why did they take them away? Where did they go?*

Later, Luisa was surprised to learn that the twins were in Neonatal Intensive Care. *The boys are perfect, the doctor said. Why Intense Care? What are they hiding from me?*

Fear energised her. She took in everything. Her head periscoped on her long neck. The world whirled around her, swamping Luisa briefly in nausea. *Where are my babies? Is it well with them? Show them to me. Where are they?*

A nurse pushed Luisa in a wheelchair. The notice outside the swing doors read: 'Push buzzer for entry'. Underneath were the words: 'Parents, relatives and friends, please wait here for the nurse to conduct you'.

Luisa's nurse draped her in a sterile gown and covered her face with a mask. She was told she need not scrub because she would not be touching the babies. A racing sensation in her chest. Luisa trembled. The nurse's voice: 'Not this time. The doctors are working on them at the moment. Once they are stable, you'll be touching them and holding them. Not yet, though.'

The nurse was kindly if a bit distracted. Luisa suddenly felt deeply tired. Her focus on her babies wavered. She noted the nurse's olive skin and the fine moustache. *You look like Baba.* Luisa missed Baba. Her grandmother would be the person to become a mother with.

They were approaching the cot. Luisa saw white coats and bodies bending over the isolette, hiding the babies. Two doctors; one, two, three, four nurses. She could not see the cot clearly. She craned but she could not see her babies.

The big bodies surrounded a perspex box mounted on a stand at breast height. Above this and around it towered bulky machines and monitors, all with blinking lights and electronic displays. Numbers flashed, morphed, disappeared and reappeared. A graph rose and fell across a screen, with peaks and valleys like the Andes. Additional graphs leaped or crawled, peaked and troughed.

Luisa's nurse brought the wheelchair to a stop at the perimeter of the huddle. Nurses and doctors stood with their backs to her, intent, crowding and peering and adjusting. Luisa felt the pounding again. The doctors moved sufficiently for Luisa to read the names on their lapels: Dominique and Theo. *Where are they, Dominique? My little ones, please, please, you are a woman, please let me see them.*

She peered around and between the huddle. She could not see her babies. Instead, Luisa saw tubing and gauges. Lights blinked yellow, red, white. A buzzer sounded and Luisa jumped. A nurse wheeled, reached up to a pole and replaced an exhausted bag of fluid. 'Ten per cent dextrose,' she said, and another nurse wrote something on a clipboard.

Luisa saw a nurse take a damp nappy and weigh it, recording the amount of urine the baby had passed. *That nappy is smaller than my sanitary pad…*

Everyone in Intense Care looked important. And serious. *Why are they so serious? Something is wrong. What is wrong? Are they alive?*

Luisa asked in a whisper (everyone seemed to whisper, urgently), 'Why are there so many cardiographs? And they are all different. Which one is correct?'

The nurse answered, 'Only one of them shows heartbeats. This one' – she pointed to a jagged line – 'is for oxygen levels, this one is respirations, that one shows your babies' blood pressures. There are three blood pressure readings on this screen – mean arterial pressure, systolic, diastolic.'

Luisa saw people in white everywhere, some entering data in laptops, others calculating dosages and drip rates on their Blackberries. She caught whispered words. The whispering unnerved her. She craned, caught words, some strange, others familiar: *C-pap. Ventolin. Phototherapy. Ibuprofen. Caffeine.* The unfamiliar words sounded like a code for all manner of unspeakable harms.

The familiar words disoriented her. 'For what is caffeine in Intense Care?'

'It stimulates the baby. It reminds the little brain to send messages to the lungs. So the baby won't forget to breathe.'

Luisa's eyes widened above her mask. *Forget to breathe? Breath is life! Such perils.*

Abruptly, Luisa realised that the machines and the tubes and the lights, the monitors and alarms and bottles, the adult people, had distracted her. *My babies, my little boys!*

Which of the many were hers? Where were they? *I am their mother. They have to let me see my babies.*

Luisa's mind butterflied back to the cockpit of the Aerolineas Boeing. Uncle Umberto made an exception and let her into his cabin. She saw all the meters and the gauges and the lights, the co-pilot and the flight engineer concentrating intently. That was Intense Care too. Uncle did not respond to her questions; surrounded, obscured at times by moving bodies, he concentrated on the dials.

Luisa felt tired again. Euphoria had faded. Her urgent need to mother evaporated. In the midst of all this authority, Luisa was a child again. A child awake past her bedtime. Blood loss and anaesthetic chemicals and opiates sapped her.

There is something I must do, something I have to remember. I am the mother, I have the right …

Luisa did not feel like a mother, not like that powerful being a mother would be.

Luisa needed to sleep. *But I am a mother, I am a …*

She slumped in the wheelchair and slept, then woke, startled, confused. *Have I had my babies? Am I a mother?*

The nurse decided it was time to take her back to the seventh floor. As the wheelchair turned, Luisa glimpsed a baby – which one? – a small pale skeleton in a white cotton bonnet and eyeshades, an albino wearing a minute nappy. Like *las ratas** at school.

Deep, deep fatigue washed through her. There was no anxiety, no joy, no question nor doubt nor fear strong enough to withstand the waves. Not even guilt for seeing her baby as a laboratory mouse could call Luisa back from her far shore.

Luisa did not stir until the wheelchair came to a stop beside the bed in her shared room on the seventh floor. She opened her eyes; her bed was a mountain. *How? I cannot climb …*

The nurse helped her into bed.

Luisa didn't register the second couple in the room, the birth-bloated young woman, the child-man on the chair, biting his nails. Their loneliness together, the mute dread.

She slept.

7. Dr Gabe and the Twins

Dr Gabe looked at the newborns. They were small, even for twenty-nine-week twins. Their limbs were filaments. Frail ribcages, bones

---

* rats

40

seen through the skin. The delicate skulls were two eggshells, translucent in the strong light. Their scalps were road maps, with large vein highways, the smaller vessels meandering byways.

Just fifteen hours after delivery, one of the twins started to show early signs of distress. His breathing was rapid and his heart rate accelerated. He moved his limbs about restlessly, as if starved for oxygen. *Respiratory Distress Syndrome?* Dr Gabe checked the oxygen monitor – the level was borderline. Not really low enough to explain agitation.

He checked the wrist band: 'Twin One of Luisa Wanklyn'.

The paediatrician worked intently, threading a second intravenous needle into a vein that showed blue beneath diaphanous skin. He secured the oxygen feed through the nostrils and fixed minute white eyeshades over the eyelids.

He repeated the painstaking processes with Twin Two. Naked save for their loincloths and shades, a pair of anorectic playboys.

Dr Gabe straightened. He had been on the wards now for thirty-six unbroken hours. He looked from one twin to the other. Fatigue eroded his doctorish being. He reverted to an older, simpler state. He saw not a couple of prems, but two brothers – two – new to the world, new to separateness.

He removed the stronger one from his isolette, cradling the ultralight human on soft fingers and palms, and transferred him to the cot of the frailer baby. An irregular action, not normal, not part of any protocol. Dimly, Dr Gabe realised he'd be answerable if anything were to go awry.

There was no shortage of space in the cot for the two. Dr Gabe laid the bodies parallel, each on a separately wired mattress, alarmed for moments of apnoea. He stood, regarding them: two very small bodies, two precarious lives, for the moment out of danger – but ever at the threshold of misadventure, a trivial irregularity that might rapidly develop into a critical event.

What's the cause of Twin One's distress? The heart rate monitor blinked, then beeped. Dr Gabe checked respirations: still too fast.

41

The minute human form moved jerkily. *What's this agitation? A seizure?* The baby doctor's thoughts turned to causes of seizures. He knew a whole alphabet of horrors and harms that could under-lie neonatal fitting: anaemia, blood disorder, calcium imbalance, cerebral haemorrhage ... *No. Please God, not a brain haemorrhage. Please.*

Dr Gabe sighed. He checked oxygen saturation levels: border-line. Sepsis? Atelectasis? Pneumothorax? Gabe spoke firmly to himself: *Don't panic. No rush for a chest x-ray. Wait and watch a bit.*

While he argued with himself, watching the brothers lying side by side in their unauthorised twin share, he saw Twin Two respond to some primitive motor reflex, shift onto his side and fling out a praying mantis arm. The limb came to rest on the ribs of Twin One. Twin One's fidgety movements ceased. His frame and limbs relaxed.

Twin Two did not remove his antenna limb. He slept.

Dr Gabe checked the screens again. Twin One's abnormal breath rate had slowed to normal. His racing heart settled and his restlessness subsided.

All busyness forgotten, Dr Gabe stood and gazed upon tran-quillity. He forgot the milligrams and the micromoles and the mil-lilitres of his doctor existence. He stood and watched the brothers: half-formed, skin to skin, complete.

8. The Naming of Twins

Luisa chose names for the babies before they were born. No for-eign names like her own; she wanted good Australian names. She consulted her guide to English, the Gideon's Bible. And settled on Noah and Jesse.

As it turned out, neither Luisa nor Bernard ever called the twins by these names. 'Noah' and 'Jesse' were confined to uterine life and to the life of official forms – Medicare, the Registry of Births, Deaths and Marriages, and so on.

Dr Gabe reacted – like everyone who saw their red hair – with surprise and delight. The firstborn he called 'Carrots'. He nicknamed the second 'Jaffas'. He wrote those names (between prudent quotation marks) on their cots and on their wristbands.

Luisa made a second visit to see her newborns. When she saw the names she was surprised. Dr Gabe's quotation marks escaped her. *Does the hospital choose babies' names in this country?*

So these were the names the babies would be called. Luisa was not ungrateful – an Aussie doctor would know what names would be suitable. And all the nurses and the doctors and the student doctors and the nursing students and the pathology collectors and the cleaners and the ward clerks and the tea ladies and the almoners and the chaplains and the families who came to visit co-tenants in the Neonatal Intensive Care Unit (NICU) – all who saw them in their intensive care weeks – called them 'Carrots' and 'Jaffas'.

Dr Gabe appeared at her elbow. 'Luisa, red hair isn't just a pigment. It's a temperament.'

Mysterious words. She would remember them: *a benediction or a warning?* In these first days, with her babies engaged in their daily struggle to see tomorrow, Luisa did not speculate on temperament. She gave no thought to the action of Twin Two – 'Jaffas' – that quieted the agitation of Twin One – 'Carrots'.

Luisa had to wash her hands with antiseptic before she could touch her babies. Did you have to do that in Argentina? She struggled with the written instructions on the chart above the wash trough. She watched and followed the motions of another new mother who seemed to be following the chart. That pale young woman, her face and body swollen, her movements slow and protective of a fresh belly wound, looked familiar. The shy young man next to her washed his hands, wincing as the water hit his raw cuticles. He looked familiar too.

Luisa washed first with water, then with the brown antiseptic liquid. *The colour of shit.* She blushed for her vulgarity. She scrubbed the brown stuff on and under her nails.

At the cribside, unattended for once, Luisa extended a hand, swollen from pregnancy, the fresh intravenous puncture still a little tender. She stretched her hand through the porthole of the isolette and touched her firstborn; she stroked the soft parchment of his yellowing skin. She whispered, 'Carrots.'

She liked it. It sounded good. It was Aussie and, what was more, it was true to the colour of his hair.

She slipped gentle fingers underneath the little torso and hefted diffidently. The baby weighed about the same as a decent-sized carrot. 'Hello, Carrots. I will nurse you and make you grow big and strong. I will hold you to my breast. I will bring you home.'

Furtively, Luisa lifted the lid of the isolette and kissed Carrots – *is this against the rules?* In Argentina, everybody kissed everybody, double-kissed actually. Perhaps you couldn't kiss your baby in an Australian hospital.

She peered at the cot to decipher the name of her second son, the hospital name, the Australian name. 'Jaffas' was half familiar. Later when she googled 'naming your baby', the nearest she found was Yaffa, a name in Hebrew; it meant 'beautiful'. She liked it. It was Aussie and it was from the language of the Bible. *And behold, my love, you are indeed beautiful.*

And a Jaffa was a type of orange. *Claro!*

Again she reached into the isolette. She stretched over Carrots to touch Jaffas. Her fingertip met his yielding cheek. 'Jaffas.' Her whisper a caress of air, a minute vibration of molecules directed to her son.

Moving slowly, gently, her finger described his contours until it reached the line of the jaw. She curved her finger under his chin, feeling for the fleshiness of grandmothers and small babies. There was very little. He was mainly fine bones.

A line came to her from the Gideons. She whispered: 'You are bone of my bone and flesh of my flesh.'

II

When Bernard visited, he accompanied Luisa to the NICU. She showed him how to scrub his hands with the brown antiseptic liquid, the *agua mierde*. They gowned and walked towards the isolette.

Passing a huddle of doctors and nurses crowding around a cot, Luisa recognised her pale roommate and the silent nail-biter. Dr Gabe was there, and an older doctor. The doctors looked serious. The young parents looked lost.

The older doctor was speaking. She paused and the young mother asked something. The doctor shook her head sadly.

No one else spoke. Luisa shivered.

She and Bernard stopped at their twins' cot. Luisa tried to shake off a dark feeling of threat. She said to Bernard, 'Our babies are ruddy like Esau. Where does this red hair come from?' Luisa played with her own jet black hair as she spoke. 'No one in my family is ruddy.'

'Yeah, we've got a bit of red-headedness in Dad's family. A lost cousin, a strange fellow. Not close. He's out bush somewhere.'

Bernard saw his babies, stark in the bright light. So white and thin and bare. *Like the crucified Christ.* He shivered. He didn't believe in signs or portents, and shook away the unwelcome augury.

Gazing at his red-headed babies, limbs entwined, wired and tubed, he wondered, were they breathing? Half-anxious, engrossed, he bent and watched their chests, the minute rise and fall. Relieved, Bernard blinked tears from his eyes. *I'm sooking. Crikey, I haven't cried since ... well, not since a day ago, when the boys took their first breaths. Now here they are breathing again and here I am sooking again.*

'You don't need to worry about them breathing.' A male nurse standing behind them was writing onto a chart. He said, 'We know their brains are immature; they can forget to breathe, so we monitor their resps. We give them tiny doses of caffeine as a stimulant.

If there's a pause in breathing, an alarm goes off and we take care of it before any harm happens.'

What harm did he mean? Bernard decided not to ask. Not with Luisa at his side. Then he looked closer and gave a quiet shout: '*Carrots! Jaffas!* Hell, Lou, those aren't their names. Who called them that?'

Luisa did not know. She said, 'Carrots must be for the red hair colour. And a Jaffa is an orange, no? But what is 'Jaffas', I do not know.'

'It's a lolly. Orangey-red. Great colour, filled with chocolate. But it's not a name.'

'But we can we change it? Is not too late?'

Bernard explained, 'Free country. Parents choose kids' names, not hospitals. *We* choose and *we* register the names with the government. No one else has the right.'

'My passport name is Luisa, but you call me Lou. I like that. It is a private name, yes?'

'Yeah, nickname … Are you still keen on Noah and Jesse?'

'They are good names, good serious names. Names for government. But we can choose our own names for nick, yes?'

'Nicknames, not names for nick. Yeah, we can call them whatever we like. Anyone can give anyone a nickname. Free country, Lou.'

They returned to Luisa's room to pack. Luisa would go home the next day. Bernard hefted her suitcase from the baggage loft. He noticed the luggage tag on her roommate's bag; it read Swan Hill.

No wonder the couple had no visitors. Bernard pictured a mercy flight by night, a young mother alone and terrified, her husband following next day by commercial aircraft. Bernard knew their baby, too, was premature, but that was not all – the face was odd, something missing. It came to him: *no ears!*

He felt lucky, blessed and guilty. *Guilty. Luisa's territory.* He said nothing. He helped Luisa pack.

The two would go home tomorrow and leave their babies behind to graze and fatten. He and Luisa would drive away from the hospital, leaving their children. They would return to their home, now an empty place.

The small apartment would be crowded with memories, memories of a father who never came home from Russia, and an image of a mother and a father who disappeared before memory secured a grasp. *What about Carrots and Jaffas? What will they remember of this betrayal, our abandoning them? What right do we have to feel anything but blessed? Doubly blessed? How can we feel so suddenly sad? Incomplete, frustrated? Most of all, confused?*

II

Carrots and *Jaffas* stuck. Bernard quickly embraced the names that were as wild as the red of the boys' hair.

Luisa took to the names at first breath. Speaking the names was incantation, the words becoming flesh; her boys *were* Carrots and Jaffas.

She hired a breast pump to express milk. Every three hours, day and night, Luisa applied the cups to her breasts and pressed a button. Her breasts took flight, the heavy flesh danced to a wild electric rhythm and milk flowed and filled two small plastic bottles. The bottles bore the names *Carrots* and *Jaffas*.

Bernard delivered the milk to the hospital where nurses checked the labels and duly fed the contents to the respective recipients, each after his own name.

And their good names from the English Bible appeared on all official documents.

9. Breastfeeding Twins

When Luisa and Bernard came to take their babies home, the lactation consultant directed Luisa: 'Treat the twins as individuals – they are simply people who happened to be born to the same mother on the same day. Each of them is a person, each with separate needs.'

Luisa understood from this that she must feed them separately. She'd keep religiously to an alternating schedule: if Carrots fed first at one feeding, Jaffas would precede him at the next. If Jaffas fed from her left breast and Carrots from the right, Luisa would reverse the order at the next feed.

She named her mountainous breasts *Ebal* and *Gerizim*.

Luisa liked the idea of a schedule. She would create a structured family life. A system that Bernard would recognise, all properly in place, all conforming to a grid. Bernard would create a spreadsheet with times and names and feeds all inscribed and recorded. Luisa felt tremors, intimations of chaos. Bernard would cover her in a spreadsheet and she'd shelter beneath it.

II

Nothing worked. There was no first and no second. There was no morning feed, no noon feed, no evening feed, no night feed: there was simply constant, perpetual feeding.

To these babies, night was day was night. For Luisa, any time was a good time for sleep snatching; left breast, right breast, *Ebal*, *Gerizim*, Carrots, Jaffas – all blurred, merged and dissolved, swamping all principle, all theory and schedule, extinguishing every abstract notion and lofty ideal. Life was the pursuit and the supply of milk, the quest for clean fabrics and bodies, the sighing, crying, laughing, fugitive hope of sleep.

Luisa laughed at herself, at the dreamer of dreams she had been just last week, or was it last month? She laughed too at the boys' facial expressions as they suckled, squirmed, gulped, burped and posseted. She laughed at her own groomed self, so quickly brought down in waves of baby vomit and smears of baby shit.

Luisa laughed the laughter of tenderness and body fluids, of manic collapse, of sleepless necessity. She imagined herself as Sarah, the mother who laughed.

But at feed times the babies did not laugh. As Luisa grappled with Carrots, wrestling the nipple into his mouth, he looked around him, questing, sucking fitfully, arching small muscles in rebellion. When Jaffas took his turn, he sucked hard once or twice, stopped, leaned backwards, craned his head, finally opening his mouth to cry. Luisa then thrust her nipple back into the open mouth, a dummy of flesh and milk, trying to forestall the crying that might rend the fabric of manic mirth.

From the time she lifted the first babe from the shared cot until both had been fed, cleaned and returned to the cot, both Carrots and Jaffas alternated suckling with crying. With a will. Gusts of pain or grief or anger, Luisa did not know which. At the end of the feedings, she laid them down, breathing a prayer. Reunited, the babies settled promptly.

Luisa pondered the contrast between the battles to feed and the peace between feeds. She studied the wall clock: her prem babies fed every three hours. A full feed cycle swallowed up two hours in every three, around the clock. The brief harmony between her body and each of her babies moved Luisa to great joy. The writhing, squirming and wrestling were a price she accepted for those short, sweet moments of contentment.

After a week or two or three of time without measure – Luisa lost count – on an impulse, or in forgetfulness or in simple exhaustion of thought, Luisa picked up both babies at once. She checked neither nappy, she forgot *Gerizim* and *Ebal*, she simply offered each baby a breast. Both sucked hard and rhythmically; both then stopped. Two small heads swivelled and searched, bony limbs extended, antennae in the void. One arm, flung outwards, came to rest on a brother's shoulder. Gazes locked, spines unarched, mouths resumed sucking, smoothly, to satiety.

The feeding took twenty minutes.

Luisa laughed long and softly, looking at her babies. Neither looked at her.

She laid the babies in their cot, facing each other. She lay down herself – for a moment – and fell instantly asleep.

II

Focal Length
The newborn baby's eye does not form a distinct visual image. At birth, the retina lacks cones, so colour perception does not occur. It is not until the age of four weeks that the newborn really sees anything with any clarity. By the age of six weeks, however, the baby is able to form an image that has depth, shape and colour. By the happy cooperation of the extrinsic muscles of the eye and the eye's innermost cells, the newly grown cone cells, the baby perceives a clear image at forty-five centimetres distance from his face. By the concatenation of these anatomic entities with the mother's anatomy, unsentimental Nature provides the nursing six-week-old baby a recurring image of an object forty-five centimetres away. That object is the face of its mother. (From *Your Bright-Eyed Baby: A Manual for Parents* by Dr Joseph Bruin.)

II

Luisa closed the book and looked down. The babies were suckling, one on each breast. Deeply content, she wondered what her boys were feeling. What were they seeing? Were they beginning to register images of their mother? An image of love? She hoped so.

Luisa guesstimated the distance from Jaffas' face to her own. She reckoned it was about half a metre, perhaps a bit less. She looked at Carrots; the distance was about the same. Luisa's face was at the apex of an equilateral triangle at whose opposite angles were the faces of her sons. According to Dr Bruin, Carrots and Jaffas could, at their present age of nearly six weeks, look up and see their mother. And love her.

Luisa watched for signs, and was rewarded. Carrots' gaze was upward and inward. He must be seeing me, thought Luisa. Does he like what he sees? The small mouth rested from its sucking, the lips parted a little and widened milkily. Luisa said, 'I love you too, darling.'

She looked at Jaffas. He took a breather in his turn. His mouth relaxed, his lips fell away from the O shape of sucking. The nipple fell free into a small sea of milk and he smiled, unmistakably. Entranced, Luisa followed his gaze, measuring a distance of a little less than half a metre. His gaze was not upwards but across; Jaffas was looking at Carrots and smiling. And Carrots was smiling back, across a distance of 45 centimetres, at him.

One prayer answered, another answered unprayed, a third unsettled. Luisa was content. Her boys loved.

10. Christening

'I don't believe in miracles, Lou, but somehow these kids feel like some sort of miracle to me.'

'*Claro*. They *are* a miracle, *querido*.'

'I've been thinking … do you want to have a Christening … or something? Some celebration?'

'Since school, I think I am not very much a Christian. I mean I don't want nuns and priests. But those tiny ones, they need a celebration. They deserve, no?'

'You mean a party?'

'Yes, why not?'

They held an afternoon tea party for family. With Luisa's few relatives in far-off Argentina, her 'family' in Australia consisted of a few close workmates from The Grand, all fellow domestics. Bernard invited all his relatives. They amounted to his mother and his sister, his father's sister and her adult son. The son couldn't come. Said Aunt Robyn with a significant look, 'He's away,' she sighed. 'Again.'

'That's a shame,' said Bernard. 'Leaves me as the only man.'

Luisa presented the twins to the gathering. She held them, one in each arm, facing the crowd of women. Skeletons still at three months, feather weights with fine skulls of papery bone, slab-faced, Carrots and Jaffas looked breathtakingly fragile, too little to be real persons. A collective indrawing of breath, a shock of danger averted as when a bus swoops past a pedestrian standing at the kerb. The women gazed, marvelled, a few trembled. Samara, Luisa's Somali friend, towered over the Filipinas, dark eyes glistening. Luisa's eyes met Samara's and she passed Carrots to her. Her friend would be remembering her own boys, snatched away by the militia.

Luisa handed the sleeping Jaffas to Bernard's mother, who was grappling with memories and thoughts of her own.

All awkwardness and reserve fell away as the women clustered and clucked and touched and spoke to the twins in various tongues.

I cannot see the difference. Luisa, how do you know who is Carrots and who is Jaffas? Luisa, they are so delicate, so small, so thin …

'It is a celebration,' said Luisa during a lull. 'Bernard is the father. He will speak.'

'Will I? We never talked about any speech, Lou. What do you want me to say?'

'Go. Bring that poem, read from the poem you read in the Twin Book.'

Bernard obeyed. He left and returned, bearing Nartik and Quim.

Hesitantly, slowly, he read:

> *Two identical individuals*
> *Suspended in the uterine bath*
> *Share separateness*
> *In a world of wordless dark.*
> *In this world no others exist; only the two*
> *Each a fragment, each partial but entire ...*

Bernard paused in the hush. He looked around uncertainly. Men friends would be embarrassed by this, but the women were nodding, all of them inward while at the same time gazing at the two babies. The two, manifestly one and the same. He read on. The arcane language worked as music, removed from the sphere of words, singing like jazz of the surreality of the twins.

The poem was long, but Bernard in his fugue, read on, unaware of time:

> *Like all who are womb-bound,*
> *The foetuses are mysterious*
> *To the already born. But once born*
> *These twain*
> *Remain enigma, impenetrable,*
> *An archipelago of two*
> *In an ocean of singletons.*

The women, too, dreamed as much as saw. The poem seemed to feed on the spirit of wonder abroad in the room.

> *The twins retain*
> *Innate knowledge of each other,*
> *Theirs alone –*
> *Of mind and body and being –*
> *A knowledge preceding speech,*
> *Transcending speech:*
> *Knowledge subtle as song,*
> *Deep as the womb,*
> *Pure as echo.*
> *Identical twins: One? Two? One?*

11. Traffic

Luisa laid her infants in their double pram. Built for full-term Australian babies, babies with a bit of meat on them, the pram had plenty of growing room even for big fleshy infants. Luisa's narrow babies swam in the pram. 'Narrow' was Luisa's word for her infants, skinny like an arrow. She said it aloud, feeling its weight and measure, as she had done with many words in English when she was new to the country.

Luisa's world had contracted to the apartment, to Bernard, Carrots and Jaffas. In that world, she spoke often to her babies, in the unselfconscious language of delight. She mapped that world and furnished it with tender terms of love and nurture. If it was a smaller world than the Grand or Buenos Aires, Luisa did not mind. It was a nest.

'Come, my slender, narrow ones, come into the wide world and see the nurse. She will weigh you.' Luisa liked 'slender' – it would signify 'slim and tender'.

She walked along her street towards the Infant Health Centre. She walked pridefully, consciously, her normal easy stride constrained by her freight of significance. *I am pushing my slim and tender babies, two babies, my own, beautiful, their price above rubies.*

Luisa walked slowly so all might admire and enjoy their beauty. She walked carefully so no harm would befall them.

She came to an intersection. The green man said *Walk*, but Luisa did not walk. A massive truck had commenced its turn into the narrow street she was about to cross. Its long, wide load dwarfed the cars at the kerbside. People came out of shops and offices to watch the great conveyance, concerned their cars might be crushed.

Luisa watched too. The truck's rear wheels rode up onto the path at her feet. She shuddered. *If my pram had been closer to the kerb ...*

She changed course, pushing her babies around the corner. She walked tentatively along the footpath. A man in a fluoro vest signalled the traffic to stop. Luisa stopped and waited. Nothing happened. She checked on Carrots and Jaffas. They slept.

Luisa looked about her. The traffic was stilled, herded into a pair of quiet lines. What was the holdup? She saw the fluoro man looking upwards, signalling. She followed his gaze to a high crane. It was a T-shaped structure, immensely high above the street. Above its lofty upright, the lengthy horizontal boom looked flimsy, unstable. The fine lines of the long vertical and the wide horizontal suggested a cross hanging above Luisa. Luisa felt her heart quicken, her breathing change.

At the extremity of the horizontal, the crane supported three great blocks of concrete, each the size of the mattress on Luisa's big bed. The crane pivoted slowly, the beds of cement swinging with the movement, swinging towards a point above Luisa and her pram.

A man stood in the sky, legs wide. He was the dogman, perched on the load of cement, riding the heavens. At that shocking elevation, the man looked absurdly minute, a stick figure, an epitome of frailty.

Luisa's babies were stirring. Carrots began to cry and Jaffas responded. For once, Luisa let them cry. She turned the pram, jerked it through 180 degrees and broke into a run, racing the babies away from the ambit of the crane and its menacing load.

She heard the sound of her breathing, sharp and harsh in her throat. She needed to cry but found she could not while running. She stopped at a safe distance. Now she cried. Great hoarse gusts of shapeless noise burst from Luisa's heaving chest, merging with the high-pitched sounds of her babies and the loud rumbles and rattles of traffic and tram.

Now walking again, walking fast, she heard a loud beeping from a point at her right, very close. Startled, she looked up. A garbage truck was backing into her path in the narrow street. She looked into its open maw. The paintwork was rusted, the interior scattered with refuse. The truck opened its dark mouth at Luisa. She saw Jonah's whale, hideous, inhuman.

Luisa strode a little distance beyond the truck. She stopped and gagged. She cuddled her babies, tried to sing them a song to settle them, to settle herself. Her voice was thick with phlegm. She laughed then, a little hysterically. She blew her nose noisily and started to walk home. They would not go to the Infant Health Centre today. *Another time, when it's safe.*

Back home, Luisa pulled her narrow boys from the pram and suckled them. They fed well. Replete, they lapsed into a milk stupor. She liked to let the babies lie and sleep at her breasts. Often she would doze too. Today her sleep wandered.

Soon, Luisa laid the babies in their cot. She prowled the flat, walked to the kitchen, opened a cupboard, bent, straightened and looked about her. She left the room. She walked from room to room – there weren't many in her apartment – finally entering the toilet. She gazed at the cistern, questioning.

No answer.

She sat down on the toilet seat, fully dressed, rose, strode into the family room. She took a volume from the bookshelves and sat down.

She leafed now with purpose, searching for something. She found what she was looking for and read a story she knew, about the woman who lost a child. It was from Kings. The book was the Gideon Bible.

She lay down the book and composed herself for prayer. And found she had no words; she could not pray. Her babies had been in danger and had been saved and she could not pray.

Luisa's Catholicism was like the traffic, a set of practical rituals. Her religion did not answer. She was in pain and alone.

12. Dreams

Luisa dreamed. The dreams began the night following her walk with the twins in the pram – dreams of small children and adult torturers. She could not see the faces of the torturers, only the faces of her children.

When she awoke, she wasted no time in feeding her hunger for horror: on the web she found torturers of all types and breeds. Most horrible for Luisa was Josef Mengele, a doctor who experimented on living twins.

She read, 'Mengele was the commandant of the largest Nazi slave and killing camp. He imagined himself to be a scientist with unparalleled opportunities for research. His theories were founded on crank genetics. Identical twins carried identical genetic material; when they arrived at Auschwitz, he plucked them from the selections for death or slavery and reserved them for experimentation.

'Mengele selected young women twins for breeding with male twins whom he had saved for this purpose. After pregnancy was confirmed, Mengele slaughtered the women and performed autopsies upon them. He believed that pairs of twins would create twins.

'Mengele had no further use for the males. Once they had impregnated the females Mengele sent them to the gas chambers.'

What did they think, those boys, how did they feel, forced into laboratory sex? Did they feel their reduction from human to lab rat? And afterwards, in the death chamber, surrounded by the naked, were they together? Did they find comfort in each other? Or did they die twice for their suffering second half?

Luisa looked at her own boys and saw visions of Mengele grinning as they walked together towards him, beneath the archway with its promise: *ARBEIT MACHT FREI.*

13. Dear Anna

I am writing to you because I have no one else. It was your therapy that helped me through the five years of my darkness. I can confide only in you.

I have the panic again. It follows me. I tried to leave the panic behind in Buenos Aires when I left for Capilla del Monte. I was look-ing for some mystic power to take me from the panic, the terror.

But the fear followed me to those mountains.

I flew a long way, to Australia. But the terror has found me again. I am alone here, I mean alone with the panic. My man is here but he is not here where the panic is; he is an Aussie male, he does not know anxiety. 'She'll be right, mate,' he says. I do not know who 'she' is, but 'she' is not me, not Luisa.

And the babies are with me, of course. And they have no fear.

I lift one baby to feed him. I put him to my breast. He finds the nipple and he sucks. He finds his brother and he smiles. Milk pools in his mouth as his smile widens; his lips are white with my milk. I lift up the second one, he searches and finds and sucks and relaxes. Both the babies are tranquil. They suck and swallow and shit. They are not afraid.

They are not afraid that my milk is poisoned by radiation from the dial of my wristwatch. They are not afraid of the meteor that is flying towards us from outer space and will hit earth one day – this moment? The next moment?

Street noises come up to our window – even on the third storey the noises reach us. Traffic noises crashing, squealing; trams grinding and clanging; and people laughing insanely. The sounds will not leave us alone.

I look out the window. Mad movement everywhere. Why are they hurrying? What are they fleeing? Is there a plague? A fire? Has war broken out?

I look at my face in the mirror. It has no colour. It cannot smile. I try to smile but I do not deceive the mirror. My mouth stretches itself, it searches for a smile. I am sorrow, my face is fear and sadness.

I look at the clean white walls for comfort, to disappear into the bland emptiness of white. To forget in a world of white. But the walls are not white, they are grey, there is grime. I cleaned them last night, while Bernard and the boys were sleeping. Four hours of cleaning and the walls are dirty. I must clean them again.

I do not sleep. The babies drink and sleep. I try to drink and sleep: a shot of vodka, a second, three, four shots. When I become drunk, still I am panicking. I come to bed and hold Bernard and listen to him snoring and count his sweet, peaceful dreaming snores: fourteen times in one minute, twelve in the next, I count minute after minute until I fall asleep.

When I wake up the street screams at me, the morning light shines in my eyes. I run a hot shower and turn on the fan. I cannot hear the street or my heart. There is just me, the water, the steam, some soap … and Bernard's razor in the shower. The fear has found me in the shower!

I run to the bedroom and cry. Bernard takes me, in my wetness, in his arms and he holds me. 'She'll be right, mate,' he says, 'She'll be right.' Here, in his arms, I will not die. Here I am safe.

Then Bernard hears the sounds of the shower running. He goes to turn it off. The babies must be awake now, it is morning. He brings them to me, clean and changed. I suckle the babies and they are quiet.

Bernard smiles. He does not know that the day is just beginning. The fight has begun again.

I am breathing fast. I cannot breathe fast enough. My heart is pumping in my chest. I hear my heart, loud and violent. The sound, the thumping of my heart, will frighten my nursing babies.

But my babies are two Aussie red-headed boys having their breakfast. They stop sucking and they look up at me and what they see does not make them cry. One's hand touches the face of the other. They smile, then suck again.

I am crying for their happiness. I am crying for their

ignorance – they do not know that I will have cancer from the sun, they do not fear the harm inside me and everywhere around.

Can they not see the window, so big, so high above the ground? The window calls to me. It says: 'Come, Luisa, come. The ground, the end, so close. Come!'

I wrestle my eyes from the window to the wall, across to the kitchen. On the kitchen bench sits the knife block. The knives, so sharp, so German, so excellent. They shine in the morning sun, winking: 'Come, Luisa, feel the keen blade. Cut, cut! Quick, clean pain, quick relief. Quick silence. Come, feel me!'

I try to make myself deaf to the knives and the windows. I try to feel like a baby, to be unaware, to know nothing, to fear nothing.

The babies do not fear me. They do not fear their mother, this mad woman. They suck and they shit and they sleep at my breast. How do they not know my impulse – to take one in each arm and to jump – all three of us together? They will not live then as orphans of a suicide. They will never know the fear, the black panic, the heavy awfulness in my chest.

I know only one way to escape these thoughts without killing myself – in sleep. But sleep traps and torments. In sleep, I dream.

In last night's dream, a tall slim man on horseback took my children away and tortured them.

I wake and I smoke. Twenty, thirty fast cigarettes to burn that dream away, that heaviness. Thirty cigarettes are not enough. Not enough to burn away the panic. Enough only to create a cancer. I feel the cells, they multiply wildly inside my lungs.

I will pass out. I will die. I will lose my mind. They will take my babies away from me. I will lose my babies. The babies will die.

You cannot help me, Anna. You are in BA. There is no help.

I am Luisa.

Amor.

14. Double Helix

Now that they were toddlers, Bernard called Carrots and Jaffas 'Watson-and-Crick'. That was his expression for the twins as a unit. He saw a double helix, two strands, reciprocal, dancing end-lessly, circling, entwining, orbiting each other – two persons, two personalities, one origin.

One destiny? – Bernard did not know.

One of the two – was it Jaffas? – seemed dreamier than the other. Perhaps the other one – was it Carrots? (at times Bernard couldn't be sure who was whom) – seemed more active, frenetic.

Luisa and Bernard were told that the boys, although similar, were fraternal. The doctors said, 'They developed inside separate bags. They were two separate pregnancies who happened to be born at the same time. They are like any other pair of siblings.'

Bernard was not convinced. Carrots and Jaffas were so exceed-ingly alike, they must be identical. Luisa claimed she could tell them apart. But Bernard noticed that she applied a dab of nail polish to Carrots' left fifth toenail.

He made a decision. He called a friend at the government DNA lab. On his way home from work he picked up a couple of swab sticks and secretly took smears of the inside of the toddlers' cheeks. For some reason he didn't tell Luisa what he was doing. He could not say why.

The tests, classified non-urgent, would take a couple of weeks. Bernard studied the boys more closely. They roamed further apart and became tighter. They were a phenomenon of physics, a sort of Hookes' Law of elasticity: the greater the distance, the stronger the mutual pull.

The two might move out of each other's sight but Bernard saw how gene called to gene – or spirit to spirit, as Luisa saw it – and each twin knew where the other might be found. 'My boys are a pushmi-pullyu,' said Bernard. 'Two heads, one person.'

The gene test was due. He called his friend, who asked, 'Mate, what result do you want?'

'What do you mean?'

'Everyone who tests a family member wants a certain result. What result do you want?'

Bernard was nonplussed. What did he want? 'I just want to know. And the boys will need to know.'

'The DNA is identical, mate.'

'That means the boys are identical?'

'Yep.'

'Thanks mate, I owe you.'

'Not me, mate, you owe the government. Two hundred bucks to be precise.'

Later Bernard told Luisa, 'The boys are identical.'

'Of course. They are twins, no?'

Neither was ever alone. They might career away from each other, veering at a tangent to their familiar orbits, but in their separateness, the absent one balanced the other. Neither ever fell from earth as they rappelled at the edges of their known world.

II

Bernard applied his mind, trained in mathematics and the philosophy of science, to the paradoxes of his offspring. He saw arithmetic paradox (*binary singularity*); optical phenomena (*each is the other's mirror and reflection*); they were irrational numbers, making sense only in relation to each other.

He saw a composure unusual in young children, especially these two, so weedy and insubstantial. They strode the earth like princes, assured, each the other's principality. He wondered, 'What does identity mean here? What does identity mean at all? Here are two persons, assuredly two – their temperaments are different; Jaffas is dreamy and Carrots never stops long enough to start to dream – but their oneness is unique, each is the missing fragment of the other.

Bernard purchased *Entwined Lives* by Dr Nancy Segal, the eminent twin researcher. Segal found identical twins were more likely to cooperate than other sibling pairs, and were more altruistic with each other. Bernard watched and wondered. Carrots and Jaffas were themselves. Were they particularly altruistic?

Bernard's babies were an endless source of questions. He pursued answers, an intellectual quest, while Luisa lived with the flesh of their lives and the spirits that haunted her.

15. Nightmare

A tall, slim man on horseback. He wears high leather boots, black. His hair is fair, his face well made. He wears a dark uniform. A face that looks good and knows it, the face of a vain man.

He is the doctor. He shouts orders. Soldiers repeat their commander's shouts. I cannot hear the shouting but my terror is enough. The big dogs snarl and bare their teeth and strain against their leashes at the people streaming from the train.

I climb down from the train and turn back to help the boys. But they tumble onto the platform. I try to help them up but a soldier with a dog runs towards me shouting: Die Zwillinge! Die Zwillinge!*

The man tears the boys from me. He leads them to the tall, slim man on the horse. I follow but the dog jumps at me, knocking me to the ground.

I try to get up but I cannot.

The man on the horse leers at the twins, at their beauty, their alikeness. He alights from his horse as I watch, my scream failing in my empty mouth. I watch as the man takes my children's hands in his and leads them away.

Luisa wakes up, sweating, breathing fast, too fast. She reaches

---

* The twins! The twins!

out to the twins' crib. They are there, but the terror in the dream will not leave her.

16. Lion Cubs

Luisa and Bernard watched the boys at play. Luisa bought toys, mainly simple objects, soft ones to cuddle, as well as geometric items in a variety of colours and textures and sizes. She watched as the boys created their own games. Disregarding the toys, the boys touched and tangled with each other incessantly.

Luisa handed a soft koala to Jaffas. He took it from her, turned, found Carrots at his elbow, stuffed it into his brother's face. Squeals from Carrots, who grabbed it and pushed the toy into Jaffas' belly. More squeals and a bump as Jaffas landed on his bottom. Then Carrots pushed the toy into Jaffas' face, Jaffas teetered backwards and fell flat, with Carrots falling forward onto Jaffas' tummy.

Luisa was on her feet, ready to rescue, to comfort the injured. But the loud squeals were of delight.

II

Luisa and Bernard bought a house in Oakleigh. They had a back-yard and a yard at the front for the boys to grow into.

Whenever they were together, the toddlers moved perpetually. They ran and tumbled, plopping onto their padded behinds, falling into and over each other. Their parents wondered that the babies didn't seem to get hurt. They were forever losing balance, colliding, slamming into walls, crashing into furniture. The boys seldom cried, delighting in motion with each other, its vertigo, its sudden checks, always touching, supported in a waterless world by the steadying substance of brother flesh.

A thump as Carrots fell heavily. A pause. Was he hurt? Mother and father tensed, waited for the gusts of crying. The boys looked at each other for a moment, laughed, paused and laughed again. They rekindled their laughter repeatedly.

It occurred to Luisa that Carrots did not feel that forcible impact with the normal unpleasantness of pain. It was a sensation caused by an action of Jaffas', Carrots' twin. Perhaps you didn't suffer when your twin hurt you?

Luisa pinched the inside of Bernard's upper arm.

'Ouch! What's that for, Lou?'

Then Luisa pinched the same spot on her own arm, hard. It was unpleasant, but not distressing.

'Bernard, when I pinch you, I hurt you. When I do it to myself, I have *dolor** but I do not suffer. Jaffas hurts Carrots, Carrots hurts Jaffas, but they do not cry, not like other babies. Are they one person in two bodies? Perhaps they pinch their own arms?'

Luisa played music for the boys. When she played panpipes the boys stopped their wrestling and listened. Jaffas was particularly susceptible to music. He could not hear it without a physical response. His body moved to the sounds and the rhythm, and Carrots followed. One held the other by a hand, an arm, a scruff of the shoulder, and swung him close. They reached for each other and leaned into the swing and the song of the pipes. The music was a further medium for connection.

The modest gradient of their weight gain levelled out. The boys burnt a lot of energy in busy movement. They played with the toys that Luisa provided, mainly as a means to the end of engaging each other.

She remembered her cousin's Labrador pups back in Buenos Aires. Those puppies never stopped pushing, nuzzling, pulling, biting each other. Fellow womb travellers, fellows outside the womb. *Those litters of puppies were large sets of twins.*

---

* pain

65

17. Mengele Again

Night-time again. Luisa fears sleep. She sits and reads from her Bible. She turns to the Book of Job and reads to keep herself from sleeping.

But sleep overcomes the suffering of Job.

Luisa sees her boys strapped onto two of four beds in the doctor's research laboratory. Another pair of twin boys lies on the remaining beds, similarly restrained. Luisa does not recognise them.

The doctor enters, wearing his white coat. He smiles. That smile terrifies Luisa. She knows that smile, she remembers it from her childhood, the day a strange man smiled and spoke to her beneath a bridge in San Telmo. Don't trust that smiling man! *But Luisa has no voice.*

She watches, tortured by that smile, as the man speaks to all four boys. None of them understands the words he speaks. The doctor plunges a large needle into the arm of one of the unknown boys. The boy strains against the straps that hold him to the bed. His mouth opens in a scream that Luisa cannot hear. Blood rises in the plastic tubing. At its further end there is a second needle. The doctor takes this needle and approaches Jaffas.

The sight of the needle, sharp, hard and merciless, terrifies Luisa. The man, suddenly savage, stabs the needle violently into Jaffas' arm. Jaffas does not look at the doctor; he gazes at Carrots. Luisa watches as blood from the first boy pours through the tubing into Jaffas' vein.

Now the doctor reverses the experiment. He thrusts a great needle into a vein in Carrots' arm and inserts a needle at the further end into the fourth boy's vein.

Luisa hears no voice. Only the doctor's mouth moves as he speaks and smiles, and blood flows out of Carrots' arm. Carrots and Jaffas stare fixedly at each other. They lie pale, inert, in thrall …

Luisa's arms thrash. She reaches to wrench at the tubing. Her arms tangle in the bedclothes. She cannot reach her boys.

She awakens, her mind coiling, reeling. Her nightclothes are wet, she smells the rank odour of panic sweat.

Luisa creeps to her boys. They sleep in each other's arms. Secure. She weeps and trembles. Sleep brings her to no safe harbour.

18. Tumbling into Speech

Carrots and Jaffas were three years old. The world sang 'Happy Birthday'. In Spanish and in English, at preschool and at home, the world sang and brought gifts.

The boys spun and whirled in wordless happiness. They didn't say thank you, not in so many words. They didn't say anything much to others. Only to each other did they sing syllables, jingles, jargon. Whole sentences of gobbledygook.

The boys spoke endlessly to each other. When one spoke the other nodded and listened. Neither Bernard nor Luisa understood what they said. They wondered what meanings the children gathered.

Bernard imagined their words might be gleanings from Luisa's Spanish; Luisa suspected they were mined from treacherous English, or perhaps from Bernard's Aussie English – a dialect that existed solely to celebrate its own obscurity. She had seen how her highly educated husband indulged in ocker speech with his boyhood friends for the pleasure it gave them all.

But no, neither English nor Spanish nor Australian claimed these meaningful sounds. Fluent, musical dancing rhythms, upward and downward, declamatory inflections, sounds that tumbled out in streams. One stream trickled, stopped, dried out, and a second flowed. This was conversation. These were secrets belonging to Jaffas and to Carrots alone.

Like the villagers of Papua New Guinea, divided so absolutely by their high mountains that the language of one valley is utterly distinct from that of the next, the two boys in a bilingual household spoke a third language, unique to their own valley. In the pidgin of PNG, Carrots and Jaffas were each other's *wantok*.[*]

Bernard worried. Carrots and Jaffas did not worry. They had facility and sufficiency; they were like speakers of Hungarian – theirs was a language without neighbours, relatives or known ancestors. They inhabited a linguistic island. They understood English and Spanish, but when those other tongues, the languages of outsiders, had to be used, the twins strained and exploded into staccato syllables.

It was not easy to do, not easy to witness. The boys preferred signs and silence. They learned the potency of the mute; withholding speech was power.

Bernard's two nieces and three nephews produced speech well before their second birthdays. The twins were three years old. Tentatively, Bernard revealed a tactful fraction of his misgiving. He was aware of Luisa's sensitivity to any question of threat to her boys. Luisa gazed into an abyss, he knew.

'Lou, don't you think they should be speaking by now? At least a little more than they do ...?'

He looked down and away from Luisa, bracing himself for an explosion. He would not enjoy it. Luisa's fear for the children distressed him, and the collapse that followed. He knew too well the sudden panic that flung his wife beyond reach, beyond speech. Within the spirals and coils of her terror, Luisa was a stranger. Luisa did not know herself.

This time, Luisa did not erupt. She gazed at Bernard. She did not cry or raise her voice or seem afraid. She sighed, as if somehow relieved. She reached across the table and rested her palm on Bernard's hand.

Finally, she spoke. 'We need a doctor to advise us. I have been

* Literally translated from Pidgin, wantok means 'one talk' or 'someone who speaks my language'. It is a term used to denote a close comrade; a person with whom one has a strong social bond, usually based on shared language.

wondering about it. And worrying. For months. I look on the web; I read so many terrible things. Such awful things can stop a child from talking. One does not name such things.'

To thwart the Evil Eye, Luisa mimed. In excruciating dumb show, she portrayed deafness. She struggled for a wordless play of autism. Asperger's defeated her charades.

'They were born too early, you know … oxygen.' She mimed breathlessness, and mental retardation. 'The wine I drank that night in the Grand, that night when we … when I became pregnant … you know, *foetal alcohol*. I feel so worried. And guilty. I hate myself.'

II

The speech therapist specialised in bilingual households. She arranged to meet the twins and their family at home. 'Hello,' she said to Luisa, 'my name is Salome.' Salome shook hands with the boys, repeating their names as she clasped their fine, bony hands. She faced them by turn: 'Carrots … Jaffas.'

Salome looked hard at the boys, searching for some distinguishing feature in their faces. She could not find anything. 'Luisa, is there any difference that you can point out to me? I should get to know them as individuals. They are two persons; although they are twins, they each have a separate identity.'

Luisa was pleased. This was respect. 'There is no difference you can see on their faces … just a bodily difference, not something you would see.' Luisa pauses, embarrassed.

Salome looked up, waiting.

'Well, Carrots is bigger in his … you know.'

Salome had a good idea. She was not certain.

'Carrots has a bigger *bulbul*. I mean longer … Jaffas is shorter in his *bulbul*, but maybe fatter.' Luisa blushed mightily for her raciness and for her lack of proper words in English.

Salome smiled. 'I'll have to watch them and learn them. They will show me their separate selves.' She was a good watcher. She produced paper and crayons for Jaffas to play with. To Carrots she gave a xylophone mounted on small wheels. Salome touched the keys with the rounded end of a little stick, creating different notes.

Jaffas looked up at the sound of the soft notes. His body started to sway. As Carrots took the stick and started belting the keys, Jaffas hurried to the xylophone. He grabbed it and started to dance with it. Carrots leapt to his feet and pulled at the instrument. Jaffas resisted. Backwards, forwards, the xylophone butted first Carrots then Jaffas in the stomach. Carrots lost his footing but held the instrument tight. Jaffas tumbled after him, falling against Carrots' body. Back and forth moved the contested toy. At each impact, the boys giggled. Rapidly, the struggle for possession became a game of reciprocal physicality. The xylophone was not a toy but a bridge, a connection. Once again Jaffas was Carrots' real plaything and vice versa.

Salome watched – it was a game without words.

The game continued, ever mutating, evolving; the boys now with the xylophone, now without, now standing, now running, chasing, colliding, tumbling, crashing, embracing. Salome saw two boys, two bodies, one idea, one guiding principle – communication by bodily contact.

After a while, Luisa brought out a platter of raw vegetables for the boys to eat. Salome asked her, 'May I feed them?'

Puzzled, Luisa said, 'Okay.'

'Carrots, which one do you like best?'

Carrots pointed at the capsicum.

No stranger to child guile, Salome turned to Jaffas, hid the platter and demanded words. 'Jaffas, tell me which vegetable you like to eat. Say the word.'

'Coocoobumber,' he said, and Salome presented the platter. He grabbed a handful of cucumber pieces.

Salome watched again. Both boys liked snow peas. Neither would eat tomato. After all the vegies had been eaten – excepting the tomato pieces – Salome took Carrots upon her knee and read him a story. He wriggled, pulled at the pages, tearing a few. And escaped as soon as the story ended.

Salome then sat Jaffas on her knee. He leant into her and sucked his thumb as she read. When she finished, he said, 'More story!'

Salome asked Jaffas, 'What are Carrots' favourite vegies?'

Jaffas looked around for the platter. It had gone. He would have to speak. Pointing would not serve. His mouth moved, tuning up for the performance of speech. Words emerged, rhythms jagged, jazz: 'Caps-icum! Peas!' Pointing to himself, he said, 'Like-coocoobumber-peas. Notlike-caps-icum!' The syllables struggled then tumbled fast, the voice straining, a high-pitched torrent running over rapids, songlike; pauses between syllables, explosions of emphasis, of triumph with word endings.

Next, Salome questioned Carrots about Jaffas' preferences. The same hyper-fluent force flowed, the same baulking at the jump from one syllable to the next in a longer word, the same bursting out of hesitation in the closing syllable.

Finally, Salome asked both boys, 'Tell me what you like to play with.'

'Lego,' said Carrots.

'Dress-up,' said Jaffas.

Then both spoke at once. Each reiterated to Salome the preference of the other. They raised their faces to the therapist, a pair of sparrows, opening small mouths widely, chirping mightily to the bigger bird.

Salome visited three times, watched and listened, questioned and observed. She said she woud not initiate therapy until she had assessed the boys' respective communication patterns.

Luisa saw the wisdom in this, but chafed as she waited for Salome's opinion. She was anxious. She confided her fears to Bernard. 'What if Salome says there is nothing wrong? We *know* they don't speak like other children! If they have no disease, will they ever speak properly? I'm scared of news – even good news!'

The report came in the post. It was relatively short and quite easy to understand.

1. Vocabulary is limited; they are three years old with the vocabulary of eighteen-month-olds.

2. They have all the speech they need for the purposes of their own relationship. Their baby talk is all they need.

3. They communicate by touch; touch fills them with pleasure; they are very happy children. They are remarkably sociable and socially confident.

4. Their understanding of adult speech in English is normal for three-year-olds – even a little above average in Carrots' case; Luisa assures me their Spanish comprehension is as good as, or better than, their understanding of English.

5. The children are: ex-prems;
   small for their age;
   identical twins;
   growing up in a bilingual household.

6. Speech delay is common in children in all these categories. All areas other than speech are developing normally; hearing tests are normal.

7. They choose on occasion to withhold speech, a weapon as unnerving to a parent as food refusal or voluntary constipation.

8. They show complementary relationship in play, as in speech. Both prefer to play – quite literally – with each other, as other children might play with a toy.

9. Jaffas has a greater love of music, of dance, of flowers. He takes great delight in beauty. He is an infant aesthete.

10. Carrots loves movement, brighter colours and stronger food textures. He is exuberantly physical, clumsy, falling

frequently over objects, sometimes falling over nothing at all. (His mother Luisa reports that she was an uncoordinated child and is a clumsy adult.)

11. The twins are unaffected by the falls and impacts of mutual play, but in the infrequent instances where one hurts the other by intent, the 'victim' suffers inordinately. At such times, after his initial screams of pain, he goes into a sort of 'shock', retreating into mute silence, locking the other out. And the offender tries to comfort the one he wounded, suffering deepening distress until distraction ends the impasse. One cannot recover until the other recovers. The wounds are always mutual.

12. The children are socially fearless, attractive and – being so similar – highly noticeable. The more they enjoy adult attention, the more confident and trusting they will become.

19. Only a Dream

Luisa wakens, sweating. It was a dream. It was only a dream.

She falls asleep again and sees the same man, now wearing a long white coat.

He walks with her small boys, away from Luisa. The boys look up, trustingly. The three enter a large, cold room. Luisa sees hospital beds with massive restraining belts. Stainless steel instruments shine in the general murk. The man fondles the instruments. Her boys are oblivious; they look only to the stranger, with their sweet blind trust.

Luisa tries repeatedly to call out a warning but has no voice. Again she tries, forcing a shapeless sound from her dry throat. The boys do not hear. They walk around a corner and are lost. 'Disappeared'.

Luisa knows she will not see them again. Already the image of their faces is slipping away. She will forget her boys' faces.

Luisa sits up, weeping. Her throat is dry. Her face in her hands, she grunts gulping sobs.

20. The Fancy Dress Parade

The kindergarten children wore fancy dress today. Mothers and fathers and grandmothers and grandfathers crowded the classroom to watch the children parade in their finery. There were a couple of spacemen, two cowboys, a bunch of clowns, some fairy queens and some human queens. And a few superheroes.

Jaffas was dressed all in yellow; his hair was daubed a canary colour, he was covered in yellow feathers and he wore a pair of delicate yellow wings. He was skinny, his bony shoulders too narrow to support his wings. They slipped downwards. He hoisted them back. Again and again the wings slipped, and the canary hitched them into position. Not the least dismayed, he looked towards Luisa, beaming. Again and again he turned towards her, smiling always. He confided in a stage whisper, 'We have to smile. Miss said so.' But his smiling was not staged; he was simply in an ecstasy of performance.

His brother Carrots, another runt, wore a pair of colourful striped pyjamas. This was the entirety of his fancy dress. He too beamed in self-satisfaction. In his many colours, he was as proud as any Joseph. This midget lacked centimetres but not self-confidence. He strode to the centre of the room and winked at Luisa. He stood, looking up to the visitors crowding the walls and the rear of the room. His stance commanded their attention. 'Welcome, everybody!' he cried. 'Welcome!' and he bowed deeply.

The children were all small. Luisa was ready to ache for their littleness. One, very diminutive, wore a Lion King costume, but he was a cub. The ambition of his outfit raised tender smiles. In his own estimation and in that of his peers, he was merely a child in kindergarten. No one in his class considered him abnormal. But already behind him, forever past, were the years of parity with his classmates. This would be his last year of unselfconsciousness, the last year before he entered the big school, where bigger kids would be free with unkind comparisons. Luisa gazed at him, concerned; she realised the child did not suffer from dwarfism – not yet.

The children left the classroom and prepared in the playground for their dance. Here they fell into two lines, one of girls, one of boys. Guided by a teacher, they soon filed back into class in pairs, each girl holding the hand of a boy. The teacher's assistant at the piano struck up a tune and the children sang. Many were the notes that they sang, some of them faithful to the melody.

Parents and elders looked on, their joy uncomplicated, un-bounded; they revelled in their posterity. Mum and dad faces, still young, shining; wrinkled grandparent faces, renovated by delight; sagging, stained, ancient, great-grandparent features transformed – every face illumined by love and pride, in every other hand a camera.

Alone among the throng, Luisa had no elders in this country. She looked away from her twins for a moment, back over her shoulder towards the old people. She took in all the satisfaction and joy, seeing old eyes shine with tears. There were two distinct scenes here to gladden – the paraders and their elders.

The children finished their song. Now they danced. Invariably, it was the girl partner who led the boy through the steps. All faces were solemn with care as they followed the movements of the teacher. This delicious gravity, this desperate earnestness, this close attention to the authority of grown-ups! The ancestors lining the wall of the classroom clucked with pleasure and excess of delight.

One boy, bulky in his fireman costume, was not happy. Hulking over the slim girl who held his hand and led him through his steps, he kept his mouth open, a little crooked, almost a smile. Luisa watched and wondered: was the child self-conscious, or was this something else? Luisa watched this child anxiously, willing him to be as happy as his peers.

The dance continued. The steps were few and not intricate: in, out, forward, back, twirl and bow, twirl and curtsey. The dancers danced, every child after her own fashion – this one trippingly, that one woodenly, but every dancer engaged, every child … save the fireman. Trailing his partner, he circled the room, his body moving, his gaze fixed, held by some eyebeam in another corner.

Luisa traced his gaze. Seated on the floor was a mother a good deal older than the average. She did not smile. Her eyes locked with the fireman's; their faces said something without words. Her boy looked back at her, watching her mouth. He shook his head. The woman semaphored her message, slowly, repeatedly, as the boy watched. Defeated now, he slumped, utterly miserable. And the woman – surely his mother – sent her message again.

The teacher waved her hands, the children burst into song. Nineteen mouths widened, nineteen voices rang. One mouth only was silent. Half open still and despairing, that mouth spoke the plight of the child who does not fit in. He was so much larger because he was a good deal older. This was his fourth year in pre-school; he did not learn readily and he did not find his place.

Luisa tried not to stare at the tableau of hurt which unfolded before her. She herself was conspicuous; she knew how uninvited attention intensified the pain of difference. Precisely because she felt this, she was unable to look away for long. She felt an awful encroaching fear – the fear of the aloneness of the child.

Luisa watched the older mother in her struggles to save him. The fabric of the woman's dress was a fashionable shiny grey material that fell elegantly into fine pleats. Her face, without makeup, was handsome. Naked, the skin revealed fine muscles that strained. Now she breathed out, looked down, and the tissues of her face folded into grey wrinkles.

Her fireman was stranded, willing her to see, to save him. At length, she lifted her face. No semaphore of speech now, no urging him to try again – a truce. The boy hulked and slid along the classroom wall, made harbour in his mother. He subsided into her lap.

Luisa watched the bulky boy and the thin woman. She saw tiredness and resignation in the mother's face, but no comfort. The face of a mother who knows the call to succour her child will not end in her days. Luisa's tenderness went out to the woman. But she was undone from her first sight of the 'abandoned' child. The lonely fireman stood as an emblem of suffering she thought she had forgotten, of unravelling in loss.

As her gift for anticipating pain filled her with dread, Luisa trembled. She applied it to her boys, blithe in their togetherness.

21. I am Carrots, not Jaffas

At preschool, the twins were a curiosity. Instantly fascinating, they were not two persons named Jaffas and Carrots: they were a phenomenon – they might be circus freaks, miniatures, a twosome without individual identities. Despite Carrots' restless energy that marked his difference from Jaffas in moments of restful inwardness, schoolmates and teachers confused them endlessly.

Luisa had requested that the boys be placed in different classes. Prompted by Salome, she said, 'They should be separate so they can develop as individuals.' Although Luisa saw the need, she feared her boys would suffer once parted.

In the event, the separation took place smoothly. Two teachers greeted Luisa at the gates. One took Carrots to his classroom while Luisa and the second teacher conducted Jaffas to the classroom next door.

Luisa said, 'Jaffas, you will be in this classroom and Carrots will be in the next room. At playtime you'll see each other in the playground.'

As far as Carrots and Jaffas were concerned, the other might just be in the toilet or sleeping in or playing at their cousin's house. They knew separateness: it was one of life's common anomalies. In their deeper reality, Carrots and Jaffas were often apart, but never distant.

At recess, the two came together instinctively and played. They had no need of others. They were a world – Jaffas and Carrots. Outsiders who visited their world were received cordially but the essential constellation was Jaffas-and-Carrots, the two whizzing in endless orbit around each other.

On the occasions when Jaffas and Carrots played separately, each was fully and dynamically absorbed in the group. But they were oriented towards each other: on the compass of each, the other lay true north.

It was at preschool that Jaffas and Carrots discovered that they were different from other children; they were different in appearing the same. They had the same red hair, a redness that shouted from their rooftops; and they shared thinness, two marionettes without strings. And both showed that precocious sociability.

Bernard called them *squirts*, *rangas*. They strode boldly into the world of people, treating adults as they did children; all were their peers. They feared no one, they had no belief in harm. They were each other's life assurance; they enjoyed double indemnity.

Jaffas' teacher had an old-fashioned pencil sharpener on his desk, an antique, a curiosity. Jaffas watched, engrossed, as the teacher inserted a pencil into the upper end of the contrivance and wound the handle at the side. Pencil shavings fell from the sharpened point into a receptacle below.

The sharpener was irresistible. When the teacher was out of the classroom, Jaffas played with it. There was no pencil on the desk, so Jaffas investigated the interior with his index finger. He pushed his finger into the opening as deeply as he could. When he tried to withdraw it he found he could not. Jaffas tried hard to extract his finger – he pulled and twisted, pulled and pushed, then pulled again. The finger remained stuck and began to swell. The finger was very stuck indeed.

When the teacher returned to the classroom, she was unable to separate Jaffas from the sharpener.

Matron was called. Jaffas was still stuck. She called Luisa. Luisa arrived and called an ambulance. The ambulance officers took Jaffas and Luisa and the pencil sharpener away in their vehicle.

Until now, Jaffas had been absorbed in the novelty of a finger that he could not see but still could feel. In the ambulance he started to cry, then to shiver.

Luisa said, 'Is it hurting, Jaffas? The people at the hospital will stop it hurting.'

Jaffas kept on crying.

Luisa tried to comfort him, to reassure him.

Jaffas continued crying.

A lady paramedic handed him a model ambulance. 'This lovely ambulance is yours to keep, Jaffas.'

Jaffas refused to be distracted.

In the Emergency Room, he caught sight of his reflection in a mirror. He stopped and looked hard. He cried, '*Carrots!*' Jaffas ran to the mirror and embraced his reflection. Only then did he stop crying.

The pencil sharpener and the boy with red hair were readily separated and returned to class.

Back at preschool, everyone continued to see two indistinguishable persons.

'Does your finger hurt you, Jaffas?'

'I'm not Jaffas, I'm Carrots. That's Jaffas over there.'

The twins confused adults and children alike. Grownups, childlike in simplicity, could not see two distinct persons. They quizzed Luisa: 'Do they have, like, this mystical thing, when one has a tummy ache in one place, and the other one somehow experiences it?'

Luisa shook her head. Nothing quite like that happened. She

wanted to say: *The boys have this connectivity-identity continuum*, but the concept defeated her English. What came out of her mouth was: 'Carrots is bone of his bone, and flesh of his flesh ...' She tried again: 'Jaffas' soul is bound up in his soul.'

Hearing this, people shook their heads.

Within the family, the boys' twinness was domestic, not exotic. But Jaffas and Carrots lived with a blindness of their own. They were slow to picture the life of persons who were not identical twins.

Jaffas had a girlfriend named Tori. Carrots wasn't interested in Tori. When Jaffas and Tori walked around the playground holding hands, Carrots paid no heed.

Just before lunchtime, Jaffas clutched his tummy. He needed to be excused urgently. The nurse called Luisa, who collected him and took him home.

At the lunchbreak, Carrots stepped into the breach. He took Tori's hand and walked into the playground with her. Carrots kissed her. Tori was not one to look a giftkisser in the mouth. This must be Jaffas.

Carrots didn't disabuse her. It was a disinterested kiss, delivered on Jaffas' behalf.

Afterwards Carrots told Jaffas about the stolen kiss. 'Tori thought it was you. I didn't tell her I am Carrots.'

The boys sat and digested the possibilities. Their eyes opened to a world of different people, people who did not understand.

Carrots was the speedier one, more physically expressive. Racing through the preschool playground, he collided with a group of girls and knocked one of them, Madison, to the ground. The child lay there, briefly amazed. She put her hand to her head. She looked at her hand.

Blood!

The child screamed, children gathered and sighted the blood. This was an emergency. Teachers were summoned. Carrots ran away and hid in the toilet.

'The boy with red hair pushed me over and hurt my head,' the girl sobbed.

Jaffas was rounded up and taken to Nadia, headmistress and hater of children, especially boys.

'Why did you hurt Madison?'

'It was a accident. I saw it happen.'

'You didn't just see it, you did it. Why did you do it?'

Jaffas did not answer. Here was another blind adult who couldn't tell the difference. Tori and the stolen kiss, all over again.

'Why did you hurt Madison?'

Jaffas saw an opportunity: the headmistress's blindness allowed him to protect Carrots without being punished himself.

'I didn't mean to hurt her. I came out of the toilet and I saw her fall over. It was a accident.'

Nadia was confused. Is the child stupid?

'Madison had to go to Matron. You made her head bleed. What do you say about that, er ... Carrots, er ... Jaffas? Which one are you?'

'Carrots,' says Jaffas.

The lunchbreak finished. Nadia took Jaffas to the classroom where she would teach him a lesson. Madison, wearing celebrity and a bright new bandaid on her forehead, sat on the mat with the other children, Carrots included. This was not Jaffas' class. His was next door.

'Carrots, what do you have to say to this little girl that you hurt?'

'Hello, Madison,' said Jaffas.

'Hello,' said Madison.

Nadia frowned. Her prominent black eyebrows met in the middle of her forehead. The eyebrows looked like Jaffas' father's moustache.

'You need to say sorry, Carrots!'

'It was a accident, Madison. I am sorry you hurt your head ... Cool bandaid!'

'Don't be smart, Carrots!'

'Excuse me, Nadia.' The classroom teacher approached the flashing eyebrows diffidently. She spoke confidentially to her superior: 'That boy you're talking to isn't Carrots. This one here on the mat is Carrots.'

Nadia, nonplussed, quickly became furious. 'Why did you say you were Carrots, Jaffas? Why did you lie to me? And why do you boys have such ridiculous names?'

'It wasn't a lie. I said it was a accident.'

Nadia seized both Carrots and Jaffas and shoved them to the door. Carrots, a practised stumbler, stumbled. Nadia grabbed him and pulled and pushed both boys to her office.

She called Luisa: 'Come and fetch your boys. Both of them! Immediately!'

Part 2

♊

22. Through Thick and Thin

Albert Burns was flying to America to visit his sister in Mt Kisco in upstate New York. They hadn't seen each other for a couple of years. On the flight his legs found little room. Sleep beckoned and slipped away: Albert had plenty of time to reflect on reunions and separations. Time for memory to roam.

The last time the entire family had been together was at Albert's graduation from Medical School at Monash. Father was there; he and Marguerite had flown from the States. Mother attended, together with her partner. Their parents observed a prudent distance.

Albert, long practised in suppression, stilled his hopes and his fears. He wore his suit of fawn and his pale mask. He had mastered the feelings of black rage. He was a controlled person, his black feelings watered down to pale greys.

Albert remembered the fawn suit he had worn. He somehow expected Father would wear his charcoal double-breasted suit with the rows of buttons at face height; but no, his father wore slacks and a blazer. The slacks were pastel. Albert was a *man*, as Father had commanded him, a man like Father himself.

II

His father wears a suit this morning. Albert recognises the suit. He does not need to go out into the hall and sight his father's suitcase to know; this will be a Goodbye Morning. The suit is of a dark woollen fabric. Albert notices the fine pinstripes that run in lines along the charcoal. And there are two rows of buttons down the front. Father closes the jacket with one row of buttons. What are the other buttons for?

Father enters the bedroom that Albert shares with his younger sister, and bends over the sleeping toddler to kiss her warm scalp. He straightens, stands for a moment and drinks in the beauty of the little girl in sleep.

Now he turns and crosses the room, sits on Albert's bed, takes his hand and shakes it. Handshakes happen only on Goodbye Mornings; his sister gets a kiss and the boy gets a shake. 'Look after your sister. Be my little man. Don't cry.'

A sober pumping of the boy's hand.

'When I come back from the Snowy, we'll have more stories. We'll start Treasure Island.'

Father is a consulting engineer to the great scheme of dams and weirs and turbines that will drown some valley towns and launch Australia into an industrialised future.

The boy is proud of his father. He will be an engineer like him. He will drive his steam engine through those Snowy Mountains. At school he tells friends: I'm going to be an Engineer.

That night Albert lies in his bed, feeling sad. No bedtime story tonight. He weeps for his missing father, a nurturing father who holds him close in the dark and tells him stories of The Thousand Nights and One Night.

This is the storytelling father. Albert was weaned onto stories when Mother became sick. She had to go to a doctor in the City, leaving a breastfed nine-month-old at home with his father. Father took the baby everywhere, telling him stories the whole time. Mother was gone, but Father was stroking his face as he worked at his desk, now reciting lines from 'Sohrab and Rustum' while driving, now reading aloud from his tables of water flow in the Murray Darling River system. Always the touch of Father's skin on his skin, the sound of Father's voice furnishing the world, filling a void.

In the mornings, Father changing his nappies. That touch again. Father stepping away to warm his bottle, the touch taken away, that voice filling the space, Father's voice singing, reciting, reading, recounting – the sounds, those vibrations of affection that affirm to an infant: You are safe. You belong. You signify. You are not alone …

Touch and voice, caress and story, father's milk.

Mother remains in a city hospital for months. In later years,

Mother would speak of those lost months, the electric shock treatment, the time without her son.

Mother comes back, tries to reclaim her baby, now a toddler. Neither mother nor son ever quite recovers the closeness of infancy.

Albert looks to Father, who cuddles him and kisses him as naturally as any mother, as his own mother cannot. Father is not yet a man in a dark suit who shakes his hand. Not yet one who goes away, taking the stories away with him. The stories that are mother and father to the boy child.

II

Father moved to the States, taking with him Albert's sister, Marguerite, still a toddler. Marguerite went to school there, later doing her BA at Wellesley. She became a teacher and specialised in sexual education. Albert wondered sometimes what influence led her steps in this unexpected direction. *Mother's sexuality perhaps?*

Once Marguerite had children, sex education gave way to the nurture of her infants. During her children's preschool years, she trained as a lactation consultant. She took up the challenge of restoring the lost arts of breastfeeding in the United States. That battle won, Marguerite joined an NGO that lobbied the UN on the rights of the child. Here she took on the multinational manufacturers of infant formula that promoted artificial feeds in the Third World. Babies died of dysentery when infant formula was – inevitably – reconstituted with contaminated water. The multinationals denied any responsibility, pursued profit and found themselves in battle with Marguerite Burns.

While Marguerite pursued her calling, Albert followed his own. He was a doctor. He was proud of Marguerite's crusades and he kept himself informed about her career. Until now, Albert had been coy about his own work. But with his sister's later interest in bowel infections, Albert saw a common career pursuit. Albert felt an urge to talk with Marguerite – face to face – specifically about his work.

He had his reasons for his long silence. Marguerite had sensed his reticence and accepted it. Between siblings, the borderlines between safe and unsafe conversation would normally be clearly lit by the blaze of fights in adolescence. Between Marguerite and Albert, these dangerous borderlines lay in the shadows thrown by their years apart.

When their parents' marriage ended and Father had taken the little girl to the United States, he left Albert at home in Australia with Mother and her lady friend.

The marriage had ended, but the acrimony between Father and Mother continued until death. The respective offspring, trapped in loyalty, found themselves in opposing camps. Over the five decades of unwilled separation, Albert and Marguerite visited each other every couple of years. Their visits took the form of cautious research projects, each of the siblings the other's subject of study.

Now, with both parents dead, loyalty no longer commanded distance. Candour might be safe. As Albert flew to see his sole blood relative at her home in New York State, he felt time was ripe – overripe, really – to talk about his work.

23. Marguerite

Albert Burns arrived heavy with meals of sludge, his body clock confused, his neck stiff and sore.

His sister greeted him at JFK. They exchanged fierce hugs.

'How was your flight?'

'Glamorous.'

'Why fly Economy? Why not Business?'

'You pay more and get the same jetlag, same sweat and grime, same fatigue. Same glamour.'

He looked at his sister. Bonier than she used to be, vigorous, she still gave a backbreaker hug. Freckles everywhere; he'd always loved them. *Glory be to God for dappled things* – was their father's phrase. And that hair, streaked now with silver, but still a burnt auburn. And the same wide-open grin – like the entry to Luna Park.

They arrived at Marguerite's home. It was a two-storey timber structure with attic bedrooms and grounds that ran down to a busy stream. Albert looked out at the waters flowing fast and clear. And clean.

He said, 'I'm rooted. I need a shower.'

The hot water ran over his head and shoulders. Albert felt life might be worth living. He took the soap and studied it; he read PEARS. He held it to his nose and sniffed for the aroma of bath times in childhood. The wet soap had no smell.

Albert washed slowly and thoroughly – his face first, his hair, then trunk and limbs; finally and methodically, he lathered genitals, buttocks, natal cleft and anus. Then he rinsed off the suds.

He stood a moment, pensive. He washed his hands a second time.

Before turning off the water, Albert held the soap beneath the water, turning it over repeatedly. He rinsed off the suds that had accumulated. He sluiced out the soap dish, replaced the soap and finally turned the water off.

II

At dinner, Albert was thoughtful. 'Marguerite, when you shower, what do you wash first?'

'My face. Why?'

'What do you wash next?'

'My limbs, I guess. Then my trunk. What are you getting at?'

'What do you wash last of all?'

'My private parts. Why the interrogation, Horrie?'

He waved away the question. 'So when you shower, the first thing you do is wash your face with soap covered in old suds from your "private parts".'

His sister looked at him levelly. She said mildly, 'When do you plan to wash your mind?'

Albert grinned. 'I never told you, but I've been interested in the spread of bowel infections forever. It's my research interest, actually.'

'Well, I'm not surprised. Whenever we've been together you've talked about bodily functions at mealtimes, bowels and stools, forever …'

'That's when it counts, sis. It's at mealtimes that the great cycle of germs from bum to mouth reaches its apotheosis.'

His sister stopped eating. She looked at the bread in her hand and put it down on the table. She wondered: *Are all Aussies so earthy, so vulgar? Or is it just me, a puritanical American?*

Albert said, 'Alright, alright. I'll stop.'

They ate for a while without more talk.

Finally, Marguerite said, 'Look, I realise you are serious about this. And I *am* interested. Let's go for a run in the morning and we can talk about your research.'

In her bedroom, Marguerite googled *Albert Burns, Medical Research.* She found there was much to read. As headline after headline jumped out at her, Marguerite blinked. She turned off her Mac and went to bed.

Ⅱ

They were up and running early. Mist rose from the stream as Marguerite led her brother along the hilly track. The sun caught the trees on the far bank. Foliage flamed gold and red.

Albert breathed hard on the hills. It wasn't easy to keep up with Marguerite. Those speckled, stringy legs were efficient. He marvelled at their definition, their beauty, actually. He made some calculations: his younger sister must have reached her sixties. *I never saw a senior citizen run so bloody fast!*

Albert gasped: 'Slow down, freckle legs!'

The legs slowed a little and Marguerite said, 'I googled your research. That's an impressive corpus of work for an amateur researcher. We'll stop at The Granary and buy some food for breakfast. Then you can tell me about your studies on medical students.'

The Granary was a series of cavernous old warehouses given second life as a food emporium. Marguerite led her brother from one department to the next, through an Aladdin's treasure-house of fresh and processed foods. The place struck Albert as unexpectedly wholesome, no polish, no spit, just a vast array of foods, mainly organic, stretching from worn flooring to a soaring roof. He imagined the building disintegrating but unable to collapse, the shelves of food supporting the entire aging structure.

They emerged with cheeses, olives, remarkably good tomatoes and fresh basil. And a bottle of fresh orange juice and a baguette warm from the oven. They crossed the road and settled down on the bank for a picnic.

'Great grocery shop, Marg.'

'Fabulous. You can get Vegemite there. Even olive oil from the Riverina. Now tell me, big brother, how did you get into toilet research?'

'Well, it all started at medical school. Between lectures we'd go out for a leak. And my friends didn't wash their hands afterwards! I was shocked. After all, we were tomorrow's doctors and we were already examining patients.

'I decided to find out how common it was. And whether it mattered. I'd duck out just before the end of a lecture, lock myself in a cubicle and wait for my classmates to arrive. I'd listen and count urinators and defecators. After everyone had gone to the next lecture, I'd count paper towels. There were always fewer towels than flushes.

So I wrote it up and published it in the journal of the medical students' society.'

'Didn't the editor object?'

'I was the editor.'

'What did your mates think of that?'

'They laughed. They called me names. It was all quite affectionate. There was quite a debate about methodology ...'

'I can imagine. But what about ethics, what about shaming your friends?'

'It was the sixties, Marguerite. We were busy freeing ourselves from all those body hangups.'

'And later, when you were lecturing to undergraduates, you studied their toilet hygiene. What did you do about consent?'

'Nothing. I needed to blind my research subjects. I set up a sort of single-blind trial. Obtaining consent would have created unsound research.'

'Unsound! Aren't there ethical rules for investigators?'

'There are. Those rules kill research.'

'So you lurked outside the toilets, swabbed their hands as they exited, wrote it up and published.'

'Yep.'

'I notice your paper didn't appear in *The Lancet* or *The New England Journal*.'

'Nope. The foundational studies had been published in the elite journals well before my time. They confirmed the euphemism: *It has always been impossible to keep the intestinal contents of one person out of those of another.*'

He paused to allow Marguerite to absorb the maxim. She pondered a moment, nodded, grimaced then smiled. 'Neat ... What about Boston? Are you visiting someone there?'

'Well, not in the usual sense, Marg. But you could say I'm going to see Paul Gauguin. There's a picture of his in Boston ...

'But back to my unsavoury research. When the elite journals rejected my papers, I realised I should publish in the *Journal of Irreproducible Research*. My work was right up their alley. I did so. And a spirited correspondence followed. All about unethical studies, unethical publishing. And a good deal of name calling by the students – everything from Dr Poo to The Dunny Spy. I didn't mind. It was fair enough.

'We primates have a structural problem. Anatomical Kismet. The eye and the anus are far apart. The wiping hand wipes, and having wiped, moves on. Contamination is human destiny.'

'Deep, very deep, Albert. But that op-ed piece – "Through Thick and Thin" – about tensile strengths of toilet tissue. That was a bit off, wasn't it?'

'Look, it's all a bit off. More than a bit off. But it matters. No one publishes much about the bum-to-mouth cycle. But every single bum-wiper has been betrayed by paper that gives way during wiping.'

'You grub.'

'Quite. It's a fact that thicker paper is stronger and less prone to perforate. It costs more, more trees go, but lives are saved.'

'You're exaggerating. Who dies of gastro? It's just a virus. It runs its course and gets better, doesn't it?'

'Generally – in New York and Melbourne. But in the third world, dysentery kills. Millions of kids die of gastro.'

'Of course. Contaminated water supplies …'

'I knew you'd get it. Your work in the UN …'

They ate in silence for a while.

'You know, Marguerite, the human species invented the spread of bowel infections. We are the sole bum-wipers. Non-wiping species have no soiled hands, no bum to mouth. It's a human thing …'

Marguerite winced but made no remark. They watched the river at their feet run down to a cascade, around a bend and out of sight.

'Marg, I've decided to leave the city. I'm going bush.'

His sister stopped eating. She looked at her brother, her expression tender, anxious now. Albert had never married, never had a girlfriend as far as she knew. Was he gay? Was her unpartnered brother a casualty of his mother's sexuality? And now Albert was burning his bridges in the city – if he had any.

'You want to know why I'm doing it?'

'No, I mean yes, why are you doing that?'

'People in the city don't want to know about bowel infections. Certainly my methods are unconventional and my interests are unusual, distasteful to many, but I do tell the truth, *and the truth matters*. Babies die.'

'But not back home in Australia, surely.'

'Yep, in Australia. Especially among Aboriginal children. That's why I'm going outback. That's where I can do some good.' Albert's words had slowed to a walking pace. He delivered sentences like newborns, with labour and deliberation.

'I mentioned Gauguin before. He did what I'm going to do. He left the world he knew; he went to an older, simpler culture. He went bush to seek simplicity. That appeals to me, I must say.'

Marguerite nodded. Albert's slower speech, his shorter words moved her. She caught his pain and his hope. His resolve.

A silence, companionable, sympathetic.

'Bertie, you obviously know about my campaign for safe infant feeding in the Third World?'

'Yeah, a little. Big Milk in the States and Europe mounting their PR counterattack on breastfeeding. They pay lip-service to the breast while biting off the nipples of Africa.'

'And Latin America and Asia. You're a bit graphic, but that's about right.'

Marguerite's freckled face shone in the morning light. Albert saw his sister's Luna Park grin. She seemed to be wrestling with her own lips, trying to arrest some escaping gaiety.

'I think I might try to adapt your research techniques, Bertie, to demonstrate the dangers of artificial feeds where water supplies are contaminated.'

'You mean swabbing people without consent? Bums of babes, water from wells, sales outlets of artificial milk, that sort of thing?'

'Well, whatever it takes, really.'

'Marg, that's unethical. I'm proud of you!'

They walked back along the bank to the house. While Albert took a nap, Marguerite went out shopping.

Later, Albert visited the bathroom. There was a fresh roll of heavy-duty toilet paper in the guest bathroom. He thought: *My little sister loves me.*

And when he washed his hands he used the brand new pump-action liquid soap dispenser on the basin. He decided, *She really does love me. It's about time: I'll ask her ...*

Albert emerged from the small room, much warmed by his sister's care. 'Marg, I've just been to the toilet.'

Marguerite braced herself. She nodded warily.

'I'm really grateful. I really appreciate what you've done. Taking me seriously. It means a lot.'

His sister smiled.

'Marg, there's a question I've wondered about ever since Mum and Dad split. I've never asked because it's ... sensitive. I ...'

Marguerite helped her brother out: 'Whatever it is, ask. If it's important to you, it's safe. Go ahead.'

'Marg, did you ever feel you weren't loved? By Mum I mean?'

Marguerite nodded. 'I didn't just *feel* unloved, I *was*. Mum wanted you. She didn't care about me so she offered me as a trade.'

She stopped and looked at her brother, a look of compassion. 'But that's not your real question, is it?'

'Well, sort of ... I suppose ... I wonder ... why Dad gave me up. He and I were close – once ...'

'Well, you were older than me. If you don't remember, I wouldn't. I don't even remember them together. But whenever I visited Australia, I ran around the family and asked all the aunties and grandmothers. No one wanted to talk about it much. In 1952, a divorce was embarrassing. And a lesbian relationship was scandalous. But everyone pitied the little girl whose mother didn't want her, so they fed me snippets. Dad *did* want you; he wanted us both. It was a legal problem that stopped him.'

'What legal problem? If he really wanted me, why didn't he fight?'

'In those days, a man could only obtain custody by proving the mother would be harmful to the child. *An unfit mother* – that was the term; at the least she had to be guilty of serial adultery. *And sleeping with another woman wasn't adultery*. It was infidelity, even a perversion. But not a legal disqualification.

'Dad consulted lawyers in Sydney, even here in the States. I know – his mum told me. The lawyers all said he couldn't win. They said all he could do was hurt us both more. I think he decided he would cop it and absorb the pain for us both.'

Albert did not speak.

Sweeping through him was the knowledge he had lacked since that last goodbye day, the day of the final handshake. He felt unsteady and sat down.

24. When Doc met Greta

A tall woman knocked on the door of the clinic in Leigh Creek. She looked thin and old, seemingly too frail to support the bundle she bore in her arms. The bundle made a low gurgling sound and the sour stink of infant excreta rose in the clinic doorway. Her bundle was a baby with diarrhoea.

The lady's figure was straight, a linear sketch. Her limbs were sticks, the hands that held her bundle almost translucent. Dr Burns noticed the pearly sheen of her skin and her fingers, long and graceful.

The old lady's voice was surprisingly firm. 'This little one, she my great-grand-niece, she very sick.' The lady bent a little to show the baby. 'Dysentery all last night, all today. My grand-niece bring baby to me just now … She young, you know, young ones don't know what to do. Bring the sick ones me. Say, *You help, Greta. You take baby, see doctor.*'

The clinic had closed for lunch. The Doc unlocked the door and brought them in. He took the baby, unwrapped the swaddling and removed the clothing soaked in liquid stool. Naked, the child lay passive, unresponsive to the blast of cold from the air conditioner onto her hot belly. She made no sound.

The examination was quick. Like many Aboriginal babies, the little girl was undersized; her skin was wrinkled and shrivelled with fluid loss. Her heartbeat was rapid and her pulses were feeble. The Doc lifted a gentle pinch of skin from her belly for a moment, then released it. Instead of springing elastically back into shape, the pinch lingered, a standing wave of withered flesh.

The Doc straightened and looked searchingly at the old lady. 'What did you say your name was?'

'Greta.'

'Hello, Greta, I'm the Doc … as you can see. What's the little girl called?'

'Ashweena. Her Mum outside, in the car.'

The Doc looked at her squarely. She met his gaze. He shook his head a little and said, 'Ashweena is very sick. Her body is drying out. She needs to be next door, in hospital.'

The old lady scooped up the baby and her wrappings. 'Little kiddie need hospital last night, I reckon. Let's go, Doc.'

In the hospital ward everything was white. The nurse was white, her uniform the same. The Doc wore a white gown and his bearded face was white. The bright overhead light bleached everything.

Baby Ashweena lay naked on the bed, the pale faecal fluid trickling from her bottom, scarcely soiling the white sheets. Her skin, dried out and deeply creased, gave no sheen. She did not move.

Greta held the little girl's hand in her own. Greta's skin looked pale and thin in the bright light.

The nurse clipped a small black thimble onto the tip of the little finger of Ashweena's other hand. She checked a meter and pressed some switches. 'Ninety-four per cent,' she said aloud and wrote something on the chart.

The nurse looked up at Greta. 'We measure how much oxygen

is in her blood. It tells us if she is strong.'

Greta could see the baby was not strong.

She watched the Doc. He was threading a pair of fine probes into Ashweena's nostrils. The probes were attached to clear tubing that ran from a tap on the wall. The nurse started the flow of oxygen, waited a minute, then studied the dial of her oxygen meter: 'Ninety-seven per cent. Heart rate still 220.'

In his hand, the Doc held a minute needle attached to some fine plastic tubing. He inspected the inside of the baby's forearm. He leaned forward, adjusting the bright overhead light. He fingered the dry skin. 'I can feel a vein there. I can't see it but I can feel it.'

The nurse handed him an antiseptic swab. The smell of medicinal spirit mixed with the too-sweet odour of hospital antiseptic reminded Greta of the infirmary at the Mission.

The Doc leaned forward, peering and patting at the thin arm. Greta watched his probing fingers. She saw the baby's arm was thinner than the doctor's thumb. Greta felt a pang.

The nurse gripped the child at the wrist and the elbow. The old man brought the point of the needle close to the arm, holding it at a shallow angle. He stood for a long time that was less than a minute, peering through his glasses. In a single slight, smooth movement, he slid the needle forward, breaching the skin.

Greta thought of her own man, the motions of his body as a young hunter stalking game – the same small movements, patient, minute, fluid, unerring. Her man had been dead a long time.

The baby's eyelids flickered at the needle prick – she mewed once, then fell asleep. She had not struggled against the nurse's restraining grip. No one spoke.

The Doc extended a hand and accepted adhesive tape from the nurse. Frowning hard, touching softly, using only the tips of his fingers, he caressed the tape into position and fixed the needle in place. He straightened, stretched his back and breathed out. Greta heard the nurse release a breath. She realised that she had not breathed for too long. She breathed hard now.

The doctor was all tense concentration again as he took a syringe and screwed it into the tubing that led to the needle in Ashweena's arm. He sucked back with the syringe. The angel-hair tubing turned red.

'We're in,' said the Doc. He straightened and stretched again while the nurse attached the tube to a bottle of intravenous fluid hanging from a stand. The Doc's face relaxed in the moment of small victory.

The baby shat a thin pale watery challenge onto the sheeting.

'Saturating at 98 per cent. Heart rate 240.' The nurse peered at meters and gauges. The Doc squirted blood from his syringe into a test tube. He handed the tube to the nurse. 'Can you do the electrolytes, fast?'

The nurse smiled sourly. 'Not here. We've got no lab here. Pathology specimens are flown out each day. We'd have got a result tomorrow if we had caught this morning's plane.'

The doctor looked at the baby. 'Ring the Flying Doctors in Port Augusta. Tell them we need them here fast. Please.'

He turned to the old woman. 'Greta, we are putting some special water into Ashweena through this tube.' The Doc indicated the intravenous drip. 'The water has salt in it and a little bit of sugar to feed Ashweena. We will put an additional salt into it as well, some potassium salt. Every time Ashweena opens her bowels she loses some of this special salt. It makes her weak. If she doesn't have enough potassium, her heart can stop.'

He broke off, plugged his ears with his stethoscope and listened gravely to the heartbeat. 'Still too fast,' he muttered.

The nurse handed him a telephone. 'It's the flight nurse for you.' The doctor spoke in medical talk for a while. Greta heard him say some unmedical things – very weak, undersized … critical … we need help – then he stopped and listened and his face fell. The doctor looked at the clock on the wall. 'It's 2.30 now. Your ETA is six hours away! She could be dead by then.'

Greta looked at the clock. The red second hand swept a steady circular path around the clockface, around and around and around. She looked at Ashweena, sleeping and shitting and breathing. How many times around that clock would the baby live? This baby was a tough little one. And the Doc seemed like a tough one. She was reassured that he looked old. An elder. She lifted her head.

The Doc was listening again. He said, 'Okay. Please do what you can.'

Greta went out to the car and spoke to her grand-niece. When she came back she addressed the doctor: 'We reckon you going to fix this baby. You, not Flying Doctor, not Adelaide hospital mob.'

The Doc smiled. He explained that there was one Flying Doctor aircraft only and it had flown to the Pitjantjatjara lands, to save an old man who had suffered a heart attack. The plane would collect the heart patient, fly him to Adelaide, then refuel and turn around and fly to Leigh Creek in the North Flinders.

A loud alarm brought the Doc's words to a halt. The nurse adjusted the oxygen thimble and the ringing stopped.

The doctor poured blue liquid into a small pot and started to swab Ashweena's private parts. The swabs moved up and down and in and out, a fresh swab replacing every soiled one. The nurse opened a white paper packet and the doctor pulled on a pair of gloves. With one hand, he opened the bleached lips of Ashweena's lower body; with the other he threaded a fine clear plastic tube into her bladder.

Ashweena did not move.

Now the Doc pushed the barrel of a small syringe and injected air. 'We need to know whether her kidneys are working. This tube will bring Ashweena's urine out of her body so we can measure it and test it. I'm squirting some air to blow up a little bubble that keeps the tube in the right place inside her.'

The nurse inserted a thermometer into Ashweena's bottom. No reaction from the baby. After a minute, the nurse pulled out the thermometer, wiped it and read the numbers. Her eyebrows shot up above her mask: '39.3!'

The baby grunted and a fresh stream of fluid shot onto the linen. The Doc leaned forward and peered. 'There's blood in that stool.'

He drew a deep breath and turned to the nurse. He realised he didn't know her name. She was quick and deft and read his needs well. She looked young; they all did. 'Nurse, I don't want to call you *Nurse* all the time. Do you mind telling me your name?'

'Lorraine ...' The young woman blushed. 'I know what to call you: you're just *the Doc*.'

'Righto, Lorraine. And this lady is Greta. She's Ashweena's great, great-aunty.'

The women nodded to each other. Lorraine smiled. The Doc continued, 'This isn't ordinary gastro, Lorraine. Could be anything, could be an anaerobe, might even be salmonella. We're going to need IV flagyl and gentamicin and ceftriaxone. And we'll have to weigh her.'

The nurse scooted away and disappeared into a drug cupboard.

With exquisite care, the Doc hoisted the baby, trailing tubing from her nose, her arm, her bladder. Her limbs hung limply from her body. Her bulk did not fill the Doc's cupped hands. He passed her, a small mammal in her nest of vinyl tubes, to Greta, and adjusted infant scales on the bench. 'Okay, Greta, just put her down carefully onto the scales.'

Greta paused before complying. She held the little simian body high in front of her chest, bent her head forward and breathed. The Doc watched, waiting. The old lady breathed audibly, rhythmically, speaking her soft sounds, sounds that ran and rumbled and murmured. She was speaking-singing to the sick infant.

Lorraine looked up at the Doc. *This break in treatment, this delay, it's taking precious time. The Doc will be annoyed ...*

But the Doc stood, silent, reverent as one in prayer or memory. He glanced at the heart monitor. The racing heart had slowed. The Doc's eyes widened.

He slid the brass counterweights, inching them along a metal bar until it was horizontal. The bar hovered above Ashweena's small frame. 'Only 3.017 kilos! How old did you say she is, Greta?'

'I never say. I not her mother. I don't know. She born in spring. Winter now. I reckon she get one year old in two, maybe three months.'

'She's awfully small, Greta. And she's awfully sick. We're going to give her very strong medicines through a tube in her arm.'

Lorraine handed the drugs to the Doc. He studied dosage schedules, scribbled some calculations and ordered doses. Lorraine drew up the medicines.

The two set up a second intravenous drip in Ashweena's other arm. The same silent concentration, the same frowning, grunting, breath-holding effort of tiny movements, studied then fluent. It seemed easier this time. The doctor could see the baby's vein. He indicated the fine blue line to Greta. 'Ashweena isn't so dry now. Her veins are fuller. I think she's a bit cooler too. The fluids in her drip are helping her. This second drip is for her antibiotics – medicines to kill the germs in her belly.'

Lorrraine took Ashweena's temperature: 'It's 37.8 degrees,' she said. 'Heart rate still fast – 190 per minute.'

The Doc squirted the three medicines into the bag of saline and set a gadget to drip feed medication at a fixed hourly rate.

The baby shat some more blood.

The red hand swept around the clock face. Greta watched the red hand. Her face was not grim.

The time was 4.45 in the afternoon. 'Lunchtime,' said the Doc. He left the room for a few minutes and returned with three plates of sandwiches. He went away again and brought back three mugs of tea.

The three ate and drank and watched the small frame on the large bed. Greta rose from her chair and leaned over the infant. A soft low sound, rhythmic, a patterned murmur, rumbled from the old lady's mouth. The soft sounds droned on, barely audible.

At length, a new sound broke the silence – the piping cry of a baby. Ashweena's eyes opened. Greta's face held close above the baby's, her voice chanting, chanting, keeping time with the rhythm and pace of the baby's crying.

The Doc watched the old lady and the baby. Greta's index finger rested on Ashweena's open palm. The baby's fingers closed around the larger one. The crying stopped, the eyes remained open, fixed on Greta.

The doctor said to the nurse, 'Those were tears. And that catheter is draining. Her kidneys are working.' To Greta he said: 'I think Ashweena is turning the corner. She's got a long way to go, but I think she's going to make it.'

'I say before she be okay, Doc. I say you fix her up okay.'

The baby's stools were still loose, but there was no further blood. By late afternoon, the diarrhoea had stopped. At six, Greta went outside and returned with Ashweena's mother, the younger woman, just a girl, her face fighting fear and the shame of failure. Her lips were moist. Greta said, 'This one, she Heloise, she Ashweena's mum.' The baby suckled hungrily then fell asleep.

Lorraine checked oxygen levels, pulse and temperature. She wrote them down, smiling. Urine flowed freely along the catheter. She struggled to suppress sudden tears. She hugged Greta and Heloise.

The Doc called the Flying Doctors and cancelled the mercy flight. He spoke into the phone, turning as he spoke, opening his face to the women in the room. He was smiling. 'We'll keep Ashweena here overnight. If she's better in the morning, she can go home.'

The Doc watched as Greta held the baby in her long thin arms. She held the baby high, a face width from her lips. The old lady crooned soft words in language, words to hold her safe.

The Doc watched and listened and trembled.

25. Playing with Each Other

Now the boys were seven years old they bathed without supervision. They loved the bath, a favourite adventure playground. Squeals of laughter, shouts and splashing reached Luisa in the kitchen where she was chopping vegetables.

The noise reached a new pitch, the hilarity enormous. Wiping her hands, curious, Luisa wandered to the bathroom doorway. Little of the bathwater remained in the tub; most of it lay on the floor. Some of the remainder splashed Luisa's sandals as she stood and watched: Jaffas and Carrots had a new game. New, that was, to the twins, but Luisa recognised it. Her small cousins used to play it too.

Jaffas pulled his brother's penis as hard as he could. Carrots did the same to Jaffas. Soapy hands slipped from small phalluses and as one lost his grip, he fell backwards, sending a further tide of bathwater from the tub onto the floor. The mutual disembowelling looked like murder, but Carrots and Jaffas were helpless with hilarity. They turned and noticed Luisa in the doorway. A pause, then, in wordless accord, they resumed the game, redoubling their attack.

Luisa entered the bathroom, took possession of the bathplug and exited. The game soon ended.

The boys were fascinated with their genitals: they touched them and talked about them endlessly. According to Luisa's child care book, this was normal. However, the book said nothing about their apparent attraction to each other's private parts. Was this a stage they would pass through and leave behind? Luisa was uncertain and uncomfortable. She didn't want to ignore it if it was a bad thing, but she didn't want to make her children feel bad about a normal thing. Maybe it was a good sign. She would ask Bernard: he was a male.

'Playing with themselves? All kids do it, Lou, all boys, that is.'

'But is it healthy to play with each other's, you know, *bulbuls*?'

'Never seen 'em do it. Wouldn't want to. You sure you're not imagining that, Lou?'

Luisa was sure, but she said no more. It was true, the boys didn't play that way around their father. But they were doing it more and more frequently when they were alone with her. Were they hiding something that was quite natural from Bernard or were they creating something specifically to exhibit to her?

These thoughts made Luisa feel more uncomfortable. Why would their father be angry? Why would the boys do something just to show her?

Thinking this way made Luisa feel dirty; they were just innocent little boys, weren't they? She realised that she would not be able to discuss feelings like these with Bernard. Nor with anyone, not even Baba. Especially not Baba, who taught her to keep her own feminine parts private. Special, somehow.

Luisa entered a spiral of anxious and guilty feelings. She wondered, 'Have I done something wrong and made my boys unnatural?'

And there was one more thing, a thing too shameful to speak of, something she didn't want to think about. 'Why can't I look away from it?'

26. Dirty Linen

Bernard did the laundry duties. He'd explain to anyone who asked how it was that he ironed and washed: 'Every man is good in one room of the house. Some are good in the kitchen, most are good in the shed, some – a lucky few – are good in the bedroom … I'm good in the laundry. I like washing and drying and sorting. I do the ironing and I'm better at it than Luisa.'

Luisa would blush and smile and agree. She blushed whenever Bernard touched on their intimate life with another. She saw how an outsider, invariably male, would grin at this laconic mock confession. She held their lovemaking close. *Secret, sacred, precious, private* – Luisa searched for the right word, then gave up the search. Their love was their own. Between themselves, Luisa and Bernard needed no words for it. Words would be for outsiders. Words could only contaminate this most private property.

Bernard recalled their first night together. Luisa had entered the suite and headed straight to a bedside lamp. She switched it on and turned and came to him.

Luisa loved to love in the light. Daybreak after that first night in the Grand saw her avid, adventurous. It became her pattern: ardent and exuberant, she'd kiss Bernard awake, caress him and bless his day.

Night times were different. Bernard happened to switch off the light and his excited woman became abruptly a scared child. It happened again the next time. Luisa was not (he understood) afraid of the dark – but *terrified* in the dark of sexual touch.

Bernard never asked. If Luisa was not saying, it was her secret; she'd have her reasons. 'Come here and cuddle, *hermosa*,' he'd say. In his arms Luisa would breathe more slowly and subside. She'd search for the little patch of naked scalp high on Bernard's head and touch it with her lips. *Buenos noches, mi querido.*

The bedside lamp became Luisa's signal to Bernard. He'd enter the bedroom at night, see the lamp glow and find his woman ready and eager. Afterwards, Luisa would smile and touch her fingertip to the bright pink spot on Bernard's scalp.

II

Throwing dirty clothes into the washer, Bernard noticed a stiffening and a sheen in the fabric of the front of Jaffas' pyjama pants. He sniffed and nodded.

Afterwards he said to Luisa, 'Those boys will hit puberty soon.'

'No,' said Luisa, 'They are only nine.'

'Well, Jaffas had a wet dream last night.'

'So, he wet his bed. That is not puberty.'

'That's not urine, Luisa. Take a sniff.'

She sniffed. Her eyebrows flew. Her stomach lurched. 'No!'

'Yes, Luisa. I was about that age when I started. The red PJs – they're Jaffas', aren't they?'

'Yes. But he is a little boy. He does not have even ten years ... it will be another six months before the boys will complete ten years.'

Luisa found herself scrutinising pyjamas. She discovered that Bernard wasn't mistaken. And Jaffas was not alone. It was happening to Carrots too.

Occasionally, she found the same sweet-smelling patches on sheets. She knew about it from Scripture: *And Onan spilled his seed upon the earth.* But Luisa was taken by surprise when both boys spilled their seed during the same night.

It became a pattern.

Both boys, at once. Was this a coincidence? Or did twins emit seed simultaneously just as a household of sisters would all menstruate together?

Luisa tried not to think about it too much. Bernard simply said it was normal. He continued to wash their clothes and he made no further remark.

One evening, Luisa nearly walked in on them. She saw what they were doing and she stopped at the doorway. The boys were intent on each other and they did not see her.

Luisa stepped quietly backward, disturbed, ashamed. It wasn't just what they were doing; it was her own feeling, something she would never put into words.

In the morning, while they were at school, she collected their underthings. They were still sticky. She lifted them up and looked vacantly at them. On an impulse she sniffed them and was overtaken by a trembling sort of excitement. She ran to the laundry and dropped the soiled things into the basket. She hurried outside and took great gulps of air. She retched violently.

Much later she consulted the web. She googled 'identical twins, sexual development' and found a good deal of information but little enlightenment. Were her sons gay? Would they graduate from sexual play to incest? 'Twincest', as some called it?

The incidence of homosexuality between co-twins was not particularly high. However, if one twin was gay, there was about a fifty per cent chance the second would be gay also. Of incest between co-twins, Luisa found no research reports, and felt relieved. But there were anecdotal reports. These played on her mind.

Flicking fearfully through the items thrown up by Google, Luisa found an essay by French writer Michel Tournier. *Each identical co-twin*, he wrote, *has an innate, prophetic, infallible knowledge of the other's body and nervous system. The two partners are immediately and congenitally attracted to each other. Thus, to a twin, mating with a non-twin partner seems like a risky and rather scandalous adventure.*

Luisa read of a real-life twin who wrote to Tournier: *Perfect twinship is surely an aphrodisiac and a spur to incest. Incest makes normal love pale by comparison.*

Luisa was distressed. She turned to Salome, the speech therapist, the one professional who had known and worked with her twins over a lengthy time.

Salome said, 'Luisa, you'd know that all little boys explore their bodies and play with them; and they always involve their brothers in the play. Your boys are approaching puberty now and they can experience real physiological arousal and climax. None of this points to a gender preference. Instead, between twins, it points to their extreme intimacy. They are literally two halves of a whole. You've told me yourself how they share everything. If one of them has a treat, unless he shares it with the other he has not had it in completeness. Now they are sharing sexual sensation.'

Luisa felt reassured – to a degree. So, all very little boys did it and shared this play. But why were her boys still doing it at nearly ten years old? And why did they seem to hide it from Bernard but display it to her?

27. The Stealer and the Stolen

My head will be right, doing this good thing. I wanted two kids, but one's better than none. It's the right thing to do, to bring kids, to steal them and replace kids stolen from blackfellas. I'm not heartless, not really. I'm not like the coppers that snatched blackfella kids away from their brothers and sisters; these two are brothers, twins by the looks of them. If the other one hadn't got away they'd have had each other for company. It's not my fault. Anyway, it's not their happiness that's my mission.

I've got to forget about them, their feelings. Got to focus on my mission, keep this perfect clarity. What I need is hubris. 'The Redeemer exhibits hubris' – that's what Wikipedia calls it. Have to hang on to this hubris.

History will remember me. I'm going to make History; I'm repairing History. People will read about me in Wikipedia: I'm a Golem. I am the One, the Redeemer. I've been studying History; I've read up on everything. It's all in Wikipedia.

I've been chosen to correct the wrongs that whitefellas have done. We stole kids from blackfellas. We did it, we never said sorry until it was too late. Broke their hearts, mums without their kids, kids without their brothers and sisters. The blackfellas copped it and we never made it up to them. That's all past, it's History.

When you pop acid your mind expands; you see how colour is a liar – all the colours explode and shift and slip. I saw red blackfellas, black whitefellas; green people turning purple, yellow, all colours. The Truth came to me when I was doing acid: colour, that's the secret of this country, the hidden secret, the secret of black and white.

I've travelled to the blackfellas' country, I've lived there among the broken families. The kids have grown up, had kids of their own, grandkids. But every generation's the same, still broken. I've been with them, in country and on the streets here in the city, in the shelters. They'll share whatever they've got, smokes, grog, ganja. Those people don't complain, they don't talk about revenge. Blackfellas ought to hate us but they don't.

They don't talk much to whitefellas, but I know, I see the wrong they've lived through. I'm the one whitefella that sees the Truth. I'm the One, the only One.

It's time for justice.

No one's doing anything about it but me. History will recognise me: I'm a Golem, like the avenger who smashed the persecutors in Prague. I know all about Prague – Smetana's country.

I found the right expression for what I am in Wikipedia: a Golem is hewn from earth, moulded in clay. Pure power and purpose. No conscience: when you're a Golem, the ordinary laws don't apply to you; you carry out your commands, you're a machine for justice. Your head knows one thing – what you have to do: a wrong has been done to the defenceless and you're going to right it, no matter who's in your way.

Hubris, that means the Courage of Destiny, the way of the Golem. The Golem's way, that's my way.

People say drugs destroy. Those 'experts' haven't tried what I've used; they wouldn't know. When I was snorting PCP, I found my path. Clarity. Clarity and hubris. When I concentrate, I can forget distractions. I can focus on my mission and forget that these kids have got a mother too … I can't be distracted by that. Need to keep focus.

I'm clean now, off everything, but the Truth is still with me. It's my mission. A Golem goes beyond and rises above. I've been chosen because I am the one that knows and cares, I'm the one who can do it.

I've been planning my move into History all the time I was inside. I've been clean ever since Remand. Did it hard – no uppers, no downers, nothing. Bloody tough way to get my head right. But I'm free now.

I meditate and my mind is the ocean, it's the Cosmos. Truth grows in me, it washes through me and flows in my acts and my words. It washes away softness. Kindness to the wrongdoers isn't kindness, it's weakness. A Golem hasn't got weaknesses. My destiny calls me to harden up.

My head is right, I have the Truth, I know I've been chosen, I know my mission: I'm the Saviour of the black people …

I kept all my allowance, I've got plenty for petrol and food. Mum's given me the car so I can go fishing. I told her I'm off the drugs, getting away from the scene here, going bush for a couple of weeks to get my head right. Mum copped that. I knew she'd believe it; she's wanted to believe that ever since I was a kid and I started smoking dope.

I've come out clean and I'm going to give her some joy. At last. Broke her heart when I dropped out of the Conservatorium. Mum always believed I'd be a great composer. Broke her heart then, broke it again every time they called her to the hospital, every time I got arrested. When they led me away after the judge passed sentence, I saw Mum's face. It sort of collapsed, just folded inwards. I looked at her and she was a crushed flower. Here I was, Mum's great composer, a crim, a pusher and an addict.

I'll make one mother sad, okay, but I'll make two happy – Greta and my one Mum.

She ought to feel proud. That's if I could tell her what I'm doing. If she knew that her boy was the Redeemer.

II

Jaffas sat for a moment, stunned. Mami had warned them about this. A man had snatched him and locked him in his car! But Jaffas hadn't done anything wrong; he didn't talk to the man, he hadn't accepted sweets from him. This could not be.

He gathered his thoughts. He must not let this happen. He shouted with all his force, 'Stop! Let me go!'

Climbing onto his knees on the back seat, he looked through the rear window. He saw Carrots running after the car with his mouth open, screaming words Jaffas could not hear. Jaffas banged the window with his hands, but the small slapping sounds of flesh and bone on plate glass did not carry.

The car turned a corner and Jaffas did not see Carrots again.

He screamed louder: 'Let me out! Take me back! Take me back to my brother!'

The car kept going and the man did not answer. Jaffas threw himself against the car door, wrenching the handle. The door did not open. He tried a second time, a third. Still the door did not respond. He rushed to the opposite door and pulled the handle upwards with all his force. Nothing yielded. Jaffas tried again in a frenzy, now screaming, now subsiding into helpless sobbing, now screaming again hoarsely. His nose streamed, his throat burned. His body was strange to him.

The door would not open. He kicked at it in fury and hurt his foot. He kept kicking, kicking with both feet until he felt his bones were broken.

Near his broken feet lay the soccer ball. He picked it up and held it with both hands. He stood behind the man driving and smashed the ball against the back of the man's head. When the car swerved off course then back, Jaffas lost his footing and the ball tumbled into the front of the car.

The man drove on without turning his head. Jaffas saw he was wearing headphones. He reached forward and grabbed at them, tearing them from the man's ears. 'Let me out! Take me back to my brother!'

He was possessed. He had been stolen, a thing not possible. He knew he was not himself. He was bad, he was crazed, he embraced madness, he would not be a good boy, the world was wrong. It was wrong to shout at a grown up, it was wrong to hurt the car, everything was wrong. He would not stop. He had even tried to hurt the man. Jaffas knew he was a bad person now. Not himself, not Jaffas. A fighting, fractured person, torn off.

But this man was a rock, something that did not move or speak or feel.

Jaffas breathed hard, he heard powerful thumping in his chest, his eyes stung. He lashed the back of the man's head and shoulders with both hands, punching repeatedly at his ears. He would make those ears hear – with the thumping in his chest and with his voice that was loud and rude. Jaffas punched hard with his strong left hand, then his right. The man of stone ducked his head, the rock had moved. Jaffas' knuckles struck bone. Now his hands felt broken. That was right, it was truth.

The man ducked his head again and this time yelled and turned around. The car swerved violently to the left. The man swore and corrected, wrenching the steering wheel, and the car headed fast towards oncoming traffic.

He struggled with the steering. Headlights on high beam blinded him, car horns blared. He swore again fiercely, hit the brakes and tore at the wheel.

II

Shit. This kid's not happy. He bloody would have been if his bloody brother hadn't got away. It's not my fault. Fuck, my ears hurt!

When Jaffas came to consciousness, he could not move. His head hurt. He smelled urine. His pants were wet. He tried to turn his head and he gagged. He tasted vomit.

Jaffas could not move his arms. Something burned his wrists when he tried to move them. His ankles were tied tightly together. He was lying on the back seat of a car. The darkness outside was a different darkness – there were no street lights, no shop windows, little traffic.

From time to time, headlights flashed as cars passed in the opposite direction. He saw the branches of trees, suddenly dark grey in a milky sky, then blackness. When there were no cars, Jaffas could see stars against the blackness.

There was the humming of the engine, and over it, loud music from a CD. Insistent, pounding rhythms filled the car. The sounds vibrated in Jaffas' chest. He felt the throbbing phrases of orchestral music, blunt and deep, echoes of another place. His father sometimes played this music, but not this loud. It was 'The Ride of the Valkyries'.

Jaffas thought of his parents and of home. Every thought led his mind to Carrots. His eyes filled with tears and he wanted to wipe them. But his hands could not move and his wrists burned.

The sounds of Wagner swelled and surged, towering tides of energy crashing to crescendo. In his grief, Jaffas, himself seething with passion, surfed the tides of grief. His head hurt. He remembered nothing of the skidding, spinning of the car that had flung him headfirst against the door pillar.

The driver, struggling to tame the vehicle in its wild careering, had not lost consciousness. He had been wearing a seatbelt while the boy was unrestrained.

The man's headphones were broken. He cursed; he would have to play the CD.

Jaffas needed the man to bring him back to his brother. He would ask the man nicely: 'Man, will you please take me home now. I want my brother.'

No answer.

'Man, man! Please take me home. PLEASE!'

He heard the man speak. Nothing about home, nothing about going back to Carrots. The voice was wooden: 'There's chocolate milk. Do you want to drink? I'll stop the car if you want to drink.'

Jaffas' mouth was dry. His throat hurt. He didn't want chocolate milk, he wanted his brother. He would say yes; it was a polite thing to say. Politeness might help. 'Yes please, man.'

The man brought the car to a stop. He got out, walked around to the near-side rear door and opened it. Cold air bit into Jaffas' face. He made to jump from the car. He would run and hide. He was a fast runner and the man would not be able to catch him. He would hide behind one of the big trees he had glimpsed, flashing past in the dark. But Jaffas' feet did not move in their tight bonds. He had believed that desire must be stronger than ties of cord. He was shocked.

The man sat the boy's small frame upright and inserted a straw between his lips. He reopened the carton of flavoured milk and helped the boy to drink. The cool milk soothed Jaffas' throat. He drank deeply and drained the carton. He looked up at the man's frowning face. Jaffas searched for kindness but found nothing. The face was closed tight. The eyes did not see the frightened child.

Jaffas saw the man's mouth move. He said, 'You hear this, son. You're going to a good place. You're gunna be with good people. And you're gunna keep everything secret – you won't tell anybody where you're from, you won't talk about your family or your brother.' The wooden voice slowed and hardened. 'You won't say anything because if you do, I'll go back and *I'll kill your brother!* Get me?'

Jaffas was terrified of saying the wrong thing. He looked at the man's face, alive now with intensity, and he trembled. In the light from the ceiling, he noticed a small goatee. The hair was ginger, like the colour of Carrots' hair. He felt a large ball of gathering sadness in his throat and wanted to cry.

The man took away the empty carton and pushed the boy onto his side. Jaffas was quiet, thinking of Carrots. The man covered the small, silent body with a rug and returned to the driver's seat. Jaffas thought he would say a polite 'thank you', but first he wanted to keep Carrots in his mind. It was dark, Carrots would be in bed. Tonight the two would not cuddle and fall asleep together. Jaffas knew he would not sleep without Carrots close to him.

II

Jaffas was deeply asleep when the car stopped for fuel in Mildura. He was asleep still at Burra when the car stopped for a second time at a service station. The man got out. Jaffas did not stir. The man went to fill his tank, but a woman came out of the office and took the pump from his hands and filled for him. She saw the boy, sleeping beneath the covers.

'Gorgeous red hair. Same as your little beard. That's a goatee, isn't it?' The man's hand moved quickly to his whiskers.

'How old is your boy?'

How old is he? How should I know? He made a guess, trying to sound casual: 'Nine … Yeah, his twin brother's got the same hair. Same as him and me.' *Shit, why did I say that? Should have kept my mouth shut.*

He paid with cash and drove around the corner to the bakery. The baker looked up as he entered by the side door. 'I'll take a loaf of sliced white and couple of those bacon and cheese rolls.' He saw a tray of sweet buns and he bought some as well. He paid and drove away.

The copper hills of Burra were great dark shapes in the pre-dawn. The hills loomed, silent prehistoric forms, elephantine. *We're all alike, the mastodon and the brontosaurus and me – the Golem. Strong like the earth, silent, pure brute power.*

He parked again, away from the town, away from the street lights. He took out his bag of toiletries from the car boot. From the bag he took a cut-throat razor. He opened the blade and looked around. The road was empty. His hand shook. He bent forward over the sleeping boy, a look of grim purpose on his face, the open blade in his hand.

He still hoped he'd be in Leigh Creek before noon. Only twenty minutes beyond the township, he'd be at Greta's. She didn't like the police. There'd be no trouble. No worries at all.

28. Bereft

Carrots opened his eyes and groped around his bed. He felt no one. Abruptly, he sat upright and scanned the room. Then he remembered: incredibly, Jaffas was not there.

Carrots ran out to the street – no Jaffas, no white car, no thin man with a red goatee. *Perhaps around the corner?* He ran hard to the corner – nothing.

Yesterday they were two. This morning, one.

'Carrots! Carrots! There you are! What are you doing outside? *Don't you understand – it's not safe!*'

Luisa, in her dressing gown, had run onto the street, her hair unbrushed, her face puffy from weeping, shouting her grief, her pain, her anger. Luisa running, running, grabbing her son, tackling him, dragging him inside.

'Never do that again. *Never* go outside alone. Never!'

Bernard, more composed, said, 'We need a guard dog.'

All that morning Carrots remained silent. The house was quiet, tense. Luisa watched the telephone, waiting. Bernard sat slumped, his hand over his mouth. He gazed at Carrots and at his wife, afraid to speak, to say a wrong word. In all the quiet, no one wondered about Carrots' silence. It was of a piece with the house – stunned, mute.

At mid-morning, Luisa looked up from the telephone and saw her child as through a fog – *who is this?* Finally she spoke: '*Tienes hambre, mi amor?*'*

He shook his head. She looked at him for a while. Heaviness overcame her and she slumped. Her hair hung over her face, a black curtain.

A policeman and a policewoman came to interview Carrots as principal witness. 'Tell us what you saw, young fella.'

The boy would not look at the policeman.

---

*   Are you hungry, my love?

The woman officer tried. She sat opposite him, spoke softly, rested a hand on his knee. 'What did the man look like, Carrots?'

No answer. She spoke again, speaking to his loss. 'Tell us, Carrots; tell me … so we can find Jaffas and bring him back.' Too tired, too old, deeply weary, the boy brought forth no sound from his throat.

A time passed. Distant from him a woman's voice floated, high, soft, kindly as song. His mother's voice? The police lady's voice? The voice floated where he used to be, where life with Jaffas had rippled and run and bubbled and burst.

Carrots was not now in sweetness or song. His mouth a dry cave. No words.

The police lady showed him photographs. She asked him to point to one that looked like the man who stole Jaffas. None of the photos of suspects looked like that man. He shook his head.

Next the officer showed him drawings of pairs of men. 'Point to the one who looks more like the man who took your brother, Carrots.' She showed him a tall man and a short man. Carrots pointed to the tall man.

Next, a fat man and a thin one. Carrots pointed to the thin one.

As the officer went through her couples, Carrots' choices created an identikit of a young adult male, red-headed, a little over average height, slim, wearing torn jeans and a small ginger goatee. A cowboy's Stetson covered his hair.

II

Carrots does not speak. He hasn't spoken since his brother disappeared. He does not sleep for a long time; he lies and whimpers, his face to the wall through the night.

No one sleeps well. His mother creeps into his bed and puts her arms around him. He stops crying, turns, feels the arms, the body, hears the voice – wrong arms, wrong body, wrong voice. He turns to the wall and breathes his soft syllables of despair.

His last words, shouted words, frantic, were of his brother, of the theft of his brother.

'Mami! Papi! Emergency! *Emergency!* The man took us … I ran away … *He took Jaffas! THE MAN TOOK HIM AND THEY'VE GONE!'*

Carrots pulled at his mother's arm, dragged her outside, out of the house into the street.

The street was empty.

The boy – crying, screaming, incoherent – pushed his mother, pulled her down the street in the direction the man took his brother. Luisa, seeing nothing, dreading all, was at a loss. She stood immobile while the small boy, bereft, gasping now, now sobbing, ran at his mother, lashing her with his hands, punching, battering her.

Carrots saw. He told, and they did not act. They did not stop the thief. They did not bring Jaffas back.

Words were traitors. Words failed. Speech failed.

Carrots will speak no more.

29. Sahara

A week later, Bernard saw the ad in a café window. A young couple had a dog to give away. Dogs were not allowed in their flats. The dog was called Sahara.

Bernard said, 'Why don't you check it out, Lou? See if he'll do to guard Carrots. If we have a dog to protect him, then we can go searching for Jaffas. And for that red-headed bastard who took him.'

Luisa didn't look up. Her voice was flat. 'Where can we search? How can we find him if the police can't?'

'Lou, the police will do what they know, but only we know his looks, his body, his walk. We have to search for him, but first we need a dog.'

Luisa visited the couple in their small apartment. They had hidden the dog as long as they could, but she gave them away with her shrill barking. Sahara barked at Luisa. She barked at everyone, at everything. The bark had a yapping quality that would drive people mad. It was something of a yelp, with that note of sudden alarm. Unusually for such a small dog, Sahara's bark had an impressive growling component. This was a dog whose language was confined to aggression and menace, out of all proportion to her miserable size.

All of this cacophony from such a skinny, low-slung creature. Sahara pleased Luisa at first sight. This hound would deter any unwelcome visitor when Carrots was home alone. Low to the ground, thin with a sandy coat, Sahara had a dark grey smudge at the tip of her tail and another around her nose. The tail whipped and waved in short, sharp movements. Luisa remembered the rats that scavenged and hunted in her *barrio* back home. With her unattractive black snout and her yellow teeth that were surprisingly large when bared (as they very often were), Sahara was not an attractive dog. Luisa thought, *You are not truly beautiful; to say truth, you are truly ugly.* Luisa thanked the young couple and took their dog.

As the young man handed her the leash, he said, 'She's a Staffordshire terrier-whippet cross.'

You *look* cross, thought Luisa.

She realised she had not prepared Carrots for the new member of the household. As she opened the door, she called to him. 'Carrots, I've got a surprise for you. A dog to keep you … to keep us company.'

Carrots looked at the dog then looked away. He said nothing. Sahara did not bark or run at Carrots. She licked his bare feet.

Sahara knitted closely and quickly to Carrots. She was drawn to the silent child who neither shrank from her nor sought to win her. When Carrots slipped food from his dinner plate to Sahara under the dinner table, the dog was won. Sahara became Carrots' shadow, erupting when outsiders approached.

The dog showed a quick, cowardly nipping proclivity. She specialised in cyclists, running at them, barking, snarling, frequently biting. She never drew blood, a small mercy which would save her on more than one occasion from the ranger and the pound.

Luisa walked Sahara in the park. Once off the leash, she'd socialise with other dogs. The newcomer would sniff Sahara's anal glands, Sahara would make as if to reciprocate, then suddenly bite the stranger on the bum. She won no friends in the park; all dogs, great and small, shied away after the first biting.

You are the Amalekite, Sahara; you fall upon them from the rear.

No one liked the dog, Luisa realised. She tried to like Sahara herself, with imperfect success. She recognised a creature that had lost home and family, an individual that no one understood. Luisa realised that Sahara's earlier owners would have been relieved to be rid of the problem dog. She menaced everyone but the members of her new household. And she protected Carrots fiercely.

Door-to-door salesmen, canvassers for charities, the postman, the paper boy, the census taker, the lady who read the meter – Sahara greeted all with clamour and bared teeth. All left in a hurry. Luisa puzzled about the dog's antisocial habits. *Wherefore is there no peace unto you, dog? What is your problem?*

She took Sahara to be vaccinated. In the vet's waiting room Sahara leapt at the small spaniel that sat in the lap of a blue-haired old lady. Luisa took Sahara outside and waited in the street for her appointment. She didn't need to describe Sahara's behaviour to the vet; she snarled and barked and darted at his ankles. The vet said, 'This is a dog that has been abused. She expects more abuse. She doesn't trust humans.'

'Perfect,' said Luisa.

'She doesn't need to be so keyed-up, so touchy ...'

'Yes she does,' said Luisa.

'I mean, we could, if you wished, prescribe a selective serotonin reuptake inhibitor to control her aggression.'

'No thank you. We need her aggression.'

'That's the other consideration, the safety of yourselves and your child. Are you safe with the dog in the house?'

'Yes. The dog is calm with us. She loves our son. He is … attached to Sahara.'

30. Doc's New Job

Leigh Creek was a mining town. Its residents were whitefella miners and their families. The Doc did not stay long in the town. It wasn't on account of his eccentricity: in the bush, people expected a doctor would be a bit different. They'd had one who wore a turban and another who was from Nigeria. No, people liked the Doc. He was old, but he was friendly and informal and interested.

The Doc left the Leigh Creek Clinic to work with Aboriginal people in Copley. He was the one who saved blackfella kids from diarrhoea and they wanted him to themselves, in their own health centre. Copley never had doctors, only a bush nursing clinic. The nurse welcomed the Doc. Her own position remained secure; she'd share the workload – which was light – and she secretly fancied the doctor.

The Doc gave notice to his employers at Leigh Creek and waited for them to find a replacement. They appointed a new doctor, a lady from Hyderabad. She had been a gynaecological surgeon in India. She wore a colourful sari and had a tiny diamond in her nose.

The new job suited the Doc. The pace of life had been gentle enough in Leigh Creek. There his patients had been the working well. In Copley, they were the unemployed unwell. He couldn't cure them; he didn't have the language – the words, the spiritual authority – to address their true malaise. The Doc came to understand their belief that there was a spiritual or a societal wrong that created ill-being. Once they became unwell, medicine – his medicine – could only patch people up.

Both the Doc and the indigenous people, the Adnyamthanha, saw the limitations of modern health practices. The Doc saw his mission as prevention, one arena where the locals were agnostic and open to suggestion.

He worked at the clinic from mid-morning to noon and a couple of hours from mid-afternoon. The rest of his time he devoted to his research. He conducted this at the library in the Leigh Creek Area School. The library held no medical texts or journals but it did have free unlimited internet. And a small treasury of books on Adnyamthanha Dreaming. The Doc found a substantial section on local history and pre-history, and works by the early whitefella anthropologists who described the traditional life of the Rock People in the days before the mine.

The Doc read about bush tucker. He was impressed and surprised to discover native pears and oranges, a sort of sweet potato, and a wheat-like grass. He read about bush medicines. He was intrigued to read of a harlequin mistletoe whose leaves were used for their appetite-suppressant qualities.

He read Dreaming stories. These he read and re-read, sensing within them an essence. The stories seemed simple, like children's stories, like Bible stories and the myths of the Greeks and Romans.

Yes, they were like children's stories; was that their essence? Perhaps, he speculated, these were not merely stories for children but were, in fact, stories connecting children with their elders. As older people told and re-told them to the children, danced and painted the same stories, the stories formed them all, connecting all to a time beyond time.

Without the Dreaming, people fell sick. To remain healthy, they needed their stories. That was the Doc's research hypothesis. He dredged and drained the library's books. Through inter-library loans, he obtained texts from city libraries. He searched the Net.

He accumulated knowledge but he knew he lacked understanding.

He needed a person with standing in the Law. It would be an elder. The person he knew was Greta.

He visited her at her house. He had news for her and he hoped she'd tell him about the emu, *warraita*, in the Dreamtime.

'Greta, will you tell me about *warraita*?'

She looked up, animated. She spoke of her totem. The old woman pronounced the word *warraiti*. All the books spelled it with a final 'a', but Greta spoke it as she knew it, as she loved it.

While she told her story, Greta trembled. Her old lady's voice gained strength, ringing with the forces of creation. Her thin hands flapped, enacting flight. Her fingers danced the gait of the flightless bird. From eager face to drumming feet, Greta's body joined her spirit in the telling.

The Doc's chest pounded. He felt his own legs drumming as he sat on the ground, watching and listening to storytelling that bordered on ecstasy. Captured by the story, he was with *warraiti*, with Greta, absorbed in the Dreaming; he was with her as she was formed and transformed by the storytelling.

The story filled his desiccated being with sap. He felt the stories capture him, carry him far from his familiar pale self – his customary greys and off-whites, now scarlet, purple, black – in the throes of the tale. He knew he hadn't felt alive like this since he was a small boy …

31. In the Flinders Ranges

Greta heard the sound of a car engine, a small one, not diesel, not her son's Toyota. She looked through the window and saw a white car, a small 2WD. The driver got out, a whitefella. Greta recognised the tattoo of *warraiti* on his right shoulder. She stood in the doorway in her thin lilac housecoat. The man with the emu tattoo looked up and grinned. Same old Greta. Same white hair, skinny arms and skinny legs. A shaky old girl, but she still had that steady way of looking at you. Those old froggy eyes that seemed to look into you.

The man did not come straight to the house. He opened the back door of the car, leaned forward and said something. No answer. He spoke again and waited. When there was no reply, he straightened and shrugged.

He turned and walked to the house. He threw his arms around Greta. The old lady patted his head with her thin hand and looked at him searchingly. 'How you going, Jimmy?' Only Greta called him Jimmy. He was Wilberforce James Reynolds. Everyone else called him Wilbur.

'I'm good, Greta. I've brought my boy. He's asleep in the car.'

'You got a son? How old?'

Shit! How old was he? 'Ah ... he's ten. Good sleeper.'

Greta walked to the car and looked inside. There, under a blanket, was a child. Only the head was visible. The face was very white. His scalp was almost hairless. Greta saw an occasional wisp and whisker of bright orange hair, like her visitor's little beard. She touched the boy's head. He did not stir.

The lined face softened. She swallowed and said nothing for a moment. Her hands trembled as she turned again to her visitor. 'You got ganja with you?'

A shake of the head. Greta, not satisfied, searched his face.

'No, Greta, honest.'

'Any other drugs? ... Grog?'

'No, Greta. I've been away, been locked up – the Big House – long time. I'm clean. No grog, no drugs, nothing.'

The muscles around Greta's mouth worked. 'It was bad last time, Jimmy. You and my grandsons. They never get off it. The young one, he gone. Swallowed too much drugs, he stop breathing. You hear about that?'

'No.' Ashamed, the man lowered his head. 'I'm sorry. I'm sorry, Greta.'

'Come into the house. Bring your boy. Put him on the lounge.'

Greta looked at the child, his thin frame, his rough-shaved scalp and his pale face.

'What happen to his hair, Jimmy?'

'Ah … cancer. He had to have chemo. He had cancer – cancer of the balls. Pardon my language, Greta. He's better now, but. They've cured him.'

Greta said nothing, her face a silent interrogation.

Wilbur turned his face from Greta, then carried the boy into the house and laid him on Greta's couch. The child did not stir.

Wilbur looked at his watch. It was noon. He had taken the boy at six the previous evening. He made some calculations: eighteen hours. More, allowing for the time difference between Victoria and South Australia.

He did not want to face Greta.

I've got a destiny that's been revealed to me – to replace old Greta's stolen sons. My vision was two kids, but I only brought one. Now she tells me she's lost a grandson, and she blames me because of my drugs. And this kid, he's sleeping too much and too deep, because I drugged him.

The man started to cry. Greta touched his bent head then withdrew her hand. She sat him at the table and said nothing. She boiled a kettle and took damper from the fridge. She made tea for them both, buttered a slice of damper and passed it to the weeping man.

She buttered a second slice and covered it thickly with jam. 'That for your boy. When he wake up. His face very white. And he sweating. And his pants is wet. He alright?'

'Why wouldn't he be?'

The man saw visions of police, an inquest, more time away in the Big House. Much more time. 'Nah, he's okay. Just tired from the drive. He'll be good after a while.'

Greta looked steadily at Jimmy. He knew he had to say something. He spoke fast. He told her the story he had rehearsed, told

Greta how the boy's mother had deserted them, how the boy went off his head with grief and made up stories, how he, Jimmy, knew the boy needed a woman's caring. He spoke quickly, filling the space between them with words. Now he stopped abruptly. His mouth was dry.

Greta looked at her guest. After a while she asked, 'What his name?'

What was his name? He thought for a frantic moment. *John Cleese ... corked hats ... the Department of Philosophy ...* 'Bruce. His name's Bruce.'

The old lady sighed. She said, 'You got a mobile phone?'

'Yes.' He went outside to the car and returned, carrying a soccer ball.

'I need phone, not ball!'

'Yeah, sorry Greta. The ball's for, er, Bruce. He likes soccer. Here's me mobile, here.'

'Dial this number.' The old lady read out the number from a magnet on the fridge. The man dialled. 'I'll talk. Give to me.'

Greta took the phone and spoke. 'We got a boy here. Little fella. Got no hair. Won't wake up. Need you to come up home, take a look at him.'

Jimmy looked up, alarmed.

The old lady was nodding. 'Yeah, I worried.' She said goodbye and handed back the phone. 'This boy need doctor. Doc going be here soon. Check him up. Doc say ten minutes, maybe less.'

The man rose to his feet. He looked at his watch. 'I'm going outside, Greta. I need a smoke. I'm feelin' pretty upset ... His mum. Your grandson ... you know, everything... Been a long drive, a long night.'

He walked out of the house and kept going. He walked into the scrub. He climbed a small hill and kept walking. After a while he sat down and took out a pack of cigarettes. He patted his pockets for his lighter. It wasn't there. He emptied his pockets. There was his mother's bottle of valium, some coins, his wallet. No lighter.

Lost me lighter. Got only one of those kids. Now they'll fret like buggery. And this one – he might die. And if he lives he might tell … everything.

The man sat down and started to cry again.

A couple of minutes later he jumped to his feet and started to smack his thighs, his buttocks. He pulled down his trousers, wrenched them over his shoes and belted the ants that crawled everywhere. He surveyed his thighs and lower abdomen and his genitals. Well after he'd killed all the ants, he belted and thwacked his trousers, again and again, against a tree trunk. Breathless, he stopped.

Through the quiet bush, he heard the sound of a diesel motor. An old Toyota troop carrier pulled up outside Greta's house. The Doc got out and walked to the door, carrying a black bag. The door opened and the old bloke went inside. Ten minutes later he came out and walked into the scrub in the direction taken by the younger man. He called out, 'Jimmy!'

There was no answer. He breasted the hill and was about to call again when he sighted the man. He walked down the slope and said, 'I'm the Doc. I need you to help me with some facts. When did he fall asleep?'

The old man was short, almost completely bald. There was white stubble on his chin. There was no accusation in his voice. He looked oldish, nowhere near as old as Greta, and milder somehow, not intimidating. The younger man decided to trust him.

He felt a sudden urge to confess. 'Sometimes I do a right thing the wrong way.' The young man's hands held his hat, worked at it, rolling it up like a crepe, unrolling it. The Doc's eyes followed the restless hands. He waited, his eyes narrowing.

Abruptly, Wilbur put the hat to one side. He'd resist the urge, revert instead to the old addict's habit of rationing the truth shrewdly. 'We left home in Melbourne about six last night. He was asleep before we were out of town …'

128

'He's got a bruise on his left temple. How did he get that, Jimmy?'

'Wilbur. Only Greta calls me Jimmy … The car took a skid and he hit the side of his head and he's been asleep since.'

The doctor nodded. 'The child has concussion. There's bruising on the temple and around the right eye. The unconsciousness means the brain is bruised. But the good news is the boy is rouseable.'

'How do you mean?'

'He stirs and he opens his eyes when I speak loudly into his ears. He can give my hand a bit of a squeeze when I tell him to. But he doesn't speak. What's his speech like normally? Does he talk alright?'

The doctor waited.

Can he talk? Can he what! He fucking near deafened me in the car. 'Yeah, he can talk alright. He hasn't spoken since he hit his head and went to sleep, but.'

The doctor said nothing. The younger man followed the doctor's gaze. What was he looking at?

The old man leaned down and picked up the bottle of valium tablets from the ground. He read the label. 'Whose are these? Who is Robyn Reynolds?'

'Me Mum. They're me Mum's. I don't take them. I don't use anything, not now. I only give the kid a dose if we're gunna be driving through the night. Otherwise he won't sleep. I gave him a bit of valium last night …' Wilbur's voice faltered and failed.

'How much did he have?'

'Ah, two tablets. Yeah, two.'

The doctor's eyebrows shot upward. The younger man noticed that the right eyebrow was much shorter than the left. 'Ten milligrams! That's five times the proper dose for a child of his weight. Valium has a long half-life. That's another reason he's drowsy. And sweaty. It lowers his blood pressure.'

'He's gunna be okay?'

'I hope so … Wilbur. It's a good sign that I can rouse him. But I'm puzzled about him not speaking.'

32. Awake

When the two men returned to the house, they found Greta sitting on the bed, cradling the boy's head against her chest. The boy's eyelids flickered. The eyes opened. An old face, lined, black, looked back into Jaffas'. A warm dry hand cradled his cheek. The boy's eyes closed.

Greta held a mug of cocoa and fed him with a teaspoon. Between spoons of cocoa, the boy slept. Each time Greta introduced the spoon, he swallowed. He did not speak. Greta did not speak to him.

The doctor watched the old woman, noting her patience, the tactful way she touched the spoon to the boy's cheek, moving it slightly upwards then downwards to stimulate him. The small mouth opened and Greta insinuated the spoon, tilting it to the spilling point, allowing warm cocoa to trickle towards the pharynx. All the while, she supported the recumbent spine, keeping the neck semi-erect to prevent gagging. The old lady concentrated on the child, the old man watched Greta. The younger man was forgotten.

The old lady sang low sounds to the sleeping child, words driving, rolling, tumbling, a bridge of words to make a child safe. A moment of grace. The Doc felt a pang, something half-remembered, lost.

Teaspoon by teaspoon, Greta continued to feed him. For some moments Greta held the child, gazing at him. A low sound, a rumble, a moan, a sigh, a pause, a soft gasp, sounds tumbling one after another, rhythmically, on, on, yearning sounds, a sort of threnody.

The men watched, listening; the song issued from Greta as she sang to the child in language, sang *at* him, sang him to health and strength.

She sighed and looked up. The doctor smiled at her and she smiled back. 'He's improved, but he needs watching. His brain is bruised. It might bleed, even now.' The doctor looked around, addressing both adults: 'You'll need to wake him every thirty minutes.'

The younger man fidgeted. The Doc looked at him briefly. He turned to Greta. 'Keep giving him fluid. Any fluid, anything wet. Call me if you can't wake him. I'll be back to see him in the morning, early.'

Greta lay the boy down and removed his trousers. She went to a chipboard lowboy and opened a drawer. She took a pair of bright red board shorts from the drawer and spoke. 'Jimmy, his pants wet. Take off wet ones. Put these on him. Dry ones.'

She watched her visitor as he pulled the red shorts up over the hips of the sleeping boy.

'You remember those ones? They belong to young fella, we lost 'im, you know, my grandson.' She did not mention her grandson's name.

Bowing his head, standing with his back to the old woman, the man did as he was bid. It was some time before he turned around. The doctor had gone. He looked at Greta and he tried to speak. 'I'm sorry, Greta.' The words were unclear. His voice was low and thick. He cleared his throat and said, 'If the kid … if you're gunna let him sleep here in your room, I'll get out of your way. I've got me swag. Alright for me to camp in the kitchen?'

Greta nodded.

It would be she who would wake the child every thirty minutes and give him fluids. It was always the women, it always would be. The men would go away and camp somewhere for a while. They'd come back later, maybe days, could be years. They'd come back, they'd be looking for a feed and a place to stay. After a while they'd go away again. There was only one who never left. He was her man. She was his woman, promised to him from her birth. Once she grew into a woman, they lived together, had the boys together, raised them in country. Then two were stolen. Her man grieved with her. And stayed. He didn't chase after grog, didn't go after other women.

He stayed until he was gone. The doctor said the tumour started in the pancreas and it was already too late. Six weeks after that, her man was gone. She'd been alone the forty years since. By choice.

This one, this Jimmy was no better than other men. He wasn't one to stay.

Wilbur watched the old lady as she insinuated the cocoa, spoon by spoon, into the sleeping child. The fire was out. He shivered, got up from his chair and spoke across the cooling room. 'Goodnight then, Greta. Thanks. I'm really … sorry …' He went to the bathroom, emerging a moment or two later, zipping himself up. *He hasn't flushed toilet. Never flushes, that one.*

The man went outside to fetch his swag. The old woman rose to her feet and thought for a moment. She took a clean glass from the kitchen and went to the bathroom. She emerged carrying the glass, now filled with yellowish fluid.

33. *Conscious and Verbal*[*]

It was bright morning when Wilbur awoke. He looked around the kitchen. He looked upward and saw the underside of a small table. He saw its stainless steel legs. Greta's table.

Greta … the kid. Shit, the kid! If he isn't awake yet, I'm gone. Fuck! If he is awake, he'll have told Greta everything. He sat up. There were breakfast dishes on the sink. The kid and Greta must

[*] *Conscious and Verbal: Poems* – Les Murray, 1999

have come in and eaten and he'd slept through. He looked at his watch. *Shit, I must have slept for twelve hours …*

He went outside. He saw Greta sitting on the ground too close to a small fire. Smoke drifted into her face. She sat with her back to him; she did not move. The boy, where was the boy?

'That boy, he better now, Jimmy.'

The old woman spoke without turning around. 'You better pack up, Jimmy. You go now. The little fella he don't need see more of you.'

'But …'

'Just go home, Jimmy. Yesterday you just about kill that little fella with your drugs. One more little fella. You no good to that boy. You not good father. Go home. Grow up. Come back when you grow up, when you proper father.'

He'd never heard Greta make such a long speech. He stood for a moment, irresolute. He didn't want to see Greta's face. She had kept her back to him throughout her speech. He didn't want to see how she looked when she said *one more little fella.*

Her voice had been heavy. Terrible.

She hadn't wanted to look at him! Greta, of all people. The only woman who ever accepted him. Never wanted him any different. His mum always wanted to turn him around. His other women gave up on him, some slowly, some fast. They saw him as a junkie and a bum. A no-hoper. He went inside and rolled up his swag.

When he came out, Greta was still sitting in the smoke. She had not moved. There was no sign of the boy.

'Goodbye, Greta.' His voice was low. She made no response. Had she heard?

He turned, climbed into the car and drove away, fast.

34. With Greta

The old lady didn't ask him any questions and Jaffas didn't have to speak. He concentrated hard, trying to recall one thought, the thought he must remember. It was a resolution he had made when the music was loud and his head was hurting. The music had spoken to him: *Carrots! Carrots! Run away from the man, run back home to Carrots. Don't give up till you're back with Carrots.* The music in the car had banged and clashed, surged and burst, again and again: *Run! Run! Run to Carrots.*

And there were the words of that man: *If you say anything, I'll kill your brother.*

The old lady had a soft voice. She said, 'Get some them little sticks.' Jaffas did not reply. He would not speak. He looked around. There were trees all around them and bits of wood everywhere he looked. He brought some to the old lady.

She smiled. 'Now some leaves, dry ones, only dry ones.'

He fetched a couple of armfuls and brought them to the lady. Another smile. A tooth missing, but kindly.

'Come close. I show you something.' The old lady held a longer stick, thin and pointed. She rested the point on a bed of dry leaves on the ground. She placed her two palms opposite each other at the top of the stick and, moving her palms quickly in opposite directions, she made the stick spin, first one way then back. 'Soon we got fire.'

Jaffas looked down. There was no fire. He looked up, unbelieving. The old lady said again, 'Soon make fire.'

The stick kept whirring in the leaves. There was no fire. But what was that grey wisp? Smoke? Jaffas looked hard: two leaves, now three, were red, now curling, shrivelling, turning black. The leaves were burning!

The old lady dropped a few of the thinner twigs onto the burning leaves. The flames grew. It was a fire. For the first time in eighteen hours, Carrots smiled. Then he winced. His left temple hurt.

The old lady sent him into the scrub to collect bigger sticks. He ran off, excited.

He heard the old lady talking; he stood still. He thought he heard the voice of the man who had snatched him. Then nothing. Was the old lady a friend of that man? Jaffas would watch and listen. He would stay quiet, ready to run.

A moment later, he heard a car door slam and the engine start. He had a moment to run back to the house, to get into the car that might take him to Melbourne. He stood still and let it go. He listened as the car sounds receded, stopped, started again then disappeared.

He collected a load of larger sticks now and brought them to the old lady. Her wrinkled face smiled, wrinkling further. She rested the palm of her hand on the top of his head. His tense body relaxed and he started to cry. 'Abu,' he said softly.

Later, the old lady led him inside, took him to the lowboy and pointed to a photo. There were two people in the picture, a young man and an adolescent boy. The boy was black like the old lady. The man's skin was white. His hair was red. It was the man who had grabbed him and Carrots outside their house.

The old lady pointed to the black boy: 'Ambrose.' She flung her hands suddenly apart. 'Gone! Dead!' Jaffas heard the old lady sniffling. Now she pointed to the young man. 'You know him, right? Father?'

The boy shook his head violently. '*Eso pelirrojo?*', he said. '*EL NO ES MI PADRE!*'**

---

*   *Abu* (*Abuela*, abbrev.) Grandmother

** That red-head? *He is not my father!*

35. On the Road to Arkaroola

Wilberforce James Reynolds drove away from Greta's house and the nearby small community. He stopped when he reached the junction. To the left was the road back to Copley that led on to Leigh Creek, then home. There was fuel in Copley and in Leigh Creek, but people knew him in both those places. He didn't want to be recognised.

He looked at the fuel gauge: a quarter full. He hadn't used the petrol in his jerry cans. With them, he'd have enough to bypass the places where he was known. He could drive on and fill up in Beltana, or better still, in Parachilna, where no one was likely to know him.

Everything's turned to shit. I had the vision, I've got my mission, I was going to do good, but I haven't made up to Greta for her two lost kids: I only brought her the one. I hurt that one kid in the car, then I half-poisoned him.

And Greta isn't pleased but bitter towards me for another boy she'd lost.

It's not fair.

Well, it is fair. The old girl has lost too many.

But she sent me away and I didn't have a chance to show myself as the Redeemer, to see her happy.

He walked the twenty metres down to the creek and reached into his pocket for his smokes and lighter. The smokes were there. Then he remembered – he'd misplaced the lighter. He climbed the slope back to the car and looked on the console.

He took the lighter and the smokes and walked back down to the creek. There it was, Italowie. *This must be the loveliest place on earth.* Its deep shade in the blazing sunlight, its greenness in all this red rock and brown scree – it moved him. And the water, always running, always cool, through dry and drought – it was beautiful.

Back in the Big House he used to meditate. He'd see that water, and the sounds he'd hear in his head were the rippling notes of Beethoven's Fourth Piano Concerto for piano. This was his special place where thought and regret faded, where the voices called him, where they spoke and meaning came, clear as that stream. In this scene of pure waters in the blazing wilderness, Wilbur heard the Call to greatness and boundless power.

He emptied his hands and sat down to meditate. This time he didn't have to close his eyes to visualise.

He finished and looked down. There at his side were the objects, strange now, foreign; he picked up the fags and the lighter and he threw them into the deepest part of the creek.

Okay. I tried to do right and it hasn't worked out. I haven't made any mothers happy. Not yet.

He climbed back into the car and started the long drive back to Melbourne. He knew his mission. He knew what he had to do.

36. Greta and the Doctor

The doctor set out early. The sun blessed its morning favourites – western peaks, taller treetops, selected folds of hill. Here and there, narrow beams probed gaps in the ranges and dowered the lower slopes with gold.

All else remained dark. No movement save for the Doc's old troop carrier, tracing the bitumen. Rivergums stood sentinel over stony creek beds, dark hills loomed silent and massive against the lightening sky. The heavens threw off their dark cap and tried on another, a metallic light blue.

The Doc rounded a bend. A pair of grazing kangaroos, creamy in the beam of his headlights, lifted their heads and hopped into the sheltering shadow. As he drove, turning off at the Copley mesas, he watched the sunlight spreading, claiming the slopes and folds and hollows, exposing sleeping scrub, surprising feeding animals in their privacy. The soft invasion of morning gathered and grew.

The Doc turned off his headlights and drove on towards Iga Warta. Before Nepabunna he left the road and followed the dirt track to Greta's camp. Slowing, he saw filaments of smoke rising from behind the hill. Greta was awake. She'd be cooking her breakfast.

He stopped at the house. There was no one by the fire. He knocked. The house was quiet. The Doc sat down on the ground near the fire and waited.

He heard sounds of movement from the bush, then a voice, Greta's: 'Grab him! Grab his tail! That the way, good! Hold him, hold him tight! Don't let him go. Now swing him, belt him neck against that rock!'

The Doc heard a soft thud. Then a second, a third.

Greta again, laughing, her old lady voice breaking, cackling: 'No, don't pat him! You gotta break his neck … Give him me. Watch.'

A single heavy thwack.

'Good. That done it. We got him now. Good fat one. You carry him now.'

A child's voice, breathless, piping strange words, not English words. The two voices came closer. He saw last evening's sleeping boy coming out of the scrub – awake, excited, flushed. Greta, following him, caught sight of the visitor. She stopped momentarily then smiled. 'You going stay, eat with us, Doc?'

'You bet. Thanks, Greta.'

The old woman took the dead goanna from the boy and flung it onto the ashes. She sat close to the doctor and answered his questions about the boy's progress. 'He sleep. I poke him, every half hour, like you said. He wake up. Drink little bit cocoa. Fell asleep. Sleep, wake up, drink. Sleep again.'

'Good. You're a good nurse, Greta.'

The old woman nodded, then fell silent, considering. She whispered, 'Another thing, this kid name not Bruce. Jimmy say he called Bruce. But I stand behind him, I yell out Bruce, he never move. Done it coupla times. Bruce not his name. Jimmy bin lying … funny fella, that Jimmy …

Doc, I need you test Jimmy piss. You know, drug test. I got Jimmy piss, inside house.' Greta shrugged, indicating the kitchen. 'I reckon if Jimmy give drugs to boy, maybe he eating drugs too. Again.'

'Well, Greta, it's not legal unless Wilbur – I mean Jimmy – signs his consent. And he's gone, hasn't he?'

Greta nodded. 'Don't want him here, not near boy. I send him away.'

The doctor pondered a moment. He enquired of his delinquent self: should he place at risk his medical licence? Greta's gaze searched him. He felt something open within, then heard his own words with mild surprise, something like relief. 'Yep, Greta. I'll do the test. Yep, that'll be okay.'

The doctor turned to the boy and motioned him to sit down. 'Ever eaten goanna?'

A shake of the head. The fire spat and crackled as fat ran from the goanna's flesh.

'Hungry?'

Another shake.

The Doc asked the boy the name of his father, his own name, his address, his phone number. The catechism of concussion. The boy did not respond.

'What is four plus four?'

The boy showed eight fingers.

What's four minus two?'

Two fingers. No words.

The doctor mused, 'You don't want to talk to me? Okay. But I heard you yelling your head off when you and Greta were hunting the goanna.'

Greta interjected, 'He call me Abo. But he say it funny. He say *Abu*.'

The aroma of cooking meat was familiar, an urgent memory trigger – Jaffas was back home, their father barbecuing, he and Carrots filching chorizo from the *asado*.* The two of them sharing the hot meat.

The two of them.

His face fell into absence. A ball formed in his throat and strangled sound. His lips framed the word: 'Carrots'.

37. Rite to Me

Dear Jaffas,

Where are you?

I know you must be a live. The polise said you mite be dead. Mami screemed and cryed and nearly fainted.

But the polise are wrong.

I know you are alive.

I know that.

The nite the man stole my head aked. Maybe your head hurt too. Next day my head was beter. I know you are not dead and not sick.

Do you rember when they put us in diferent clases?

i always knew where you were. They said Carrots and Jaffas are to close but they coodnt stop us.

I always knew where you were.

Jaffas you are not dead. But lost. I am lost when you are lost.

I serch for you in my mind. i serch in Papis atlas in all places in the mountens or in the desert or across the sea.

I lie in bed and i wander why you dont rite to me, jaffas or

---

* barbecue

call me. You know our number and our adress.

I think you must be across the sea. I think the man sold you to pirates. Like josefs brothers sold him to the ishmelites, in Mamis red book.

If you care you would rite
i am afraid you dont care any more. thats the most fritening thort that i think.

Yours Lonely
Carrots

38. Greta and Warraiti

'You no talk much. Not like whitefella kid. Whitefellas talk too much. You talk funny. Not English.'

'*Espanol.*'

'But you watchin' all time, listen all time.'

The old woman and the boy sat close on the ground, their thin bodies a pair of parallel lines, vertical against the low brush.

A sound, a sudden movement at a close distance. A tall bird flashed from the scrub across the clearing. Jaffas started – he had seen that bird before: it was the bird in the tattoo on the man's arm – the man who stole him!

Greta lit up. '*Warraiti*! Sit still. Little minute we see *warraiti* mate. Every time two, never one alone.' More sounds from the scrub and a second emu bounded after the first.

'See? All time two. *Warraiti* and his mate. Never see him alone. Need mate. Too lonely without mate. Understand me?'

He nodded.

Greta saw tears in the boy's eyes. 'You lonely? Homesick?' Her voice was gentle.

'Carrots,' he said.

Greta rested her hand on the boy's shoulder. 'You wanna hear *warraiti* story? Why he run but he never fly? Important story, that one.'

Jaffas blinked tears away. He nodded.

Greta's voice trembled, her face alight. She looked up in wonder and began, 'One time, long time, *warraiti* have big mob of chick; and *walha* – that bush turkey – *walha* she got big mob too. Too many baby, not enough tucker for all them chick.

'*Warraiti* say to *walha*, "We gotta knock the chicks on the head, your mob, my mob, then we both only got two babies."

'*Walha* say: "Alright, I kill them."

'*Walha* take her chicks and kill him, kill him, every one, only two left alive. But *warraiti* trick *walha*. She put babies under wings, she hide them. After *walha* kill her little ones, *warraiti* drop hers on the ground, let them go. *Warraiti* still got that big mob of chick.

'*Walha* see *warraiti* cheat her. She very angry. She shout at *warraiti*, "You still got all your mob, your chick. You bin lie to me. You my sister, but you lie, you make me kill my kids. Now you still got your big mob and I only got two."

'*Walha* she stay angry, every day still angry. She get an idea. She say to her two chick, "Come with me, see *warraiti*."

'*Walha* say to her chicks, "Now I cut your wings shorter. Little bit, not much. Mine too. Then I tell *warraiti*: 'I cut all our wings off. No more flying. Walking better.' That what we say. Not fly now, just walk."

'So *walha* and her two chicks walk all way to *warraiti* and *walha* tell her that whole story, that big make-up story.'

Greta rose abruptly to her feet. She waddled this way and that, making as if to peck the ground. The old lady incarnated *walha*, the bush turkey who pretends she cannot fly. '*Warraiti* see that bush turkey coming, all walking, all getting tucker on the ground. She say to old lady turkey, "Why you mob walk, not fly?"

'So *walha* tell *warraiti* that whole story – "Better on ground, better this way, that why we cut off our wings." And so *warraiti*, she pick up *yurdla* knife, she cut off all her chick wings, then she cut off her own wings too. They all just stand there, blood coming out everywhere, all that mob been cut.'

Greta leapt to her feet again, spread her arms as if to take to the air. 'Then *walha* fly up into the air with her chicks and she start to fly away.'

Jaffas sat, appalled. He pictured blood. Treachery between friends defeated his imagination. He looked up, out from the tale, up at the teller, who had herself taken flight.

Greta resumed: '*Warraiti* very sad. She call out, "*Walha*, my sister, you cheat me. You say you going always on ground. Now you mob all flying. And *warraiti* and all my mob only walk on the ground. Never fly any more."'

Greta finished the story: 'Now *warraiti* never fly. All other bird fly, *warraiti* never fly. That why, that the story.

'*Warraiti*, you call him emu, you know? Very strong spirit. *Warraiti* he the Law Man. He protect the Law. Plenty mob – blackfella mob, whitefella mob – eat *warraiti*, but not me. Never me. *Warraiti*, he my dreaming, my father. You get *warraiti* fat, good cure for skin. If sick in the head – you know, crazy – *warraiti* fat good medicine for that one.'

Greta had finished the telling. She turned and faced Jaffas. She spoke with slow emphasis, didactic now. With each phrase she nodded her head. 'Important story, that one. My story.'

Jaffas bent forward; he looked down. His fingers closed on a stick, dropped it. He probed the leafmeal, found nothing, probed again. He groped, looking for something. Voice, words. His voice, when it came, was unfamiliar, low and indistinct: '*Es mi historia, tambien. Es porque no volo, nada.*'*

Jaffas and Greta leaned into each other. They sat close. For a good while, neither spoke.

---

* It is my story too. That's why I don't fly.

39. Doc's Visits

The Doc visited often. The old lady welcomed the whitefella who truly wanted to understand. 'You come here, you listen, you not talk.' Greta became the Doc's local expert, his librarian of country; she introduced him to her own research text, which was the rock country. She took him on short walks, seldom more than a hundred metres or so from her house. This was quite sufficient to open him to country.

Once or twice a week, Greta took him out and showed him a tree, a bush, a prostrate plant. All the flora evoked a story; every growing thing hid or fed or depended upon another living thing. Greta turned the soil with her foot, peeled bark from a tree, shook a sapling – revealing a bird, a worm, a grub. All life, the soil itself, all was essential.

There was that word again, *essential*.

The Doc decided that the prevention of disease among the Adnyamathanha must depend on their learning their own country. Greta knew it, that is, she knew her own Dreaming stories. Others owned other stories – different stories. Those who knew were old now and few. Their sons and daughters had not learned. He asked Greta why.

'They chase after drink, you know, grog. Too much drink.'

The Doc wondered, 'What about drugs?'

Greta shook her head mournfully and did not speak further. She was silent. Inward. Impregnable.

Something private.

Was it the boy, Ambrose, that she remembered? Whom she lamented? The Doc did not press her.

Later he learned some of the facts. Of early death, he already knew more than he wanted. Of madness and mayhem, of degenerative disease in young adults, of under-nutrition and of over-nutrition: of all these he knew much. And of premature death, often sudden, violent. These were medical facts, but they were effects. The Doc was pursuing causes. And on the way, he was learning family stories.

Late one evening, he visited Greta at her shack near Nepabunna. She was sitting outside, sitting on the ground by a small fire. She held her head on one side as she listened to a small radio. The Doc stood and listened too. Greta was listening to *Awaye!*, the indigenous ABC radio program.

Her listening caught the Doc's interest. There was an intensity, a totality of attention, that took him aback. The woman gave her senses, her entire awareness, to the sounds of the voices from that small radio. The voices were Aboriginal voices.

At length, the program came to an end. Greta switched off the old transistor radio in its 1960s leather case. She greeted the Doc: 'You wanna hear more stories, maybe *Tjukurrpa* stories?'

'Well no, not Dreaming this time. This time, maybe your own stories, stories from your life.'

Greta waved a dismissive hand. 'My stories just little ones. *Tjukurrpa*, I mean Dreaming, they big ones, they important.'

The Doc nodded and said nothing for a time. Greta waited. Finally the Doc spoke, somewhat diffidently, his face to the earth. 'It is a personal question, Greta, maybe too personal. A big, big story.'

Greta lifted her face. The Doc looked up. Greta's face was open. 'Can you tell me whether any children were taken away, you know, by the Welfare, years back?'

Startled, Greta sat silent. The Doc's question pierced her, a shaft that penetrated hidden recesses of feeling and memory. A violence, that question, intolerable from any but a friend; the directness ill-mannered from any non-intimate quarter.

Greta collected herself. She considered; she seemed to wrestle with the question. She nodded and said nothing for a time. She looked steadily at the Doc, taking his measure. Then she made her decision. 'Lot of kids taken. Stolen, you know. Welfare come, police come, grab children, take 'em away. Never come back. Mother never see 'em again, maybe when they grown up. Sometime never...'

Greta's flow stopped. She looked down.

'My boys, they take two my boys. Never come back. I reckon they big fellas now, fathers. Maybe grandfather. I never see them. Maybe they die, maybe they just lost.'

The old lady looked at the Doc. 'That what happen. That what they do. Steal 'em.'

'How old were your boys, Greta?'

'Big one four, little fella two. They my littlest fellas. The big ones, their brothers, when the Welfare come, they run, hide.'

The Doc had met Greta's remaining children, now in their sixties. He had treated their diseases. They were far less healthy than Greta herself.

Greta spoke again. 'I had one more boy, 'nother one. He not my son, that one, he my son youngest boy. I say he called Ambrose. Not his real name. No one say real name, not now. I raise Ambrose. His mother bring that baby to me. She say, "You take this baby. I cannot have him."

'I tell her, "You keep him. He need you ... a boy need mother."

'She say, "I can't."

'I tell her, "You go away, maybe you change mind. Child and mother gotta be together. You listen me: I *know.*"

'My son wife bring that baby back. She say, "You take him. I cannot."

'She go away, Port Augusta, go for grog. I take Ambrose. I am old, too old for baby, but he make me happy. First he a baby, he grow, he start become man. Go bush with the old men, go into Law, into men business.'

Greta paused. Her smile died. 'Then he go into drugs, drugs and grog. Get sick in head. One night, too much drugs. He stop breathing while he asleep. In the morning I see him lying down by campfire. He not move, he not wake up. I say "Ambrose!" I yell

"*Ambrose!*" He don't answer. Ambrose dead.'

Greta stopped speaking. No more words.

The Doc had no words.

The old woman sighed. She nodded her head slowly. 'Now I stop here. I stop here, in country.'

She looked around her, raised her head, surveying the horizon. Finally she looked upwards. Abruptly she said, 'Night time come. I see my father.'

The Doc emerged from the blanketing sorrow, from his sense of his own, his ancestors' implication in those endless journeys upon seas of grief.

She sees her father? Has grief unhinged her?

'That *warraiti*, see 'im in the sky. Night time, I see 'im ... You wanna stop here now, have feed? The boy eat already. He sleeping. After I show you *warraiti*. No moon tonight, you see him. Easy.'

The Doc was glad to stay. He fetched a can of baked beans from the Toyota. Greta baked damper and they ate together by the fire as the night came down.

There was no moon, no sound. The two sat in a small clearing at the top of a rise and watched the stars emerge.

After a while, Greta pointed upwards: 'That *warraiti* head.' The Doc looked and recognised the Southern Cross. Greta indicated an area of dim light, separate from the Southern Cross, a little to the left. He could trace the shape of a bird's head. Now Greta pointed out some dark clouds trailing out along the Milky Way towards Scorpius. 'That his body, there his legs. *Warraiti*.'

The old lady shone in the fireglow. She said again, '*Warraiti*. My father ... You father, still alive?'

The Doc shook his head.

'What about woman, kids?'

'No.'

Greta's voice was incredulous, almost indignant.' No kids? No family?'

A shake of the head. 'I lost my Dad. I never wanted to lose anyone again. I've got a sister in America. For a long while, I half lost her too.'

A half laugh.

The Doc threw wood onto the fire. He pieced together the story of Ambrose and the story Greta had told him of her stolen children. Her words and her silences, like a dilly bag, a reticulum of threads and gaps. The loss of her children; the loss two generations later of another precious child. How these losses seemed to connect to the *warraiti* Dreaming: all were stories of mothers cheated of their young.

One connection endured, Greta and *warraiti* – they existed on account of each other.

For a good while, the Doc and the old woman sat and were quiet. The dying fire flared briefly and the Doc saw Greta's curls catch the crimson light. Suddenly moved, surprised by unexpected beauty, the Doc did not know himself. Clouds gathered, covering the stars.

Greta's voice crossed the dark space. She said, 'You wanna stop here with me?'

The man followed the woman inside.

Part 3

♊

40. The One Story of Albert Burns

With his white beard and his big head, the old doctor looks like a gnome in a storybook. He has large ears, a huge nose and a long, wide jaw. He is a funny-looking man. Jaffas tries not to stare.

In the early morning, the school is quiet and still. The old man leans against a slab of stone outside the school library. Despite himself, the boy does stare. It is the first time he has seen the old doctor since Greta cooked the goanna. In the bright light, in his white shirt and trousers, in his pale, old-man skin, the man is a shape, a part of the rock, one of the large boulders that mark the paths of the school. The ferrous stone is pastel in the bleaching light. The old man is bleached too. He looks weathered, ancient.

He says, 'You're the boy from Greta's place, aren't you?'

The boy nods.

'What's your name again?'

The boy points to the name on the badge pinned to his school shirt: Bruce.

'Bruce? Good to see you again, Bruce. I'm the Doc.'

The boy looks at him. The old man's face is wrinkled. There are lines around his eyes and his voice is cracked and dry; it crackles like the scree that moves under his school shoes. The old man smiles and the lines around his eyes move up and down.

'You here for the library, Bruce? You like stories?'

The boy nods again.

'Me too. But the library won't open for a while yet. Want to hear a story while you wait?'

The boy, uncertain, watchful, retreats imperceptibly. His shaved scalp glows in the light. The old doctor notices a patina of gold on the pink. He falls silent, watching the boy who has disappeared into himself, wondering. The boy inserts an index finger into a nostril. He excavates for a while, pulling out a payload of black mucus and dust. The doctor watches the index finger at its work, notes it is the boy's left. *Black snot. Coalminer snot or city snot. You're no miner, so you brought that snot with you from somewhere. And you are a left-hander. And a red-head.*

These feel like elements in a puzzle, clues to the silent boy's identity. They fall into a slot in the old doctor's recent memory. He remembers something – what did he read somewhere about a red-headed boy? A left-hander? Where was it he read it? Or did he catch something on the TV? He cannot remember. He wonders whether it was important. Lots of things nowadays are just beyond the reach of the doctor's recall. They generally come back to him later. *I've got a lot of good ideas. I just can't think of them sometimes …*

His mind returns to the boy before him. Seemingly, he has forgotten his offer of a story. He asks again, 'Do you like stories, Bruce?'

The boy nods.

'Well come over here and I'll tell you one.'

There is another pause, before the Doc looks up and speaks. 'I'm trying to choose a story to tell you, young fella. As you go through your life and your days, you meet so many stories. And your nights too: sometimes night stories are the best – bedtime stories, dream stories, even nightmares. The story of Joseph is the story of a dreamer and his dreams and of other people's dreams. All those dreams are night stories.'

Jaffas nods. He knows the Joseph stories, favourites from Mami's red book.

'I'm about a thousand years old, young fella, so I've come across a lot of stories. I'm built of stories. And the reason that I'm here, I mean in the Flinders, and with Greta, is to learn the stories of this country. There are always more stories to hear and learn and tell.

'All human groups have stories and they all preserve and tell their stories. The stories preserve the memories of the group. Really, the stories keep human groups alive. Human children need stories like they need milk and light and air.'

The old man falls silent. After a while, Jaffas wonders what is going on. Is the old fellow asleep? Or sick? Jaffas looks up – the old man stands, silent, apparently quite well, in fact, *very* well, for on his old face Jaffas sees a smile that lights up every one of his many wrinkles. The old man's face shines, sweet as a full moon.

Jaffas waits.

The old man speaks at last. 'So many stories, so many, many good and beautiful stories, more than I can count. I have been going through some of the best ones in my mind, trying to choose the very best to tell you. And then I realised the great truth about my lifetime collection of stories – I don't have so many really; in fact I have only one story. Probably no one has more than one. My story is called, *Where do we come from? What are we? Where are we going?*

'That's the story that Adnyamathanha people (that's what the old people call themselves – it means "Hill People" or "Rock People") tell and paint and sing and dance. Obviously, I'm not the first person to tell that story. A French painter named Gauguin told that story in a painting in 1897. He learned the story in turn from his teacher, a French Bishop in Orléans, by the name of Felix-Antoine-Philibert Dupanloup. Dupanloup – funny name, isn't it? You know what? I bet there's a good story locked up in that funny name. I bet there's a story in your name too, young fella ... er ... I'm sorry it's slipped my mind at present.'

41. Were are You?

Dear Jaffas,

Were are you?

I wonder all the time were the man took you.

I watch and I lissen.

Every nite I lissen. I here a sound and i think Jaffas, Jaffas is here. Jaffas has come back to me.

I call to you, in a wisper. Do you here me?

Do you call to me?

Yours sincerly

Carrots (your brother)

42. The One Story – Fossils

'G'day … Brian. It is Brian, isn't it?'

Jaffas shakes his head and points again to his lapel pin.

'Oh, Bruce … right. Goodo, Bruce, this is a story about the fossils that were first found around here. It's a story of *Where do we come from?* Most of the stories around here are like that …

'Fossils are echoes in the rock. Some fossils around here echo the oldest life forms that ever had bilateral symmetry. Do you know what that means, Bruce?'

A shrug. In truth, Jaffas has only a vague understanding of words like *fossils, symmetry* – but there is a music, a poetry in the old man's voice that Jaffas recognises. It is the romance of science that he remembers from his father's accounts of the life of work and of life outside work. Jaffas is used to stories where hard words appear, obscurely, and fall into place late in the telling, borne on the music in the telling, in the movement.

More than this, the dried-out old man is transformed, irresistible in the telling of his story. As he listens, the Doc tells his overture.

'Symmetry means both sides look the same – like mirror images. Once you've got symmetry, you can have a front and a back. The front end of a creature advances into the world ahead of the middle and the back. Makes sense doesn't it, Bruce?'

A nod.

'And the front needs to know what's ahead of it – is there a threat, is there food, a mate perhaps? So the front develops antennae – soft wobbly fingers of flesh that work like little radars to spy out the environment. They smell or feel what is ahead and they send back information to the tiny creature.

'Now, the tiny little living thing needs to make sense of the messages that the "spies" are sending. So nerve cells, excitable, electrical cells and filaments, start to gather at the front end of the *creature*. You know what that means, don't you?'

'Bruce' is not sure. He looks up, eyes wide. The old man's voice is no longer a dry crackle; it sings and rings, it pauses, rises, falls. The face, animated now, glows golden. As the old man speaks, the boy rests his back against the warm rock, closer to the story-man.

'Brains! This little creature in the Flinders Ranges starts to develop a brain. It's made of nerve cells, it's a brand new organ. No other living thing ever "thought" of making a brain before. But up here, in these hills, a little creature starts to create this organ for processing information. Processing information is another way of saying *thinking*. For a while, these little complex organisms are the brainiest creatures in the world.'

'Bruce' moves nearer. He enters the world of pre-Cambrian creatures. He wonders about their lives.

'If these species had been ambitious, they might have ruled the world. Instead, they lived domestic lives, untroubled by predators. As it happens, fossils like these – they're called Ediacara – have also been found in Mexico and in Russia and Canada.'

The boy stands hard against the storyteller now. They lean their backs against the same rock. Both have forgotten the world – they live in the tale, it carries them away, they travel together.

'Of course, these ancient intellectuals were dorks – spongy forms like jellyfish or tubes or discs. Some of them were like mattresses or mud-filled bags ... It's the same among modern humans; quite often the thinkers, those who are originals, look different. Take a look at that Scandinavian bloke up at Lyndhurst, that sculptor fella. Or Finnegan at Copley: like the Ediacara, they live in their heads. They don't care much how they look.'

A long silence. The sun has warmed the rock. The two emerge slowly from the echoes of narrative. The old man moves to the library door. It is nine o'clock. He says, 'See you later, Bruce. If you like, I'll tell you another story next time you're here. I'm here every morning.'

The boy has a voice. Quiet, tentative: '*Gracias, Abu.*'

The old man stops at the door. He looks at the boy, inches away. 'I've got some stories that are mine alone. Everyone here, everyone who is new, has a story. The story of what we left behind and what brought us here. All these stories are part of the great story. You know, *Where do we come from ...*' Jaffas' eyes widen.

'Stories of adventure, sometimes heartbreak. And bravery. And deaths and births ...'

Jaffas is swimming, drifting fast in the swirling currents of storytalk. He moves with the tidal dash and weave of the telling. He doesn't want it to stop.

The story seems to end with the old man's final words: '... and suffering. And loneliness.'

Before Jaffas makes the shore, this dumper from the old man: 'What's your story, Bruce?'

Jaffas clutches at the door jamb. The old man looks at him benignly.

Jaffas shakes his head.

43. The One Story – Untold

Next morning the Doc finds the silent boy outside the library. 'You waiting?'

The boy nods.

'Library doesn't open for a while yet, er … Bruce.'

The boy nods again. He has come for the newspapers he sighted in the library. The papers might have news of his abduction, maybe of his family, of Carrots. He does not speak.

The Doc decides it is time for a story. 'Bruce, I'll tell you a story about a little girl I just visited in the hospital. This one's a *Where are we going to?* story. It's about a killer.'

Some pressure of vicarious pain, some need to discharge, drives the Doc to share the story. Then he stops abruptly, shakes his head. 'No, Bruce, I can't tell you this story. It's not mine to tell. It's confidential – that means it's a secret. I made a mistake. I'll find another way, another day. Not today.'

44. I am not Me

Dear Jaffas,

They say Carrots why dont you talk.

I do talk.

I talk to you.

At nite i wisper so only you can here me.

I dont talk in english or in spanish. just our own talk, our old talk like when we were babys.

I feel diferent when i talk to you.

Same when i rite to you.

I feel reel when i am talking with you jaffas. Other times nothing feels reel.

I am not me.

I know that your my twin and i am your twin. Thats what i know.

Jaffas and carrots, thats us.

Come home jaffas. I am not me without you

Yours cinserely

Carrots

Your twin brother

45. The One Story – Killer Germs

Jaffas haunts the library. There is a newspaper delivery every day except Mondays. Jaffas searches all of the papers for reports of his own story. Nothing. The papers are the national broadsheet and the Adelaide paper. Neither cover the non-news from Melbourne. The non-recovery of a red-headed twin child is the non-news from Melbourne.

Both papers offer additional material on the internet. A search of their files would throw up a feast of distressing information for Jaffas. He would read speculation that he had been raped and murdered; he would learn that his body had been dismembered and disposed of piecemeal, in dumpsters; he'd learn that his kidnapper was one of a number of known paedophiles. He would read of his twin's collapse into muteness and malnutrition, of his mother's rumoured breakdown. Brothers in a religious order were incriminated, their ranks closing against investigation like a gang of criminal bikies. The closure of ranks was the clincher of that theory.

He would discover that the reporting, almost all of it false, came abruptly to a stop when the juicy scandal surfaced of a cabinet member and a prostitute.

Jaffas does not consult the Net.

He finds nothing in the papers. He *has* to contact Carrots. But Jaffas will not ask a grown-up for help. The man has threatened – *if you say anything, I'll kill your brother.*

Jaffas writes in code.

mi hermano

estoy vivo, robado, en Egipto.

su hermano

José

He folds the letter and puts it into his pocket. He will find someone to give it to, someone who will deliver it safely. *Who? How?* Jaffas doesn't know. He keeps the letter close and checks it every night.

⚏

Jaffas comes every morning to the library. It is in one of the school buildings. He comes home later and says quite truthfully he has been to school. Greta is very strong on schooling.

And he meets that old man storyteller while he waits.

The old doctor looks at the boy. The faint golden haze on the shaven scalp has grown. The hair is red. Unmistakably red. He recalls a schoolmate with hair like that. What did they call him? The nickname surfaces on the Doc's lips: 'Carrots'.

Jaffas jumps: '*Que?*'

The doctor says, 'Hello, Bruce. I've worked out how I can tell you a little of the forbidden story, the part that isn't anyone's secret. Look at this …'

Jaffas, his mind still reeling from the sound of his brother's name, stares at the Doc. *He knows! I never said anything. How?*

But the old man shows no interest in discussing Carrots. Instead, he reaches into a ragged old canvas rucksack and produces

159

a small bottle of goanna oil. He opens the bottle, pours two careful drops onto his left palm and rubs his hands together. He closes the bottle and takes from the rucksack a packet of silver sparkles. He opens the sparkles and shakes some onto one oiled palm. He extends the hand to the boy: 'Shake hands with me Bruce.'

Bemused, the boy shakes.

'Look at your hand.'

He looks. His hand is oily and sparkling with tiny silvery particles.

'That's today's story, son. That's the story of how the enemies of human beings get inside us and make us sick. One enemy is the streptococcus that can destroy your heart or your kidneys. Another is a bowel virus.'

The boy looks at his hand, looks at the old man. He doesn't get it.

'This is the story of human fate, human history really. It's the story of how bugs get from one person to another. Just like your hand only had to touch my hand for the sparkles to pass to you, that's how bugs spread from one person to another. It's the story of how the Adnyamathanha get sick, how bugs kill their children.'

Jaffas' mind races, stumbles: *Carrots – what does a killer have to do with Carrots?*

The doctor notices the child's anxiety. He says comfortingly, 'Don't be afraid, Bruce. Kids are safe if we teach them to wash their hands right.'

The boy looks lost.

The Doc rests an old hand on the child's shoulder. 'Do you know Greta's little great-great-niece Ashweena?'

Jaffas shakes his head.

'Well, she's just a little baby. A bowel virus almost killed her. Ashweena nearly died from diarrhoea.'

A frown on the boy's face.

'Ashweena nearly pooed herself to death.'

The old storyteller man tells the boy about the tides of the long struggle to save Ashweena. When the baby shits blood, the boy's hand flies to his mouth. Otherwise the boy listens without moving. At the end, with the baby suckling, the boy cries inside himself.

'If that virus had killed Ashweena, I think Greta might have died too. Her heart would have broken. Greta has lost too many.'

The story has nothing to do with Carrots. The boy relaxes. He thinks about the doctor who has saved the little girl. The Doc is the person who looks after all of Greta's people. He made that baby better and he saved Greta.

The boy speaks, shyly. He says, '*Gracias, Abu.*'

46. The One Story – People of the Rock Country

When the Doc arrives the next morning at eight, he finds the boy waiting. The child waits there every school day. He never finds his own story. He waits for the storyteller and *his* stories.

'I'll tell you something, Bruce, something about stories. You're new here, aren't you?'

A nod.

'And everyone else in Leigh Creek is new.'

This doesn't make sense to the boy; there are kids at school who were born in the town, their parents too. Some families have worked the mine here for generations. They aren't new. The only newcomer he knows is himself, Bruce, as people call him here. The boy looks confused.

The old Doc is speaking again. 'But these hills are old. Very old. In Brachina Gorge, out Parachilna way, you can actually see age lines of country. Like this – look at my face.' The Doc points to wrinkles that furrow his forehead.

'The sides of the gorge are layered, age upon age, epoch upon epoch; time is compressed, eons are buried. Those hills are twice as old as time.'

Where is this going? The boy says nothing. 'Epoch', 'eons', new notes in the strange music of Doc's geological storytelling. The boy does not move. He will wait and anticipate translation or conclusion or resolution.

But the old man looks energised. Something has excited him. 'There are hill people who've been around here for thousands of years. They've lived off the land. The land fed them and clothed them. It taught them everything they know, everything we ...' – the man points to himself and to the boy and to the township in general – '... everything we don't know.

'From the air or the road, this country all looks pretty much empty, just dry stones. Not much growing here, not much happening, not much to see or to eat or to do. But for the Adnyamthanha, these hills are an emporium. And a university. And a theological college.'

The old man pauses. 'I don't suppose you've heard the mountains calling to each other up near Arkaroola ...'

The boy's eyes widen.

'Well, up there you can hear the Gammon Ranges as they groan and cry out. The Adnyamathanha have their stories about that.'

A barking gecko bathes in the sunshine, stationary on the rock, just beyond and above the bleached old man. The boy watches the lizard. The old man stops talking, looking intently at the boy. He leans forward. 'The Adnyamathanha are old; that's why I say we are new, all of us. And the old Adnyamathanha stories are full of the magic of beginnings.'

The boy's mouth opens.

The old man continues, 'That's the old people and their stories. But all of us new people – the coal miners and the mineral prospectors and the goat farmers that wanted to be sheep farmers; the nurses and the coppers and the teachers; the derelicts and the drifters and the seers and the seekers – all us new ones, we all have our own stories.'

Stories again.

162

'These hills have stories that are almost incredible. The ancient plants and animals here are unique. I told you, didn't I, that this is the place where living things first learned to think?'

'*Si.*'

The Doc looks at the boy. He raises an eyebrow. 'This is dry country, not much rain, not much water. But up near the Beverley uranium mine, you'll see pools that never dry out. And if you watch, you'll notice the hill people never touch those waters, they keep their distance. They call them "bad waters", "sickness waters". Those waters are *permanent* waters. Permanent waters in an area where it mightn't rain for years.

'I was at the local church here in town …' – the old man hitches his thumb over his shoulder towards the biggest building, which is the hospital, and towards the little church that nestles at its side; his old man's voice changes as he points to a time past from within his own remembering – 'It was my fourth Christmas Day here, hot and cloudy. Unusual weather, humid. Suddenly there was a hell of a racket on the roof. The minister interrupted the service and told the children to go outside. They would see a miracle happening.

'We all went outside. The ground was wet, streaming. Water was falling from the heavens. Great drenching fat drops fell straight downwards on to the congregation. Kids stood in wonder. The water soaked them. They touched their clothes, they stretched out their little open hands, palm upward, caught the water and tasted it. They looked at their parents in amazement. The adults smiled.

'I saw a few old farmers who wept quietly, their tears falling onto the streaming earth. There were children there, six years and younger, skipping, running, kicking up the bountiful waters, splashing wantonly in the very stuff they'd been told all their lives to ration. Those were kids who had never seen rain. Have you seen rain, Bruce?'

The question takes Jaffas back to a different time, a different place, another life. The boy nods, pensively.

'Well, that's how dry it can get here. Years without rain.

Waterholes dry out. Life recedes and shrinks into the drying mud. But those waters up at Beverley are always there, always bubbling away. And the local people, I mean the old people, the Adnyamathanha, they've always had those waters. *But they never go near them*, those "sickness waters". These people knew the danger, thousands of years before we whitefellas discovered radiation. The little Polish lady who discovered it in France had to contract cancer to know what the old people here knew forever. From their stories.

'You want to know those stories, Bruce. We all need to learn those stories. We have a chance here to learn important things – learn our own country.'

47. After Jaffas

Luisa had lost one son. She would not lose a second. She or the dog would always be with Carrots.

Bernard had lost his firstborn, chief of his strength. He saw his wife withering, her juice drained. He would find the boy and bring him back. He would get his wife back.

Carrots lay on his bed and breathed. It surprised him that his breath went in and came out. He decided he would stop breathing. But soon his breath came in, hard, unbidden, unwelcome. And went out again. In, out. In, out. He could not prevent it, he could not understand it. There was no reason; there was no Jaffas.

The psychologist came. She spoke to Carrots of loss. 'I know it seems like a part of you is lost, Carrots.'

He looked at his hands. He clenched his fist. The fingers furled then relaxed. He shook his head. *Why?* His feet worked too. Carrots looked at them, perplexed. What was the point?

In the kitchen, he tried an experiment. He took the fruit knife in his left hand and regarded it. *Jaffas is left-handed too.* He drew the blade along the back of his right hand. He saw a line of red rising, filling, overflowing from the non-dominant hand. Carrots looked at the red line and felt the hot pain. It was a sensation at once sharp and remote. He looked at the blood. In the blood and in the cutting, for the first time since the man took Jaffas, Carrots found a glimmer of meaning.

He put the knife down and walked quietly to the bathroom. All of his movements were quiet now. Carrots was a shadow; his physical presence reduced. An agile wallaby, he passed like a breath.

Luisa, eyes red, nose streaming, came into the kitchen for the tissues. She saw the knife. Fat splotches of blood on the bench and the floor led to the bathroom. She stifled a scream and ran. *I saw thee weltering in thy blood!*

She gasped, grabbed the boy's wrist and elevated it. She looked closely at the wound: it was wrist-wide, but shallow and clean. Luisa held the wound under running water. As the cold water hit the fresh cut, her son did not blink. Where was he?

She held her son's slab-shaped head hard against her chest, held it there long. The blood of her son ran, thin, diluted, pink onto the white of the sink. *And I say unto thee: 'In thy blood live!'*

The dog Sahara smelled the blood. In a moment, she was at Carrots' side, her spare body insinuated between him and the woman. The dog's eyes fixed on Carrots' face. She growled softly, lifted her face and began licking at the boy's arm. The boy cried then.

48. The One Story – Arkaroola

'And the dingoes. Why aren't there any dingoes any more up at Arkaroola? All the other grazing properties have dingo fences – to keep their stock safe. But not at Arkaroola ... not any more. Why do you reckon that is ... er ... Bruce?'

The storyteller has trouble with the boy's name. Greta had mentioned something about the child not responding to 'Bruce' when he first arrived. But that was before he had recovered fully from his cerebral contusion. No, there is something else, something in the boy and his distance from the word. As if 'Bruce' were a new label. Even so, by now a kid should have learned to connect to a label, make it his own. But this boy, from some obscure intent, stays distant, seeming to hold himself outside that label.

'Arkaroola is at the top end of the Flinders. Just before you come to the end of the ranges, the hills there are the most spectacular of all. Rugged. Great gorges and ravines, broken rock faces, dizzying vistas. And heat. Arkaroola holds the record for Australia's highest minimum temperature. A hot place, a hard place. The cauldron of planet earth. Dramatic, historic, older than history.

'The first people there were the Adnyamthanha. They tell how the monster, Arkaroo drank up all the water in Lake Frome. That lake has no water now, just salt, a sea of salt. Arkaroo drank it dry. After that, he crawled up into those mountains and he took a piss here, took another there, relieved his bursting bladder everywhere. There are waterholes wherever he went up there. Arkaroo's bladder created them – as well as Arkaroola Creek.

'Where there's water, there's life. Whitefellas farmed Arkaroola, but their stock struggled. Their cows and sheep had to compete with feral camels and donkeys. And the dingoes loved the new diet of mutton and beef.

'Arkaroola has just about every mineral anyone ever wanted to mine. At Paralana Springs, a bit further north, water is heated by rich veins of uranium ore in the rocks. Water trickles constantly, releasing carbon dioxide, nitrogen, radon and helium. Any creature that stays there long will get sick. Amazingly, there is an exception – you've heard of algae?'

Jaffas doesn't think he has. He shakes his head.

'Well, there's an algal mat there they call an extremophile; it can live in the hot waters – the temperature is 62 degrees – and in the high radioactivity. Scientists nicknamed it "extreme slime".

'There's a great whitefella story about the discovery of uranium up at Arkaroola. In 1910 a young fella called Smiler Greenwood discovered an unusual mineral while he was chasing a goat for the family's dinner. His dad sent it (the mineral that is, not the goat) to the Department of Mines, but no one there could identify it. It was just left in a cupboard. Then the world-famous Professor Mawson returned from a visit to Europe where he had met Madame Curie. She told Mawson to be on the lookout for unusual bright yellow or green radioactive materials. When Old Man Greenwood asked Mawson to check out his strange chunk, it turned out to be uranium.

'There was a gifted academic, a disciple of Mawson, who studied the soil and the rocks and the land. At first he was at a university in a city. But soon he was in "country"' – when the old man used this word, Jaffas heard it in quotation marks – 'and the Professor became a friend of the Rock People, the Adnyamathanha, who had always been here. *In country.* That Professor was Reg Spriggs.

'Spriggs bought Arkaroola and made a radical decision – *to return it to nature.* The professor got rid of the skinny sheep. The dingo fence went too. He mustered the mountain goats and he sold them. Now there was nothing much to attract dingoes. And Arkaroola returned to its natural state. It's still a sanctuary, a nature reserve. Australia's first ecotourist venture? Maybe the world's first.

'Finally, the land went back to how it always was, how the Adnyamthanha found it. I reckon if we want to go forwards, sometimes we need to go back to where we started, Bruce.'

Jaffas emerges from a reverie of sheep and goats and dingoes and extreme slime. His head falls at the Doc's closing words: *We need to go back to where we started.*

49. How to Search for Stolen Boys

Every weekday Greta listens to *'Awaye!'* The Doc observes the ritual. Greta sits with the radio at her left, the volume turned up loud. Her eyes pierce the unseen scrub as she listens with her good left ear.

The Doc watches Greta, the hunger in her eyes that subsides whenever the red-headed child is near. He hears her moaning softly in her sleep, watches her lips move, shaping words unheard.

The boy awakens and Greta opens like a flower to the light. The child returns at the end of the school day and the old woman is younger, quietly animated.

Without this boy Greta hollows out.

The Doc returns to the Net. He googles 'Stolen Children'. There is much to read. He finds the lengthy government report *Bringing them Home*. It brings him for a time undone. He narrows his searches to the Flinders Ranges. He calculates and guesstimates: *Greta's two youngest ones would be in their late fifties – I know the oldest ones; they are about sixty ...* How do you search for boys who must be men, who lost language, tribal name, country when they were small children? Men who do not know their stolen selves?

The Doc tries 'Protector of Aborigines, South Australia'. But the Government of South Australia has sealed its lips on the times of the Protector. The *Adelaide Advertiser*, on the other hand, is garrulous. The Doc finds an entire archive of microfiche of *Advertiser* copy from the sixties. Day after day, following storytime with the boy, the Doc fishes for names he knows from today's Adnyamthanha.

Day after day he returns to Greta and remains silent about the silent past. The past that moans in Greta's sleep and hungers in her waking eyes.

50. I Pull Out My Hair

Dear Jaffas,

I have got a big long cut on my hand.

I cut it with a knife.

I didnt stop the man. He took you.

I cut myself.

i dont know anything, I dont know if you are ok.

they ask me am i ok. I dont anser, i dont know.

I pull out my hair and I eat it.

My hare is missing, my redhare brother is not here.

Ive got a sore on my hand.

I dont know anything.

I know i miss you.

Come back to me jaffas, come back, come home.

Yours sincerly

Carrots (your brother)

51. The One Story – The Father of Stories

There are moments during the telling of a story when the Doc senses the boy withdrawing, shrinking. The story has taken storyteller and child into new worlds, different times – they journey together. In the course of the telling, the child leans against the adult, the two bodies merging as the carpet flies on through a wide universe of wonder.

But when the narrative touches on loss or separation the boy's face falls. He draws the event inwards. The Doc feels a lessening of the leaning pressure and body warmth as the boy retreats. His eyes unsee, his neck folds and he faces down. Only the red hair flies on, a flag, defying absence.

The Doc witnesses this and experiences an obscure distress of his own. Memory fragments, shards of old knowledge break a surface. Buried remnants, jagged edges scrape and tear at the old man's composure. His eyes sting, whether for himself or for the boy, he does not distinguish.

II

Father returned from the Snowy very early yesterday morning. Mother did not expect him until today. It was still dark when Father's kiss gently abraded Albert's cheek. Father crept to little Marguerite's bed and kissed her awake. Then he tiptoed into the double bedroom to surprise Mother. He surprised her and the person lying with her who slept there while Father was away. So Mother wouldn't be lonely.

Albert heard voices raised, crying, shouting. A slap. Then the front door slammed and Father was gone.

Marguerite was frightened. She cried and called for Father. He did not come.

Albert comforted his sister – while Father was away he would be a little man.

Albert came home from kindergarten at lunchtime. Father's big car was parked outside the house. Albert ran inside.

Father in his dark Goodbye Suit, standing near the front door, his suitcase at his side. Marguerite high in his arms.

Mother grabbing Albert, holding him close.

Mother speaking, 'Say goodbye to Daddy and Marguerite. They are going to live in another house now. You will be here with me … with us.'

Albert looked at Father. He had shaved; there was a small cut on his cheek. Father kneeled down close, the two rows of buttons next to Albert's face. Father took Albert's hand. His face was pale excepting around his eyes where the skin was red and swollen.

Father said solemnly, 'Don't cry son, kiss your sister now. And be a man.'

Albert felt his father's large hand pumping his smaller one. His own hand was not big, not like a man's hand. Tears flowed from Father's swollen eyes.

Then they were gone.

Albert stayed with Mother and with Shirley the maid, who slept with her so she wouldn't be lonely.

52. The One Story – Bluebird

'Just across the ranges from here are the salt lakes. Usually the lakes are great shimmering sheets of solid, crystalline salt. Blue on the maps, off-white in the sharp light. Dry lakes. Dry and cruel. The great monsoon rains soak the north of the continent, while down here the dry persists. The Great Dry.'

Jaffas hears the words as the Doc pronounces them, capitalised. The boy is inside the great cycles of nature.

'Now, just at this moment those lakes are full. They're teeming. Afterwards I'll ask you the Great Question, not yet though.'

Capitals again. The boy recognises the intonation.

'Ever hear of Donald Campbell?'

A shake of the head.

'Amazing man. Set world records for speed on land and on water. He travelled at speeds that no one ever travelled before, in his cars and his boats. He had the one name for all his vehicles, *Bluebird*. You've travelled in a Bluebird: that's what I call my old Toyota. In honour of the other Bluebirds.

'Anyway, Donald Campbell looked for a place to create a new land speed record. He needed a really flat surface. It had to be uniform in its texture and as free as possible of friction that would

171

slow him down. One of the traditional places was Bonneville Flat in Utah, in the USA. A very flat, very fast surface. But Campbell chose Lake Eyre, just across the hills from our own biggest one, Lake Frome. They're all the wrong names, you know. All named for explorers. As if those people discovered something unknown … The Adnyamathanha knew, of course.

'Anyhow, Donald Campbell chose this patch of South Australia. He was British, a Scot actually. The British liked to do their big thing on our soil; their own land was too small. Like Woomera, like Maralinga. Space rockets, atom bombs. As if the land were theirs. As if it were empty.'

The old man's voice has dried, slowed, taken up a heaviness. Jaffas senses the change.

The tale picks up its former pace. 'Campbell set up his record attempt. The Bluebird was ready … Teams of mechanics, official timekeepers, weather forecasters. The weather would determine success or failure, not to mention life and death.

'If the wind was strong, the Bluebird wouldn't set out. That's because a record time had to be averaged over two successive runs, one in each direction. If Campbell started with a strong following wind, the time wouldn't qualify; and on the return leg, that same breeze – now a headwind – could make the Bluebird literally take flight. You see, Bluebird was, for its time, extremely light, and literally the fastest land vehicle in history. It might fly, then crash – no Bluebird, no world record, very likely no Donald Campbell.

'And there was a limit to the number of attempts the Bluebird could make. Its engine, all of its parts, were engineered to a point of exquisite perfection. There was no capacity, no tolerance, for wear and tear.

'So they waited for ideal conditions. They chose the right season, nice and cool in the desert. They waited for the wind to drop. Lake Eyre is not very far from windy Lyndhurst.

'Campbell waited, the team waited. The team was divided into

Engineers and Cowboys. For the engineers, waiting was natural; waiting meant measuring, minimising risk. For the cowboys, risk was life, waiting was death.

'We were in the century of explorers like Scott of the Antarctic and Edmund Hilary, of British victory in two World Wars, of great risk and great Britons. Campbell's own father raced Bluebirds to world speed records. It was the era of Very Great Britain.

'They felt a strain in waiting. They needed to wait enough, but no more than enough. How the teams negotiated the strain of waiting would determine the outcome of the mission: success and survival – or the reverse. So they waited.

'Every morning the team prepared the car. Campbell prepared himself. Each morning, before he joined his teammates or went near the Bluebird, he read from a book which he never showed to another soul.

'The wind dropped, the call came, Campbell put away his book. Only now did he join his team. He climbed in, strapped himself in, fired the ignition. The great British engine roared, the vehicle shook as Campbell wound it up. The tachometer needle sailed smoothly through the hundreds of revolutions per minute. Up, up, up towards the red line. Campbell held her at the red line, then edged the motor to its limit. Under unbearable strain, the great thoroughbred thrashed itself, its engine held in neutral. Unnatural. Painful for machine and man alike.

'Thumbs up from the Chief Engineer, thumbs up from the timekeeper. Campbell thrust his own thumb aloft. Then he heard in his earphones: "Abort! Abort!" The weather forecasters had registered a shift in the wind – it was rising, it was too strong.

'The engine slowed and stopped. All the humans unwound. And waited.

'And waited again.

'The strain between Cowboys and Engineers increased with every delay. Eventually, the weather stabilised. Campbell boarded the Bluebird and went through the routines and checks. The engineers and timekeepers checked and cross-checked. The weather watchers watched the weather.

'This time the conditions were perfect. They contacted the Giles Weather Station which had the latest aerial weather probes, balloons and so forth, with the fullest data. Giles signalled all clear.

'The Chief Engineer raised his thumb, the timekeeper raised his, Campbell's thumb was the third. The engine engaged, the car trembled, leapt from its leash and flew! Campbell kept the Bluebird grounded, held her true as she flung him to his destiny. They flashed over the salt surface that held firm and flat. They traversed the measured distance faster than any earthbound human conveyance had ever travelled before. They flew across the line that marked the end of the measured mile.

'But Campbell had further tasks. His work was not yet half completed – he had to repeat the run, this time in the opposite direction. Before that, he had to hold the careering Bluebird in line and bring her to a stop, safely. Technically, this was as difficult as the processes of acceleration to maximal velocity. In his half-triumph, in the heat of achievement, he now had to nurse the beast into a tame and gentle canter, into a trot, slow to a walk, finally come to rest. Then quickly, before the wind rose, before the blood cooled, Campbell had to turn the Bluebird around and do it all again.

'Quickly, quickly. But not too quickly. All safety checks, every meticulous detail of routine, everything that would bring bird and man back in safety. Campbell went through his mental checklist, his lips speaking the words silently.

'The ritual was complete. Three thumbs rose, Bluebird thundered and once again was away. The tacho needle sailed through the red line, and Bluebird held her line; the beast beneath the bonnet bellowed, breathed deeply on air and aspirated fuel as thousands of explosions took place every minute inside her cylinders.

'Bluebird crossed the Line. She had set the record.

'Campbell slowed the car, gently, gently. To overturn now, to crash and burn, with the record in hand, would be too sad, too futile.'

♊

The old man's voice too now comes to rest. The boy does not immediately look up – their gazes do not meet too quickly. They share this moment of perfect suspension.

When they do relax, when again they breathe and speak normally, the boy feels his heart slow down.

53. They Took Me to the Hospitel

Dear Jaffas,

They took me to the hospitel. They put some water into a tube in my arm.

I forgot to eat or drink. I ate my hair. I got to thin and i fell on the floor and i fainted. They made me stay for a hole day and a hole nite.

I tryed to run away.

To be home in case you came back.

If you looked for me and i woodnt be there you mite think i wasnt waiting and wanting my brother.

I do want you back, jaffas.

I promised them i will drink and eat so i wont faint again. I was reely promising you, so i wood be home and not away in hospitel when you come back.

They make me go to scool. But I am waiting, always I wait.

And when you come home I wont let anyone steel you away again.

With love from Yours Sincerly
Carrots (your twin)

54. The One Story – Sugar

Greta demands that Jaffas attends school every day, no exceptions. She makes sure he arrives early. He falls into the practice of waiting for the library to open. The Doc will be waiting too with his One Story that is a thousand stories.

There is a story about Doug Spriggs and the propeller of his Avro Anson aircraft.

And a story about Murti Johnny, the longest-lived Australian.

And another one, about Talcum Malcolm the Danish sculptor.

And stories about the old-time whitefellas and their relics that you find in caves and mines and ghost towns.

The stories of old Finnegan, formerly of the Ireland, latterly sexual entrepreneur of Copley.

'And talking of Copley, Bruce, there are the mesas. Those great big tabletop hills, they're full of hints and hidden meanings …

'And there's stories about Lyndhurst: that's where the bitumen ends and the outermost outback starts. You know, Lyndhurst almost has too many stories for its size. The local population is only twenty or so. By comparison, Copley is a great city. Most of Lyndhurst's stories are fables of loneliness. The lost and the lonely find each other at the pub. Stories here, you could tell stories every day of your life and still there'd be stories to tell.'

Jaffas catches himself thinking, *All my life? Lucky me. We'll never finish …*

'All those stories told *Where from?* Young fella, this story could tell *Where to?* It starts with what killed most of the Aborigines but it could go on to become the story of how they stopped dying. And it leads to how they need not keep dying.'

A shake of Jaffas' red head. He knows nothing of Aborigines killed.

'It wasn't only shooting and hunting and starving them off their lands ...'

Jaffas is alert.

' ... and stealing them. That was the cruellest. That's what took the living from the living.'

Jaffas' heart pounds.

The old man falls quiet for a time. He clears his throat and resumes. 'More than all of those it was our diseases. At the beginning the blackfellas caught our smallpox and our measles. Later, it was alcohol that caused new diseases. Some of the elders and the grandmothers saw the harm that grog can do, and they voted it out of their communities.

'Nowadays, it's sugar that's killing the blackfellas. And no one can vote sugar away. Look,' says the Doc. He stops talking and pulls a couple of small bottles of drink from a cool pack he carries. 'I'll show you something.'

Jaffas recognises the two different labels. He likes both cola drinks.

The Doc says, 'Close your eyes.' Jaffas puts his hand over his eyes. The Doc pours a little from each of the bottles into separate cups. He passes one to Jaffas' and he drinks. The boy likes the sweetness and the way the bubbles bite the back of his throat.

The Doc takes the cup from Jaffas. 'Now try this one. See if you can tell the difference.' Jaffas drinks.

'Which drink has the sugar?'

The boy can't tell.

'You see,' says the Doc, 'One's a sugary killer, the other is just as sweet but it doesn't cause diabetes. Sugar kills. If people are "sitting down" – I mean, if they aren't hunting and gathering anything except welfare and royalties – if they sit down and they eat and drink sugary foods, they get sick with diabetes.

'Every day, they drink their favourite sugary cola, they become diabetic and they die young. I've tested these cola drinks on lots of people; they are like you, they can't tell by the taste which drink contains real sugar. They all go by the label.

'Now I'll tell you this, Bruce, if someone would just secretly swap all the cola labels, everyone would win – the company and the store and the people. There'd be less diabetes, teeth would be healthier. People would live longer.'

The Doc's eyes shine. This sugar story is different from his sad stories about sicknesses that kill people. The Doc seems excited. Whatever diabetes are – or is, Jaffas couldn't work it out – the Doc is *grinning*, bursting with some mystery. He keeps looking at the boy. He winks.

Jaffas feels confused.

The two finish off their cola drinks and the Doc says no more on the subject. He winks again.

It's almost time for the bell. 'Bruce, remember the story about Campbell and the Bluebird? Just before you go in to class, I'll tell you about my two great questions – one about Nature, the other about Man.

'Firstly, the Nature question: how do all those tens of thousands of waterbirds, how do they know on their salty coasts where these inland waters are, far distant, when the lakes are filling, where they'll find their foods, where the grasses and the fishes are? Lake Eyre can be dry for a decade, more. When the rains fall, southern Queensland floods, the Cooper floods and the salt lakes fill and freshen. The Murray fills, flows, and floods, the Coorong comes to life. How do the birds know? And so soon? And know it so securely that they will hazard all on a flight inland across the continent, a trip that can kill? That's a secret and as far as I know – it remains their secret. For me, that's the great story of our knowings and unknowings.

'And you know what, Bruce? Sometimes I like a question more than an answer.'

Doc then asks, 'What do you think is the second question, the question about Man?'

The boy shakes his head.

'My question is: what is the book that Campbell reads every morning of the campaign? He shows no one, he shares that book with none of his team. What would you think it was, Bruce?'

Jaffas thinks of his mother's One Great Book. His mind flies then from the Gideons to his mother, to Carrots. There his mind stops. Thought collapses, swamped by pain.

'What do you reckon, Bruce?'

Jaffas can barely shake his head.

'Well, I don't know either. No one knows. Campbell's mother was English: she thought her son read Kipling's *If*. His old man, a flag-flying fascist, said it would be the poetry of Ezra Pound, his laureate. Or else Robbie Burns. His old school padre was sure it was Campbell's Confirmation Bible. His first sweetheart believed it was a book of her collected letters of unrequited love, written and posted to him in the course of his many campaigns.

'He read from it every day of every campaign. Now the book is lost. His diary entries declare blandly: *Read and meditated* – on every morning of every campaign. No one knows and no one ever will, because he destroyed the book. After his final campaign, he burned it. He said afterwards, "It was always going to be the book or me. I always intended that only one of the two of us would survive. That book gave me the world records. It gave me my success, my life. And I survived. Afterwards, I sacrificed it as my thanksgiving offering."

'The irony, the tragedy really, is that Campbell did crash and die. In a later Bluebird, at a different time. What do you think of that, Bruce?'

55. The Copley Mesas

Classes begin at 9 am. Jaffas notices something odd: the Aboriginal kids don't always come to class. They're there one day, absent the next, sometimes present for a week, then away for a week. It's different from what he knew in the city, where all of the kids turned up every school day.

He calculates, takes a risk, speaks in English. Four words, quietly. He asks Kendall, the Aboriginal girl who sits next to him, 'Where were you yesterday?'

'Business.'

What does that mean? Is Kendall telling him to mind his own business? Jaffas hears that word, *business*, quite often. He realises the tone of voice is not unfriendly. Blackfella kids mean something else when they say 'business', something understood. Something more urgent than school.

Jaffas lives with Greta in an Aboriginal household: *so I should have business too*. Jaffas decides he'll take the occasional day off from school.

He thinks more about his business. There is something, something important he's been neglecting. Whole days are passing without him thinking of Carrots. His business is his brother. His brother is half of him. While he, Jaffas, is missing, Carrots will not be alright.

Every school morning, Jaffas visits the library to search for his own story in the newspapers. He never finds the news he is looking for. But there are storybooks and CDs and videos and DVDs. And a reference section where the books have no stories. Jaffas never looks at these; if there is no story, there's no point. But Jaffas stumbles on an atlas, misfiled under Fiction. He leafs idly, stopping at the familiar form of the map of Australia. His eyes, ever searching in this place for Carrots, finds Melbourne at the bottom right-hand corner of the map. He can't see Leigh Creek.

The librarian points out the Flinders Ranges.

Nursing the atlas, Jaffas walks a distance from the librarian. Melbourne looks close. Jaffas plots his course, a straight line. And decides he will walk back to Carrots. It is probably a long way. He'll need to train himself; he'll take some long walks.

II

At 9 o'clock on his first morning of *business*, Jaffas hides behind the farthest shelves in the library. He waits until well after the bell rings for class. He peers from his hiding place – the library is still. Only the Doc is working at his usual desk among the computers. Jaffas walks quietly from the library and out of the school grounds. He climbs the steep hills behind the golf club and looks around. To the west and the east, he sees flat brown earth stretching to distant brown hills. To the south, the hills of Aroona cluster around the green life of the creek and the dam.

He turns north. Two tabletop hills shine bronze and massive in the morning sun, dwarfing the scattered human structures of the hamlet of Copley.

From the heights above the golf club, the mesas look very close. Jaffas knows they are five kilometres away. He'll walk there and back, that will be ten kilometres, good practice for the big walk to Melbourne, to Carrots. And he'll climb up to the top. He'll get fit for the hills on the walk home to Melbourne.

It takes Jaffas over an hour to walk to the massifs. The heat drains him. He wears his schoolbag with the damper and the drink bottle that Greta packs every morning. He always eats the damper, but he never touches the water. There are plenty of taps at school. But Greta insists he take the water bottle. 'Hot country, this one, dry. Need water. Whitefella kids maybe can't find water. Take bottle, take every time.' Jaffas drinks, grateful for once for Greta's insistence.

He skirts the rocky tumbles that guard the hills, looking for a way in and up. He can't see one. He climbs one of the smaller rocks, sliding on the loose footing. He falls backwards a little and lands firmly on his bottom. He breathes hard and rubs the bone above his butt cheek then tries again, this time bending forward, climbing hand over hand. He straightens when he gains the top of the small rock, cranes, looking for the flat tops that beckoned so beguilingly from the golf club hills. He cannot see them; only rugged rock upon rugged rock, and steeps that speak darkly of things hidden, of country where he is not welcome. The land has locked him out.

Dizzy, he tries to recall the old man's words about the mesas: did he say *secret* or *sacred*?

Jaffas sits and looks down the further slope of his small rock. There, winding before him, is a hint of a line, not a track so much as a flattening in the scree, leading into the tumbles and upward. He grabs his bottle, throws his schoolbag over his shoulder and follows the wallaby track. Here, perhaps, is a way to the top.

He doesn't make it to the summit. Instead he follows the almost-track. It leads him up, around, down. *Down! How will I get to the top? How will I find the Secret?*

Jaffas faces two towering walls, sheer, unclimbable. There is no way up, no foothold. No way around either. Once again at a loss, he looks down. There, at his feet, a shadow, a lessening of the light leads his eyes to a small fissure between the rock walls, small enough for a wallaby, small enough for a boy, if the boy bent and crawled.

Jaffas crawls. Into darkness.

Something disturbs the air at his side, something not seen nor heard, but somehow felt. There it is again, a whooshing, a fleeting sweep of air, an eddy. Disorienting, disturbing.

He stands without moving, ducking occasionally as the whooshes approach and recede. His eyes accommodate to the blackness and he sees the bats, horrible blind black stealth bombers. Disturbing, somehow significant, speaking of the hidden, the not seen.

Behind the squadron of bats, on the far wall, a suggestion of colour, of colours in the plural, mutating, shifting: the Secrets!

He makes his way across the cave. The floor is powdery. He kicks up dust and sneezes repeatedly, a volley of shrieking explosions that bend him double. The bats flee into the dark.

He sees more clearly now. A painting, a number of paintings in shades of rust and white and cream and black, with patches and streaks of purple. Jaffas makes out a large bird and its many chicks, all walking. Another bird, smaller, with only two chicks, flying above them. The biggest bird, the mother, occupies most of one panel, her feathers spiking from her odd, egg-shaped torso, her legs long thin sticks that end in wide chicken-toed feet.

The paintings are large. The big bird that walks strides across her space, massive, dominating all.

This is a story, a story Jaffas already knows. Secret, certainly, but *sacred* too. He stands for long moments. Then walks out backwards.

II

After school, Jaffas tries to keep out of Greta's way. Greta unpacks his lunch box, finds his water bottle. She shakes it: empty. She corners the boy. She takes in his coating of dust, of ochres – pink, mustard, white. And the smell of dried batshit from his shoes.

Jaffas does not want to meet Greta's gaze. Her voice is quiet, clear, the words even slower than usual. 'Thirsty today. Maybe you been walking? Big walk?'

Jaffas shakes his head.

'You been with *warraiti*. Today. You been see him.'

The boy stares at the woman. Habitually mute in English, he can't find any response in Spanish; he cannot now, even silently, conjure words to account for himself. He looks up at Greta. For the second time that day he trembles.

'You been see secret thing. Special one.'

Her old face is shining. Her gentle voice softens, slowing further.

183

'Good!' A pause. 'Now you got him secret.' She beams, nodding approvingly. 'And I got your secret. Walking one. Big walking. I keep him secret. Now you gotta keep *warraiti* one secret!'

56. Every Nihgt

Dear Jaffas,

Every nihgt I stay awake. I wait. Then I fall asleep, i cant help it.

If i dreem of you I feel happy. In dreems we are together we walk or talk or swim in the creek.

Last nite i dreemed we playd murder in the chookhouse, i was so exited. I woke up and my PJs were stiky, the sheets to.

You felt close in that dreem. I cood feel you. My arms and my boddy miss you, Jaffas.

I woke up and I felt arms around me, reel arms, not a dreem. It was papi. I closed my eyes and pretended it was you and I tryed to be happy.

Yours Faithly,
Your twin brother, Carrots.

57. The Sculptor of Lyndhurst

Jaffas hears or dreams a jingling sound. He opens his eyes. It is morning. The Doc and Greta are up and dressed. The Doc's car keys jingle in his hands as he paces.

'You want a story this morning, Bruce?'

184

Jaffas rubs his eyes. He nods.

'Well, grab some clothes. We're going to Lyndhurst, to Talcum Malcolm. It's his story, he's the one who tells it. Greta reckons you need to know this story.'

Greta says, 'You listen that story. Big story, that one.'

II

'G'day, Greta. Gentlemen ...'

'Gentlemen.' Papi calls me and Carrots gentlemen ... sometimes.

The speaker is a short, stocky old man, maybe as old as the Doc. His wild and rampant beard is a thicket. Jaffas recalls a limerick:

There was an Old Man with a beard ...

The old man shakes hands with Jaffas. 'Call me Malcolm – Talcum Malcolm.' Malcolm offers them a seat in the shade, an area with a brush roof supported by rough poles. Outside, dozens of sculptures, all of them milky white, burn in the sun.

Malcolm is a sculptor. He wears ragged shorts and a shirt without sleeves. His hair is long and wild. He has a soft way about him – a soft, crackling, old-man voice, a soft handshake, a breathy, confidential sort of voice, a singsong with a funny accent.

Jaffas looks at the old man's outdoor sculpture gallery. One life-sized sculpture holds his gaze, all soft curves, lines and planes that flow and merge and fold: a mother and her infant.

The Doc says, 'That lady is Matilda. Malcolm, tell Bruce your Waltzing Matilda story.'

The sculptor looks at the boy. 'You like stories?'

Jaffas nods.

'You know how the song goes? *Once a jolly swagman ...* ? A swaggie comes to a billabong, he steals a sheep, he's about to be arrested, but he jumps into the billabong and drowns himself. You know how it ends – *The swagman, he upped and he jumped into that billabong / You'll never catch me alive, said he ...*

'Well, that's nonsense! Who would kill himself for a sheep? Do you know where all this took place?'

Jaffas doesn't know. He looks at the Doc.

The Doc says, 'Winton, wasn't it? Out in the Channel country?'

'Yeah. They say Paterson wrote the words in Winton. But before it was called Winton, people called the place Pelican Waterhole. The actual drowning occurred at Combo Creek. I reckon Pelican Waterhole and Combo Creek might be the same place. Anyway, the truth of the story is hidden in that name, Combo Creek. Combo means "combination". You know what a Combination Man was?'

Jaffas does not know. He looks at Malcolm expectantly.

'A combination man was a whitefella bloke who combined with an Aboriginal woman. People looked down on it. I'm a combo man myself. The swaggy was a combo man. That made him an outcast.

'His wife gave birth to a child. The whitefellas called the baby a half-caste. The police took the child away. Stole him. That's what they used to do. They stole children. And the swagman, well, he up and he jumped into that billabong. He couldn't bear to live without his child that had been taken away. By that time he'd already lost his wife. Ever since, they've called that billabong Combo Creek.'

Jaffas wilts. *A child was stolen and a parent killed himself.*

I was stolen. I am alive. But what about my parents?

Suddenly afraid, he starts to cry. He cries, 'Mami. Mami.'

The old men and Greta look at him, snuffling, choking on his muffled syllables. He repeats them, over and over. The men turn their gaze away from the boy, respecting his secret grief. Greta takes in his form. His skinny body, lightly muscled now, his scalp covered in dense red hair; his freckles, darker and more plentiful. The boy's body predicts the man he will become. Greta shakes. She stands at his side, her translucent hand resting on his head. The boy weeps on. *A parent killed himself after a child was stolen. A parent, a grown-up person!*

Jaffas has witnessed Luisa as fear overtakes her. He sees her now, her child stolen. He sees Mami, collapsing, despairing. Jaffas forgets all manliness. He cries out loud, he rocks, his face running with tears and snot.

186

He lets go, he cries for his mother. He cries for the Combo Man, for the man's wife, for their stolen child. 'Mami, Mami! Mami, Mami!'

He cries, in the end, for Jaffas.

58. Greta Dreaming

Samuel! Samuel!

Jaffas wakes from his sleep. It is very dark, not the time to be awake. What was that sound? Silence. Jaffas turns over and burrows into the swag.

There it is again: *Samuel! Samuel!* The voice is loud in the small house, a voice familiar but strange. Wide awake now, he recalls Mami's story, the one she read from her Red Book about the small boy in the house of God – *Samuel!*

Is God calling him, Jaffas?

Again the voice: *Malachi! Malachi!*

Malachi?

A new voice, a man's voice. It is the Doc. 'Wake up, Greta, wake up! You're dreaming.'

Greta's voice, choking: 'My boys, Malachi, Samuel. I see 'em, I call 'em. They not come. They not hear. They walk away, whitefella take them away. I watch, I call … My boys, I not see them again … My boys, my boys …'

Jaffas hears Greta's great gulps of grief, the Doc's voice, soft, speaking soothingly, speaking in language, in Adnyamthanha.

Confused – *how does whitefella Doc know Abu's language?* Frightened – *why is Abu crying?* – he wants to go and investigate. He climbs from his swag and hesitates. He has heard a grown-up woman crying in the dark before – Mami. The memory burns. He stands, irresolute.

Now the Doc speaks in English. Jaffas catches words here,

phrases there. *No luck ... internet ... whitefella books.* The weeping subsides, resumes.

The Doc again: *Someone, somewhere must know Samuel or Malachi ... Maybe Shepparton, Ballarat, Bairnsdale, Warrnambool ...*

The weeping, the odd soft gasp, the blowing of a nose – the boy listens, hears it all.

Quietness falls again on the small house. He peers through the doorway. A single dim shape in the quietness, an agglomeration of shadow, a single fullness in the swag where two are become one.

Sleep does not come quickly to the frightened boy.

II

When Jaffas awakens, it is bright outside. He hears Abuela talking to Abuelo. He looks out the window and sees Abuelo eating damper, hot from the ashes of last night's fire. Abuela, wearing her lilac housecoat, looks at the damper in her hand. She holds it as if she doesn't know what to do with it. The old lady has been crying. She speaks, not loudly but emphatically, shaking her head. The words are heavy, she heaves them painfully from deep in her chest. *That boy ... he don't belong us ... he got mother somewhere ... She need him. Boy gotta be with mother. We gotta be find mother ... give him back.*

The effort of giving birth to her last words exhausts the old lady. Her head falls forward, her spine folds, her hair falls from her face towards the earth. She looks no bigger than Jaffas himself. Wisps of smoke hide her face momentarily. The old lady does not move.

The old man sits at her side, his arm around her skinny back. He nods his head, nods again. 'You're right, Greta. You're right. I'll search the web – again.'

Disturbed, Jaffas withdraws. He returns to bed. When the Doc comes in, Jaffas looks as if he's sleeping.

59. Ochre Pits at Lyndhurst

Another early morning excursion in the Doc's troop carrier. Greta, wakes early. There's no time to waste. She insists the boy always arrive in Leigh Creek in time for school.

'School important. Grow you up man. Learn you man. Writing, computer, everything. Gotta learn, gotta go to school. School important.'

They drive to Lyndhurst, last town on the bitumen. Beyond Lyndhurst the dirt roads wind and bump all the way to Birdsville, to Oodnadatta; and the Sztrezlecki leads to Innamincka – dusty highways into the real outback that stretches north and east, stretching into silence, into immensity and enigma.

Five kilometres north of Lyndhurst, they arrive at the ochre pits. Craters and mounds and hollows, ghostly white, mustard, magenta, cream – eerie, quiet, quiet, the only sound the sighing wind.

They climb from the troop carrier. They gaze upon the silence.

Greta steps into the wasteland of bleached white and powerful pastel. She leads the Doc and the boy, winding a track between unearthly forms to a mass of stone that looks like all the others. She stops and straightens. She points: 'Look this one.'

They gaze at the rock. Greta caresses the smooth roundness. Her long bony hand slides, stops abruptly at a point where the soft curves of stone give way to hard lines and chipped planes. 'Here. Here Adnyamthanha people take white stone. Make powder, for paint, ceremony.'

Greta straightens, opens her arms wide, encompasses the vastness, then folds her arms inward, gathering unseen multitudes. 'Adnyamthanha mob, all blackfella mob, all come for ochre. All blackfella gotta paint, all gotta dance. Gotta come here. Adnyamthanha country.'

Greta fixes her eyes on the child, pauses dramatically, making sure Jaffas is attending, then flings a fist suddenly skyward, shaking it at some foe. 'Sometime, another mob need ochre. Might be fighting. Maybe fighting our mob long time. Come here, come Adnyamthanha country, want ochre. What we going do? Fight 'im? Send 'im away – "no ochre, you mob our enemy"?'

Greta is asking Jaffas. He does not know what to say to this fist-shaking Greta. *Abu* is suddenly a warrior, fierce, intimidating. Every mob gotta have paint. Gotta have it. For dance. Gotta let him get ochre.

'Big one, that one. Important. You see that, you remember that.' Greta slows, she points at the boy, she wags her finger at him. 'We not fight him. Him not fight us mob. He come, he get ochre, he go home, own country. Gotta do that way. Big Spirit make ochre for all blackfella.'

Greta shines with her great truth.

Jaffas recalls Greta in her dreaming stories of *warraiti*. In the stillness and the whiteness, surrounded by mute mounds of ochreous rock, Jaffas tingles, the electric current of Greta running through him.

They drive away. The Doc ensures Jaffas arrives at school in Leigh Creek right on time, at nine o'clock.

Part 4

♊

60. One Twin at School

The therapist said, 'Carrots, you need to go back to school. It's been more than a month now, since … since Jaffas hasn't been here. You need to learn. And you need to be with other children.'

Carrots knew his need was otherwise. He said nothing.

The next morning, Luisa took Carrots to school. Carrots did not resist. He sat in his seat and did as he was told. Not now the Carrots of the past, he of perpetual motion; Carrots was now a slow, silent child who sat when he was told, who stood, drew, tidied up as directed. He was no trouble, this new Carrots.

Headmistress Nadia did not speak of the absence of Jaffas or of the change in Carrots. All the children, however, saw there was only one twin at school. Some had seen the news item, others had heard parents speak of it. The word spread that Jaffas had been stolen. The school revived its 'Stranger Danger' program.

No one now confused the twins. Jaffas was 'gone' – whatever that might mean. The twin who remained at school was Carrots. Carrots was that boy island, thinner, if that was possible. And here and there he had bare patches on his scalp. Carrots frightened people. He was a silent warning.

The reality that you could be in school one day – red-headed, brother-knit, buzzing, sparking – and the next day you were gone, absolutely, definitely gone and gone *indefinitely*, stunned the entire school population. Teachers, classmates, parents, all experienced a rupture in the natural order. No one knew what to say to Carrots. No one dared think too much about Jaffas. There was abroad a global paralysis of the explicit. This suited Carrots.

One person acted differently, one who missed Jaffas as a person. At playtime, Tori began to wait for Carrots outside his classroom. When, as often happened, Carrots did not go out to play, Tori would walk quietly into the room and sit down at Carrots' side. She said little. Tori seemed satisfied to be near to Jaffas' twin.

Quite often, Carrots simply failed to come to school. On these occasions, he was seeing the therapist; or sleeping, having missed sleep the previous night, writing to Jaffas; or simply waiting, listening for his brother.

On the days that Carrots failed to arrive, Tori became quieter.

There came a day when Carrots spoke: 'I should have saved him.'

Tori was still.

'I saved myself, I ran away.'

Tori shook her head, started to cry softly.

'I'm the strong one. I should have stopped the man.'

Tori's body shook silently.

Carrots stopped speaking. Diffidently he extended an arm and rested it on Tori's shoulder. Tori's body stilled. She nestled against Carrots' arm. An occasional shudder disturbed the stillness, then subsided.

Carrots did not speak again of self-blame.

II

School was altered – Jaffas was not there; he might never return. Carrots was there, locked inside himself, with Tori his only visitor. Or Carrots was absent, with Tori observing a silent vigil.

The school was not itself. No one wanted to speak of Jaffas or his absence. The air was still and dull. All felt the slowing of the metabolism of the school community. Children and adults alike experienced it as a paralysis that numbed and gagged them. No one broke out of the muteness and the heaviness.

61. The Mother of Carrots

Bernard came home from work. He found his wife, searched her face, gently kissed her dark face. No light. 'How's Carrots been?'

'His soul is bound up in his soul.'

Luisa's 'Bible talk' used to amuse Bernard, the archaic words and phrases of the Gideons. Over time, her English had 'naturalised', capturing something of local cadence, if not its informality. The Gideons still spoke through Luisa when she was moved by strong feeling. It was instinct, not intent.

Since Jaffas' disappearance, Luisa was never far from those depths. Bible talk was the sound and the proof of her disintegration, of the family's. Would he too fall apart? Luisa's *bibliolalia* – would that be the correct term? – drove him crazy. It drove them apart.

The old nightmares became Luisa's daytime thoughts. Sometimes it was Mengele torturing Jaffas. Now a paedophile had him, now he was dying of neglect somewhere, untended, unloved. She saw Jaffas captive, disoriented, not knowing himself, disintegrating. She saw him pining for Carrots: *his brother and his flesh.*

Fresh horrors came to her from the news: visions of twin sisters at 'The Family Shooting Center' ... 'They practiced for an hour until confident of their accuracy. They took aim, and on the agreed signal, they fired at each other. One perished. The other was less fortunate.'

The name, the '*Family* Shooting Center'!

Real life supplied endless vehicles for her guilt and her fear. She needed no power of imagination; the daily news sufficed: today, a parent drove his children into a dam. The children drowned, the father survived; another day, a second father drove his two children to the top of a high bridge. He stopped the car and threw one child to her death. *He took one of two.* He left the second to survive, to suffer.

Closest of her terror parallels, a pair of identical twin brothers in Belgium, deaf since birth, was informed that presently they would both lose their sight. Rather than lose this unmediated communication, the twins chose to die.

The bad dreams that came at night now were all biblical, text-heavy, lament-laden. Whole passages of dialogue disturbed her sleep. She'd awaken, sweating, with the words burning her tongue. *But he sent not the brother with his brethren, for he said, 'Lest there happen unto him harm.'*

Luisa wasn't sleeping and Bernard, Bible-bashed, retreated to Carrots' bed. He lay there, pressing his face against the boy's unconscious back, feeling the small body warm, alive, present. His tears dampened Carrots' pyjamas. The child slept on. Bernard released pent-up love for his boys, and grief and rage for his torn wife.

Luisa woke again suddenly and sat upright, quivering with unformed fear. *What will happen?* It came to her then: *No point in fearing anything worse; the worst is actual. No, no, not quite the worst – worse still might follow, something – someone might harm Carrots.*

After such an awakening, Luisa tried to remain awake, but sleep crept up on her and she'd rest for a time, innocent and unfearing. Then, hammering at her mind: *Have ye a father or a brother?* O, Jaffas, dear Jaffas, bereft and alone! *Surely he is torn apart, and I have not seen him until now.*

Sometimes the Bible words brought Luisa a bitter comfort. They had borne her into English and now they bore her grief. Their power was equal to her pain. Old friends, sad allies from her single days, the stories were her companions now in loss. Luisa lived in them, retreated to them. She had no place here, among the present: *The child is not, and I, whither shall I go?*

She did not deserve the sweetness of sleep. Hers it was to be mindful of Jaffas. *If I forget thee, let my tongue cleave to my mouth.* If she stopped thinking of Jaffas, would he exist? If she forgot him, would he remember? Luisa, unworthy of living connection, turned inward to the stories and retreated. Bernard and Carrots inhabited far reaches of her mind.

62. Tracking

The sun rose. A long shadow and a shorter one moved steadily along the perimeter of the backyard. The moving shadows left behind them a trail of trample, black against the silvery glisten of the dew.

The shadows followed a thin boy and a thin dog that walked silently, automatically, around and around the yard. They had been walking for an hour. Every time he passed the driveway, the boy stopped and looked up and out to the street. Boy and dog, both still, eyes and ears to the road. The moment passed. The boy's head fell and the two resumed their circuit.

Inside the house, a man prepared coffee for his wife. Soon he would wake her, they'd drink coffee and go out to search.

Bernard looked out at his back garden and watched the steady shadows in their circuits. He waited for the boy to reach the drive- way, he saw him pause and lift, saw him slump and resume.

He shook his head. His own body sagged and he turned away. But at every circuit he watched anew. He had to watch. He needed to keep faith with the son keeping faith with his brother.

The sun lit the pale dog and the thin boy. Suddenly ablaze, the two looked down at the grass at their feet and walked on.

63. Luisa, Avenger

Eventually, man and wife talked. Bernard said, 'I'm lonely. I miss Jaffas.' He lowered his voice, absently moving his hand up and down Sahara's spine. 'I miss *Carrots*.'

He looked at last at Luisa. His voice cracked, a rustling in his dry throat. 'And I miss you, Luisa.'

Luisa looked up at Bernard; she saw him. She drew a long breath and leaned forwards. The daughter of a smile, another long breath, a look, as of resolution. 'I explain to you now. The day I meet you, I decide: this man I can trust. I showed you a mark on my leg, but until now I never explain.' Luisa pointed to the mark behind her knee. 'There was a man … when I had only twelve years. He raped me. He had a knife. He cut my leg when I ran away.'

Bernard's gaze had moved to Luisa's leg. At the word 'rape', his head jerked upward. He stared at Luisa, his mouth open.

Luisa continued: 'Please do not be angry for my silence. And do not feel sorry for me, Bernard. I do not need sorry, and I cannot bear it now. I can forget any hurt anyone does to me. I learned that, after that man, beneath the bridge in San Telmo … Not straight away; it took five years of therapy. I was seventeen before I decide that that man and his acts do not define me. They do not really relate to me. I was the occasion, the location.

'I am Luisa, a person. Not connected with that creature. There is nothing for me in remembering. He is nothing to me, he is less than nothing. But so long as I held him in my thought, I was that man's prisoner. He was free, unmolested, he never served time.

'It took five years for me to know I was serving time. Then I was free. I will always be free of anyone who ever hurts me. I will forget hurt. I learned how to forget.' Luisa smiled. She looked again at her husband. Her features softened, she rested her hand on his.

'That decision to forget, that was before. Before a man stole my child, before I discover my limits.' She lowered her voice, breathing the words. 'I see Carrots every day, suffering, withering. Carrots is a shroud, not now a child.' Luisa wrenched her eyes from the spectacle before her. 'I think of Jaffas – who can know his pain? I see him dead. I see him dying of loneliness. I have visions – he is a child broken. He searches faces for the one face that is his reflection. When these images start, I see Jaffas in every extreme, every misery. Now I see him dying of starvation, he is bones and skin. His hair is somehow coarse and grey; now I see my child injured, bloodied and torn, his bones broken; now he is maimed, his body crooked from broken bones unset.

'And then I see the kidnapper raping my son; I see the man's face, I recognise him. That face, it comes back to me from the darkness of the shadows under the bridge in San Telmo ... You know when you play music from opera, always I leave the room. I explain now.'

Bernard, confused, waited. Luisa continued, 'I explain: before the rape, I am walking in San Telmo, my legs walk towards the bridge but my eyes look across the road, looking at the opera house, at the beautiful, terrible picture of the next opera. It is Theodorakis' *Medea*. The picture is of Medea. She holds her two small sons, she is about to murder her boys. I see the beauty. I feel the horror. I do not see the man who sees me. I walk under the bridge into the shadow and he ... I cannot go to opera, I cannot hear it.'

Luisa stopped, her head in her hands. Bernard watched her fingers claw at her head, the nails press hard into her scalp.

'I see visions of the suffering of our boys. They flash and fly away. Other visions – all bad – follow, they do not end. My mind spins; madness calls me, it calls me back, it tempts me. No! I will not go mad; Carrots needs me. I learn to anchor myself in hatred! I steady myself by hating the man who took Jaffas. When I picture myself revenging, I can unpicture Jaffas: *If one person steal another, and the stolen person be found in his hand, he shall surely die.*'

Bernard recognised Luisa's slide back into Bible talk, the resort and habit of her deepest feeling. He looked across the room empty of one son. He saw the remaining son, Carrots, the boy's face unpresent. He saw Luisa's face, a face not empty but working its rage, a face full of feeling, olive skin darkening, cheeks tensing and collapsing.

He remembered for a moment the beauty of Luisa's face in tranquil moments. How those cheeks when smooth seemed to rise gently into rounded hills, her mouth slightly open, hinting a smile, her eyes glowing – he saw this beauty, this beauty lost.

Bernard did not recognise his wife, this woman, this face not rounded but long, the eyes narrowed, the mouth cruel. The woman moving her lips, framing words.

'*Surely he shall die.* Surely. I kill him myself. *I kill him.*'

64. The File on Wilbur

The Doc walks through Greta's shack, collecting soiled clothes, towels, tea towels to launder. He checks the pockets of Jaffas' shorts. He finds a scrap of paper, grimy and tightly folded and re-folded. Curious, he unfolds it and reads the childish script:

mi hermano

estoy vivo, robado, en Egipto.

su hermano

José

More Spanish. He wonders what it means.

The Doc checks the curious text in the library. He clicks 'Spanish into English'. 'Prisoner in Egypt' tells him nothing. The piece of paper seems to be significant to the boy. *A mystery.*

The shorts dry quickly on Greta's clothesline. The Doc replaces Jaffas' scrap of paper in the shorts pocket.

Doc has news for Greta, and he feels close enough to her to ask a question he has suppressed until now. 'You and Wilbur are old friends?'

'Not friend now.'

The Doc raises an eyebrow. 'What happened?'

'Jimmy bring drugs. Used with young fellas, with Ambrose, all time. All time.'

'What sort of drugs?'

'Sniff some, swallow some, drink with grog. Sometime use needle, you know. One time Jimmy real sick. I call ambulance, he go in hospital.'

'Here? In the Flinders?'

Greta nods. She stands and turns away. 'Jimmy come out hospital, more drugs, all sort. Ambrose too. When Jimmy see Ambrose not wake up, he run away. Real quick. He don't want see police. He run. I glad he gone.' She paused. 'This time, when he come back, he bring this little fella. I send Jimmy away.'

'Greta, why do you think Wilbur … Jimmy … brought this little red-headed fella here?'

'Don't want talk about Jimmy.'

'Well, I'll mention one last thing, some news you'd want to know. That urine test you wanted me to do … Jimmy's test. It's negative.'

Greta regards him, digesting doctor words.

'His urine was mixed with water from the toilet. It was diluted; that meant the drugs could be harder to find. So I did some sums and made allowance for toilet water. I tested it four different ways – no drugs. That means he's clean. But just to be sure, I sent the urine to the forensic lab in Adelaide. They test for rare drugs, fancy ones – all negative. No drugs. No ganja, no speed, no coke, no benzos, nothing …'

Greta stares, shakes her head. 'Funny fella, that Jimmy.'

The old lady grunts, 'Too late. Jimmy clean now. Too late …'

II

201

Wilbur's urine is negative, but maybe drugs hurt his brain permanently – I mean forever.

The Doc consults the hospital records. He finds no file for Wilberforce James Reynolds. He tries the three names in various sequences: no record of a patient admitted with a drug overdose by any of those names.

Google is more fruitful. Records of convictions, of court cases, of a number of aliases, of misappropriation of a Medicare card. The stolen card was of a Gil Israel.

The hospital holds records of Gil Israel's admission in a stupor. A thirty-year-old man was found unconscious. The patient was a known drug user. Toxicology tests done in Adelaide were positive for a remarkable number of illicit drugs and prescription drugs, including LSD and PCP.

The latter is new to the Doc. Wikipedia lists side effects: *paranoia ... belief in messianic status ... ideas of superhuman powers ... eclipse of the superego ...*

The Doc sits for a while in thought. He closes the computer. *So the messiah has come and gone. He's fulfilled his historic mission, his destiny. All the grand biblical imagery, the great themes: he's brought the boy here, a sacrifice, a lost lamb, a lamb found. A child restored to a lamenting woman ...*

He opens the computer again.

Perhaps it's not too late to find Greta's boys.

65. Early Morning

Mum's car's too risky: someone might recognise a little white Honda. Safer by train, then a walk.

Wilbur took an early train and alighted at Oakleigh. He paced nervously, looking for the toilet. *Where's the dunny? I need to piss.*

He emptied his bladder and hurried from the toilet. He walked briskly through the early chill. Since Wilbur left the Flinders, he had avoided this area. *Shit, it feels likes years since I watched and waited while those kids played soccer in their front yard.*

He had kept Italowie in his mind. The pure vision, the clarity gave him resolution. He knew what he had to do. He reminded himself repeatedly: *I'm doing what I have to do. Bringing the second kid is the only way to make things right.*

Wilbur heard a car motor in the still dawn. He hid behind a tree at a distance on the far side of the street. A silver Subaru wagon emerged from the driveway of the house where the kids lived. Wilbur drew field glasses from his jacket pocket. Through his binoculars he saw two figures in the car: a man and another adult, darkly clad – a woman?

As the car drove away, he searched the back seat for a child's face or body. The rear was empty. He checked his watch: 0600 hours. He looked up and down the street. Empty, everything slept.

Where are they going? How long will they be?

He sprinted from one sheltering tree to the next, pausing to peer and catch his breath, then sprinting again, melting in and out of view of the house. Wasn't this the way he recalled Greta's grandsons' stalking game?

Wilbur stopped. He had gained a hundred metres. He congratulated himself. Thanks to his bushcraft he had not been detected. In truth no traffic had passed. No blinds lifted, no curtains parted.

Quickly, Wilbur crossed the street. Outside the Target Premises now (he liked the cool operations jargon of his action comics), he crept to the driveway. He heard a sharp yapping, saw the sign: *Attack Dog*. And bolted.

Back behind his tree on the opposite nature strip, Wilbur composed himself. And prepared for his next Operation. *Better buy some Schmackos for that dog. I'll cook up a valium syrup out of Mum's sleepers and soak the Schmackos in it, knock the dog out …*

He sat and waited for the Subaru to return. The kid would have to go to school. They'd come back some time before nine, he reckoned.

At 0850, he heard the sound of the Subaru. He sheltered and peered through the field glasses: two adults, a man, and now in the brightness of morning, definitely a woman.

He walked away fast.

66. One Red Hair

Every weekday morning, Bernard and Luisa spent the early hours searching. Bernard, awake before the alarm, dressed in the dark. He'd have to get dressed for work anyway. Getting up early to search filled in the hours when sleep was a fugitive.

At 5.45 he brought coffee to Luisa and woke her. She drank and dressed quickly, choosing clothes that Jaffas would recognise, thinking, *strangers will not notice me …*

Bernard never spoke the words – *this is hopeless*. Searching was something to do. Something he could do together with Luisa, a small bridge they could build without words.

Luisa never spoke the *hopeless* word either. To speak the word would be to create the reality. This she knew from instinct. And from the Bible: *Let there be light … and there was light.*

Neither Bernard nor Luisa ever gave voice to the guilty fact: searching was relief from the unbearable company of Carrots.

They did not speak the words. They tried to resist the thought.

They left at 6 am. Carrots stayed home with Sahara. *Safe.*

II

Bernard had created a system. He thought himself a man of systems.

Our best chance has to be where we'll see the most people, busy places at busy times. Rail stations first. Peak period, lots of people. Before I have to go off to work myself.

The Dandenong Line was busy and close to their home, close to where the man had snatched Jaffas. It was a straw to clutch at, as likely a prospect as any other. Today Bernard and Luisa searched at Oakleigh Station.

They arrived at 6.15 and positioned themselves just inside the barrier, standing opposite each other, both facing the gate.

They would know their man by his small red goatee. If he hadn't shaven it off. And if there was an accomplice, he, or she, might betray guilt.

Bernard searched faces for oddity. He held a belief that faces were eloquent. He looked closely, straining to learn what a face might tell. He was alert for commonplace oddities – furtiveness, fussiness over detail, undue nervousness. He was after the person who was hiding something.

This meticulous blonde woman, precise, tidy, systematic in her commonplace acts: validating her ticket, checking her hair in her mirror, snapping open her handbag, replacing that mirror fussily; now snapping the bag closed, re-checking the clasp one more time, now running her tongue over her glossed lips. That was the sort of attention to detail you'd need to cover your crime.

Bernard stared hard at the woman, piercing her being, willing her to show her guilt. She surprised his staring scrutiny, smiling candidly, speaking pleasantly, as if she knew him. 'Good morning.'

He half smiled, half responded, then looked away. He felt absurd.

Back at the gate, here was someone with something to hide. A thin adolescent, probably male, wearing a jacket many sizes too large, bent down and picked up an expired ticket from the bin. He sneaked past the attendant, hurrying into the gathering crowd. A tattooed forearm emerged from the loose sleeve and a hand with dirty nails brushed overhanging hair from pale features. The eyes moved constantly, scanning faces – for what, for threat? Authority? Opportunity?

In any one of a number of ways that Bernard could imagine, the street child was almost certainly on the wrong side of the law, but it (he or she) was not the criminal Bernard was watching for.

Here was a portly man showing every sign of tension. Gulping coffee, sucking smoke from successive cigarettes, stabbing numbers on his mobile phone, speaking fast, looking repeatedly at his wristwatch.

Everything about the man spoke to Bernard of a man keyed up to his limit. The sort of man he was looking for: but he was not the lean figure of Carrots' identikit picture. More than that, Bernard did not recognise him. Bernard's systematic mind sought a familiar face – *most crimes against persons are committed by another person known to the family. I might recognise someone.*

Luisa had no time for systems. 'I have instinct, I feel. I know wickedness and cruelness.' Bernard did not correct Luisa's English. So Luisa watched for a cruel face. The child stealer would be heartless, an adult; that much she knew from Carrots' last words: 'The man took Jaffas!'

Could there be a female accomplice? Luisa's children always trusted women. But she, Luisa, knew female cruelty. She remembered the nuns in school in La Bocca. Luisa scanned bodies. She quickened – that small stunted child in school uniform. Could it be … ? But he was one of the busy throng, his face merry. Not Jaffas' face.

Luisa scanned adult faces for images already formed in her

mind. She searched for thin Eichmann lips, Mengele looks. She would recognise a child torturer.

She saw everyone but herself. She arrived immaculate and, she imagined, incognito. There were the giant sunnies, the long fringe and a loose poncho, less for warmth than for shapelessness. Luisa did not relish notice. Back in BA, to be noticed invited trouble – from the nuns, from the police, from people like the man who jumped her when she was twelve.

She did not see her distinctive self, this tall, bat-winged, dark sentinel creature, body poised, angled, the face of a pointer, restless, swivelling.

Luisa saw no one, man or woman, who answered her image of the face of cruelty. She had arrived upright, alert, ready to accost the stealer of her child. She would challenge, she'd attack, she'd reclaim her child.

Two fruitless hours later, she slumped, her tall frame infolded, shrunken. She spoke old words that spoke to her loss: *O my son, my son, would God I had died for thee* ... She prowled the yellow line, muttering her own incantation: *Wherefore do I not jump before the train?* And Bernard, seeing Luisa near that line, worrying, wondering, fearing her impulse, insinuated himself between her and the track, cradled her, a collapsing concertina, against his own frame. His body felt her despair, the slackening in her muscles.

Did she see, or did she dream, as her man held her, a flash in her peripheral field? A shadow, a furtive image, a tall thin male with red hair?

Later, Luisa would wonder and worry at the fragment of image. Lost now in her incantation, chanting her grief, Luisa reserved no strength for a wraith.

By 8.30 am on that sixty-fourth day, the morning rush was slowing. Bernard and Luisa were exhausted. Bernard pushed Luisa a little apart, searching her expression. Her face was drawn. He rested his hand on her cheek, then behind her head. He cradled it for a moment, then gently leaned her head forward again onto his shoulder.

Neither spoke. It was hopeless.

Bernard's bladder called urgently for relief. He'd resisted the signals for hours. 'Gotta take a leak, Lou. Back in a minute.'

Luisa stood, deep in unthinking litany. She was with the Gideons: *I sought him whom my soul loves: I sought him but I did not find him.'*

There was something odd about the urinal. Bernard pondered, then realised: the place was unusually clean, unusually unsmelly. The cleaners must have been in already. He was the first customer of the day. No, not quite the first – there was a hair, a solitary dark hair, standing out against the whiteness of the Doulton.

Bernard had finished. Somewhere between the shaking and the zipping up, another thought came to him: *That hair's not black, it's red. Even wet with urine, it's a bright colour.* He turned to go, stopped, looked back. There was something else. The hair was straight, dead straight, and long. That was unusual. Lavatory sheddings were never straight, always curly, always short and curly.

Bernard stood, his mind racing. *Red hair, dead straight. The twins have that. Well, they used to have it. Poor Carrots: ever since Jaffas, he pulls and twists at his hair. Never leaves it alone. When he thinks no one's looking, he eats it. His head is a mess, orange stubble and desert scalp.*

Someone else … who else? Someone I once knew had that blazing red hair, dead straight.

Bernard bent forward, reached out and took the hair, moist with his urine, and dried it on a piece of toilet tissue. Once dry, the hair was brighter, a lighter colour, ginger.

Bernard remembered: the cousin! Fingers shaking, he folded the toilet tissue and placed it carefully in his wallet. He hurried back to his wife. He tried to appear calm.

Luisa was pacing the platform, muttering: *I sought him but I did not find him. I asked the watchmen: 'Have you seen him whom my soul loves?'*

Bernard took her by the arm and guided her to their car. He said nothing but she felt the urgency in his grip. Luisa looked at him. His face was intense, bursting with a suppressed wildness. He looked as if he was about to explode. How he looked at 'the vinegar stroke', as he liked to call it.

'What? What? Who did you see?'

'I didn't see anyone. I found a red hair in the urinal, and it reminded me of someone. A sort of cousin, the son of my father's cousin, to be exact. At the twins' christening, remember? We invited my entire family. Everyone came except for that one cousin. And he couldn't be there because he was in jail. You made that remark, something about the witch in the fairytale who took revenge because she wasn't invited ... I wonder whether the cousin's out. And when he got out? I need to get a photo of him to show to Carrots ...'

Luisa, affected by Bernard's urgency, saw a flash at the edge of memory. Excited against her will, confused, she asked, 'Why him? What has he to do with Jaffas and Carrots?' Then dread: 'He's not a paedophile, is he?'

Bernard shook his head. He explained about the straight red hair. He added, 'That cousin went to jail for dealing drugs. He's been hooked on one drug or another since he was a kid. His mum is Dad's cousin. She's a sort of aunty or something. She says underneath it all, he was always a good kid, smart too. Says his brain has been pickled by too much dope and speed and prescription drugs. He'd take uppers and downers, mixes, matches. He'd end up in hospital, in the watch house, his parents would be called at 2.00 or 3.00 or 5.00 in the morning ... He went crazy for a time. Never really recovered, always twitchy, nervy. I think he went bush at one stage, spent a long time in the outback, amongst the Aborigines ... I need to find a picture.'

Luisa felt sorrow for her man. This was not evidence of any-thing. Excepting that Bernard's cousin who had been in jail might now be out of jail and – just possibly – urinating at the rail station. She did not say to Bernard what she thought. That he was clutch-ing at a straw. A hair, to be precise. One red hair.

She wept quietly.

Once home, Bernard raced to the family photo albums, throw-ing open the heavy pages, one after another, in a fever of bright be-lief. He discarded volume after volume, coming finally to a smaller, older-style book. Its pages were a dull grey-brown. The corners of the pictures were secured by small adhesive stickers. They were old-fashioned photos, perhaps half the size of a postcard.

'Here!' Bernard's finger stabbed at one photo repeatedly. 'Here! This fella, third from the left. That's him, that's wotzisname … Willie, Will Something, my Dad's cousin's boy.'

Luisa looked at the image. The face she saw was one of five small faces, five schoolchildren. She recognised Bernard's adoles-cent features as the oldest of the five. The child's face that excited Bernard looked a good deal younger than his. Luisa reckoned the boy's age was nine or so … Carrots' and Jaffas' age. In the black-and-white photo his hair was dark. Black and white. Quite useless.

Luisa said gently, 'I'm going upstairs to check on Carrots.'

Bernard didn't look up from the photograph. He replied, 'I'm going to see his mum, Wilbur's mum. Wilbur, that's his name! I'll go and ask her about Wilbur. I'll get a recent photo of him. And I'll get something personal, a hairbrush or something, something with his DNA.'

Later, Bernard visited the Forensic Institute. He made his way to the office of the same friend who had tested the twins' DNA. Bernard handed him two sealed and labelled, ziplocked plastic bags – one contained a used comb with fragments of reddish hair and dandruff; the other contained a single red hair, dead straight.

'I can rush them through, mate. I'll start them once everyone goes home after work. It's a foreigner, so I can't do it while anyone else is around. The basic lab work takes twenty-four hours. It'll be indicative only. It won't be good enough for evidence in a court case. But I'll have something for you tomorrow night. I'll give you a bell after work tomorrow.'

Bernard thanked his friend and went on his way, whistling an old tune his dad's parents had sung in the War.

At work he began to prepare his Missing Person site. He had a photo of the red-bearded cousin. And something more, some information – Aunt Robyn had told him she lent Wilbur her car after his release from jail to go fishing. 'He went out west, to the Darling. Menindie Lakes, he said.' Wilbur was away fishing for five days, a little less than the week he intended. He left the day Jaffas disappeared.

While he wrote on the website, Bernard was still humming:

We'll meet again,
Don't know where,
Don't know when …

67. www.lostchild.com.au

Lost, stolen from home, our son, aged nine.
Answers to Jaffas.
Left-handed.
Might be in the company of the adult in the photo (see link).
Speaks Spanish and English.
Very thin little boy, has brilliant wild red hair – see link to photo.
His twin brother, Carrots, is pining and unwell.
We will give anything for information about Jaffas or the man in the picture.

Email Jaffas@lostboy.com.au

Or ring Sergeant Jeanette Jolley at Oakleigh Police.

Large reward.

II

The Doc laboured long over the wording of his notice.

www.stolenchildren.com.au

Stolen by agents of the South-Australian Government, c. 1960, two boys of the Adnyamathanha People, brothers, named Samuel and Malachi, then aged four years and two years.

The stolen children would now be in their early sixties. They showed family resemblance to their older brothers and to their mother (see link to photos of those relatives in childhood and today. See also black-and-white photos of the stolen boys with their bigger brothers).

Their home country is the North Flinders Ranges, where their mother and their brothers long for contact or information.

In the first instance please contact The Doctor, Copley Clinic, Copley, SA

He deliberated longer on how to approach the very numerous state and federal government instrumentalities, the schools, orphanages, departments of infant welfare, departments of Aboriginal affairs, the churches, missions, and adoption agencies that he could imagine might know, had once known; retained or destroyed records; be willing or unwilling; be constrained by official secrecy or have decided to break free of such. He knew well the nature of officialdom, but he also knew the nature of human regret, the promptings of remorse, the nagging of a conscience too long stilled.

Prepared for anything and for nothing, the Doc could not say what response he expected to receive, beyond, 'if any'.

Finally, he drew radial lines on a map extending from the North

Flinders towards all the Aboriginal communities that he knew had their own medical clinics. His lines spread south to Adelaide, Whyalla, Port Augusta; east to Broken Hill, Redfern, Newcastle; and south-east to communities in Victoria, where he knew of Lake Tyers, Bairnsdale, Ballarat, Shepparton, Warrrnambool.

The Doc wrote to his brother and sister physicians in every clinic, begging for any help, any idea. He made himself naked, closing with this heartfelt plea: *I am a friend of the mother of these boys/men. I see her suffering, I hear her call to them in her sleep. For sixty years she has been longing. I cannot bear to see it any longer.*

Brother and sister physicians wrote in their numbers, letters of regret, of support, of compassion; letters promising to ask around.

One letter came from Mount Gambier:

Dear Dr Burns,

I have practised in this area since 1970. I inherited files from my predecessor, who started the practice here during the War. I have searched those files and my own for any Aboriginal kids named Malachi or Samson, without success. However, I found old correspondence from the Matron of an orphanage that operated here until the late 1960s. Matron speaks of 'half blood' children sent to Mount Gambier from South Australia by the Protector. The correspondence suggests that the children were to remain in the Gambier orphanage only until adolescence when they were to be sent to Victoria. There they would be concentrated in the large communities at Warrnambool and the Gippsland Lakes prior to being sent into service.

Unfortunately I found no medical records of individual Aboriginal children.

Finally, I visited the cemetery. We have numerous unmarked graves here in the section marked 'Heathens'. Some of these appear to be graves of small children.

Some are named, but I am sorry – and relieved – to tell you that none match your names.

I do hope you find Samson and Malachi.

Yours ...

68. Death of a Twin

He's a big bloke in all directions, tall and broad. His round face smiles widely as he enters the Doc's consulting room. He has an open gaze. The Doc makes room for the big man to pass.

'Thanks, Doc.' He offers a large hand. The Doc's hand disappears inside his patient's. The grip is manly, firm but gentle.

'My name's Alexander, Doc. Call me Alex.'

'Good to meet you, Alex.'

'I've got hypertension. Need a repeat of my tablets.' He smiles, his jowls rise and shine and recede. He tells the Doc he is sixty-six. A man who invites conversation.

The Doc asks Alex where he lives.

'Port Augusta. Been there forever. Born there. Father met mother there, in primary school. They're long gone. I've got a sister, a good bit older. I had a brother – we were twins ...'

The glow on Alex's large face gives way to something deeper as the man slows his flow. Something is happening. The Doc waits.

At length he asks: 'Were you identical?'

Alex nods. 'And close.' He clears his throat.

'What happened to your twin?'

'Cancer.'

In Alex's mouth, the word is a sentence. 'You know, we only saw each other three times in the last thirty years, but we were close.'

The Doc looks at him.

'Very close ... Thirty years back he went to New Zealand for a fortnight and he stayed. He came back to see me, stopped with me here, for twelve months. Here we are together.' Alex fishes in his wallet and pulls out an old colour photo. Two large round men in their thirties sit in a small fishing boat and smile goofily into the sun. The light bleaches their faces and sets fire to their hair. One of the men rests his hand on the other's shoulder.

'After that year he went back to New Zealand To his friends and his life. Then he got sick and died. Cancer.'

'It was tough?'

The serious face recedes inward for a moment. The Doc is forgotten. Alex is alone with memory of the feeling, with feeling returned. He looks at the Doc. 'Knocked me around something terrible.' He stops, shakes his head. 'People used to ask us, 'What's it like being twins? We'd ask each other, "What's it like not being a twin?"'

The Doc looks away while the other man composes himself. At length, he resumes. His face is earnest now as he searches for words to carry feeling. 'You know, I lost my son. Suicide. My wife and I only ever had the one son … terrible … I wouldn't wish it on anyone. But it's my brother I think of. Half of me is gone.'

Alex's eyes are wet. 'It's been seven years …' A pause as he searches for dates. 'Seven years and one day. There wouldn't be a single day when I don't think of my brother.'

The large man takes his prescription and shakes the Doc's hand. He conjures a smile for the Doc and he leaves.

Alex's story and his losses stay with the doctor. Every day, as he drives from the clinic to Greta's shack near Nepabunna, the photograph of the old man with his brother knocks gently on a partition in the Doc's mind. The Doc wonders about that picture; he cannot divine the teaching the photo wants to give him.

Every day the Doc checks www.stolenchildren.com.au for news.

69. Yellow-footed Wallaby

The Doc's old troop carrier pulls up at Greta's shack late in the afternoon. Before he can honk, Greta and the boy appear at the door and the Doc understands it is learning time. Some afternoons, it is Greta's story, and the man and the boy follow the old lady into the bush and learn to look and listen to the stories the bush is telling.

Other times, they all drive off in the troopie and the old people show the boy secret and hidden things.

Greta directs him to the Aroona Dam and the protected area for the rare yellow-footed wallaby. The Doc explains to Jaffas, 'The numbers of this endangered species are few. There are locals here who use the dam every weekend, year in, year out, for recreation, who've never sighted one.'

The Doc parks the Bluebird in the parking area. Greta leads the Doc and the boy along a wallaby track, a line between rocks and she-oak undetectable from the car park. The sun is low, the shadows long.

Greta stops, looks around, wets a finger with her tongue, finds the wind. She leads them a short distance away, downwind from a shallow pond in the dried out Aroona Creek bed. They ensconce themselves in a cleft in the rock that defines the upper margin of the track.

'We sit here, sit, wait. Soon wallaby feed, drink.'

And indeed wallaby arrive: in the plural – a slender buck and his smaller doe, yellow of foot, fine featured, sniffing, craning sentinel ears for movement. The buck drinks while the doe keeps watch. Now the doe bends to the water. The buck stands erect, alert. He surveys his domain, a secret aristocrat. The light dims, his fair fur darkens. Soon he is a silhouette, a statue.

Jaffas tries not to breathe. How long do the three sit and watch? It is a time without measure. Five mammals in the hushed dusk, the watched and the watching. Three humans in reverie.

The dark comes down. A feeble crescent of moon appears above the horizon.

The night is alive with unexpected sounds. Jaffas listens, wondering – surely the wallaby will take flight. He hears the soughing breeze, the warning calls of night-birds and, joining these, a new sound, low and rhythmic, now rising, now falling.

Jaffas listens, rapt. Finally he recognises the Doc's stertorous breathing in sleep.

After some time, Greta rises. 'Wallaby gone. Time we gone too.'

70. The Return

Greta's funny today. When Jaffas wakes in the morning, he catches her in the bathroom. He walks in for a pee and there she is, looking intently in the mirror, fixing pink plastic things in her hair. She looks funny – her eyes are red. And her white hair with these half balls of pink plastic everywhere. Strangest of all is how long it takes Greta to notice him and how she jumps and covers her head with her hands. And blushes.

He backs out of the bathroom and goes outside to pee.

All day Abu behaved strangely. She talked a lot. At the end of the afternoon she said, 'You go off now, catch bit of tucker. Reckon you hunt without me. I not strong today. You go hunt alone this time.'

But Greta is strong. She spent the afternoon gathering quandong, pushing from bush to bush, wrestling the fruits free, shoving them into the dilly bag that Jaffas carries for her. It was hard work just to keep up. In her fever of harvest, Greta did not seem weak.

Why is Abu pretending to be tired?

Jaffas' mind is busy. He stumbles over a bush turkey. He chases the bird, closes on it, anticipates its flight, grabs it as it takes to the air. He wrings its neck and returns.

Jaffas has been away only ten minutes or so. He notices Greta at the mirror again, looking at her hair. *She looks different, her hair is all curly.* There is Greta's purse and her pension card in the opening of her dilly bag of quandong.

Greta plucks the bird while Jaffas makes the fire. They eat alone. The Doc does not come. Greta says, 'Doc busy tonight. Been read at library, been busy at hospital, got meeting there. He say to me he come late. You know, meetings, doctor things.' A lot of words from Abu.

Greta hurries Jaffas to bed. 'Better get big sleep, son. You get sleep.'

Why aren't we sitting by the fire and watching the sky for warraiti?

Lying in his swag, Jaffas hears the Toyota well before it pulls up. Greta hurries outside. She and the Doc speak in low voices. Something – he can't hear what – has excited the old people.

II

The Doc whispers, 'I was right, Greta. It is him! It's definitely him!' His words race away from him. The old man is an excited child. 'I found his picture on the net. And his twin: they look just the same. The family posted a notice; they're offering a reward. And there was a photo of Wilbur, you know, Jimmy.

'I searched the papers. The family lives somewhere in Oakleigh. We'll need the boy to take us to his street.'

Greta speaks, her own words quiet, intense. ''Nother time I going lose a boy … this one got funny hair, talk funny … This boy love story, love country … 'Nother boy gone …'

Soft crying. Then Greta blowing her nose. 'We gotta give him back … Boy need mother, father, brother … He gotta have them …'

The Doc speaks again. 'I took this tablet from the dispensary. Safer if he sleeps while we travel. I'll only give him one. Last time he had a couple and it was an overdose.'

Meanwhile, Jaffas keeps his eyes closed and tries to control his breathing.

The Doc is at his bedside. 'Here's a nice cup of warm cocoa.' The boy drinks. The cocoa is very sweet. At the edge of the sweetness there's a funny taste, familiar. The old man stands over Jaffas as he drinks. He takes the mug and turns off the light.

'Good night, son.'

'Good night.'

Jaffas closes his eyes again and imitates sleep.

Outside, the Doc's whisper is loud enough for deaf Greta to hear. It carries through the window to Jaffas. 'Valium takes a couple of hours to work properly.'

Abuela's soft footsteps and Abuelo's heavier ones enter the house; a slower, heavier tread recedes outdoors. He opens an eye. At the end of the corridor, the two old people lug a large box. The Toyota door clunks closed and they steal back inside.

Jaffas falls asleep. The Doc tiptoes into the bedroom, bends close to the bed and picks up something from the floor. It is the soccer ball that Jaffas never kicks. The ball he keeps to connect him with Carrots. The Doc says to Greta, 'Eight o'clock. I've set the alarm. We need to cross the Murray well before dawn.'

He climbs into Greta's swag. They are both dressed in their day clothes.

II

A short distance before they reach Mildura, the Doc grows tense. 'The border is the one place we can get into big trouble. If the border people see the boy with all that flaming hair, they'll remember him. If they recognise him, we'll be suspected of kidnapping.'

Greta, indignant: 'We not stealing any child! We bring him back!'

'Doesn't matter. We'd be guilty of withholding information from the police. As well as unlawful imprisonment. Obstructing justice. The usual catch-alls.'

At the mention of police, Greta loses her bright sense of rightness. 'No police. I don't want …'

'No, Greta, there's no border police, just the fruit fly people. They stop cars and check them for fruit. What I'm saying is, if the fruit fly officers see the boy they'll likely remember him. And they'll have film of the car and its rego. They could tell the police later. They'd trace us easily.'

'Maybe go different road.'

'Yes. But there's a simpler way.'

'What that?'

The Doc slows, drives the 4WD well off the road and into some bushy scrub. He extinguishes the Toyota's lights. 'Greta, hop out and lie down in the back. Get under the rug with the boy and make as if you are asleep. Cover his head with the rug. Just make sure he can breathe.'

Greta smiles and nods. She climbs into the back and holds the child close. The Doc starts the engine and drives. Five minutes later, they reach the fruit fly checkpoint. The boom gate is white in the headlights, pointing upwards at the silent stars. The post is deserted.

The Toyota proceeds to the border and beyond into Mildura.

'Greta, you want to come up front again?'

'No. This my last chance hold this boy. Going lose him tomorrow. Same I lost Ambrose.'

II

The sun shoots a horizontal beam through the car window. Greta wakes and listens to the boy's breathing. She hears the hum of the engine and the song of rubber on bitumen. She opens her window a crack and listens for bird song. She watches the trees, river gums, she-oak and other trees that are strange to her. She takes in the flat terrain. Good country, but no hills of red rock. Not Greta's country.

They travel like this for a long time, quietly.

Greta sees movement between trees, a brown-green shape, then another. '*Warraiti!*' she shouts. '*Warraiti!*'

The boy stirs, rubs his eyes, struggles himself upright.

'*Dónde? Dónde está el warraiti?*' *

The Doc slows, pulls over and climbs out of the vehicle. 'I need to take a leak.' To the boy he says, 'Want to come with me?'

Greta heads back a distance and disappears into the scrub. The Doc goes off in the opposite direction. Jaffas follows him.

'Jaffas.' Abuelo's soft voice is thunder in the boy's ears. He jumps. 'We know.'

The old man's smile is kind. He reaches for the boy's hand. His bony handclasp is warm, his old skin dry. 'We've had a good idea for a while.'

The boy does not speak. He stands, poised, alert, all lines and angles – a spear ready for flight, ready to impale the moment, this moment he has awaited, this moment he has feared.

'Don't be scared, Jaffas. No need to be afraid. We're taking you back to Carrots.' The old man starts for the Toyota.

The child holds back. He speaks, a wordburst: 'Carrots!' He starts to cry. He shouts, '*El está en peligro. Peligro! Peligro!*' **

The old man reaches again, folds and holds the boy in his arms. He squats, facing the weeping child. 'We're taking you back home. Don't be frightened, Jaffas. You're safe.'

'*Yo no estoy en peligro****. Carrots! Carrots *está en peligro!*'

The Doc walks the boy to the car, cradling him.

Greta is waiting. The old man says, 'Abu knows everything. Both of us know, but no one else does. It's a secret. Your mum and dad don't even dream you're coming home. And Carrots doesn't know either.'

The boy shakes his head wildly, his long hair flaming, lashing his head. Tears run and mingle with snot as he cries again and again, '*Esta en peligro!*'

'Jaffas, you don't need to hide in Spanish anymore. What's frightening you? Try to say it in English. Tell us and we'll help.'

---

* Where? Where is the emu?

** He is in danger!

*** *I* am not in danger.

The child is silent. He takes a breath, makes as if to speak. A sob bursts from him and breaks the quiet. He looks at the Doc, at Greta, looks into them, measuring faith against risk. He takes another breath and says softly and clearly, 'The man said ... he will kill Carrots ... if I tell anyone ... anything.' Another sob. 'I have told you now –'

There is unfamiliar steel in the old man's voice: 'We'll go straight to your place and we'll make sure he's safe.'

Through his tears, Jaffas sees a face set in resolve – not an old man's face, the face, almost, of a warrior.

They drive the remaining hours without conversation. Jaffas sits in front, between Greta and the Doc. Greta holds him against her. Every few minutes a sob shakes his body. Gradually his stiff frame relaxes.

He turns to the Doc. The old man of stories. Abuelo. Jaffas rests his head against the Doc's arm. Greta holds the boy gently, ever so gently, against her coming loss.

The Doc hears crooning sounds, sounds Greta made over Ashweena in the hospital, the same sounds of that first night when she held this boy, a pale stranger, ill, stuporous, shorn. The boy lost, found then in Greta's arms, in her song. After today, the boy will be lost again to them. Greta's low song rumbles along slowly, softly, endlessly; it rises, a slow moaning, falls and rises again, an unbroken ribbon that pulsates and drones. On and on, the quiet cradle of song throbs and trembles. *How does the old girl keep it up? When will she take a breath?*

The Doc looks away. He listens, hears the song that was at once lament and comfort for the child. He shakes his head, wipes his wet eyes and squints at the road, muttering motoring polysylla- bles, directing them to the dashboard display: *Fuel okay. Engine temperature. No warning lights. 90 km/h ...*

Then he reads road signs aloud ... *Wedderburn ... Kyneton ... Craigieburn ... No Overtaking: Narrow Bridge.*

Jaffas peers at the road ahead. He leans to his right, sitting hard against the Doc. He pulls Greta closer to his left side and burrows into the folds and hollows of her bony frame.

71. Wilbur's End

0830 hours. The small white car arrived outside the Wanklyn family home.

Carrots and Sahara remained at home while Luisa and Bernard went out searching again. They would be back soon to take Carrots to school. They didn't let him walk by himself anymore, not since Jaffas.

A car turned into the driveway. Carrots heard the sound of a car engine. It was not the sound of his parents' car. He looked out the window. Recognition, imprecise but strong, vibrated wildly. A tall thin man stepped out of the car. Carrots knew the man: the man who stole Jaffas.

Fearless this time, driven, Carrots flew from the house, flung himself at the man in the driveway and wrapped his arms hard around his legs. The wire door slammed behind him.

The man staggered back a step or two with the force of Carrots' tackle. He steadied himself. He grabbed Carrots by his arm, speaking urgently: 'You want to see your brother? Come with me, quick. I'll take you to him!'

Sahara had heard the car too. The back door slowed her. She nosed it ajar, growling, and bounded after Carrots. She showed her teeth. The man heard the dog. He reached for the snack in his trouser pocket with one hand as he pulled Carrots with the other. He tried to hurry Carrots into the car, but the boy would not release his legs. The dog was almost upon him, snarling now, a sandy blur, narrowing the gap between them.

Wilbur tried to run. Carrots held his legs fast. Wilbur did not like the sound or the look of the dog. It was small, ridiculously small. But nasty, all aggression. He leaned down to peel the boy from his legs. He overbalanced and the dog was upon them.

Sahara went for the man's throat. Wilbur fended the dog off with his hands. The dog bit down hard on Wilbur's right hand. The man pulled, the dog's teeth dug deeper into the flesh. Wilbur looked at his hand in disbelief: it was in the mouth of this stupid hound, blood was spurting from it. The dog would not let go.

Wilbur's left hand went to the rescue of his right, leaving his throat exposed. The dog released the hand and Wilbur observed his thumb that projected at an unfamiliar angle, hanging from the hand by a narrow isthmus of tendon and skin. How could this be?

The dog's maw was at Wilbur's throat now. He tried to pull the dog away, but his right hand would not do his bidding. His left hand flew to the back of the dog's neck and pulled violently at the collar. Wilbur heard snarling, felt the hot mouth at his throat. He pulled with all his force and there was a new sound, a cracking and tearing, horrible, then air roaring from his ruptured larynx. Wilbur wrenched the dog; the dog pulled at Wilbur's throat; Wilbur gulped air, huge gasps roared out of his torn throat.

He heard the sounds and wondered why his breathing was not working. His brain, oxygen-starved, soared. Visions came and raced; he saw Greta's country, there was Ambrose, his round open face, the boy's gap-toothed grin.

Wilbur commanded his hand to pull the dog away from his throat. The obedient hand redoubled its force. It wrenched the dog's head backwards but the dog's jaw was clamped, tearing carotids. The man tasted blood, saw his hand, saw the dog, felt the wrenching at his throat: *Shit! I'm helping the dog rip my throat out. It's a fuckup!*

Carrots released the man's legs. He had to save him from Sahara. This man alone knew where to find Jaffas. Carrots raced for the garden hose, turned the tap and directed the force of the water at Sahara, aiming for her eyes.

There was a yelp, then another as Sahara released the man and peered through the torrent towards her master. The water kept coming and Sahara ran away, whimpering. The man had grabbed Carrots and it was her job to save him. What was Carrots doing?

The man did not move. His body lay in the driveway, his throat torn open. Water flowed red from the body to the lawn and onto the flowerbed beyond.

Carrots looked at the inert form. He ran into the house and dialled triple zero. A woman's voice said, 'Fire, Police or Ambulance?'

Carrots had no voice.

'Fire, Police or Ambulance?' – the female voice insistent.

Carrots gulped air. A voice emerged: '*Mi perro ...*'

'*Fire, Police or Ambulance!*'

'My dog bit the man. He's bleeding, he's lying on the ground. The dog bit the man's neck. Hurry!'

Carrots flung the phone away and ran outside. He looked at the man's throat, all bloody and torn. He looked at the white face, silent and still. Carrots' hands clenched in tight white futile fists. He threw his head backwards, his mouth open in a soundless roar. 'Jaffas! Jaffas! I'll never see you again.'

Sahara licked the boy's face, spreading blood and salt tears, smearing Carrots' face red.

The sound of the ambulance siren penetrated Carrots' despair. Two ambulance officers hurried from their vehicle, lugging heavy bags of gear. One spoke to the child, 'Next time you call 000, son, give us your name and address. We'll get here quicker.' The second officer asked, 'Where's the man with dogbite?'

II

At the rail station, Bernard checked his watch. 8.40. Time to collect Carrots and take him to school. He showed Luisa his watch.

He took her arm and led her to the car. Neither spoke. There was nothing to say.

Two blocks from home they heard the harsh klaxon of the ambulance. Luisa's hand flew to her open mouth. Bernard turned to her, his reassurance a reflex, denying his own vague alarm. As they neared home, alarm became urgency. Bernard ran a red light, screamed around the corner and braked hard outside the house. An ambulance stood at the kerb, its doors open, lights flashing.

Luisa saw blood on the driveway. 'No, no! Not Carrots! Not him too!'

They squeezed past the white car blocking their driveway. At the end of the driveway, Carrots, his face bloodied, stood with some ambulance officers, shaking his head at their questions. Luisa ran to her son, saw the blood was not his own, held him hard. Bernard saw a body lying on the ground before his son. He ran towards the body and saw the goatee, grotesque, orange against the white. He roared: '*Wilbur!* You cunt!'

The body, lying white and lifeless, drained Bernard of hope. He threw back his head and roared again. Wilbur was dead – no one alive could help him find Jaffas.

A terrier-whippet cross with a sandy coat, black snout and black tail slunk around the corner, confused. There was blood on Sahara's snout.

II

In the side street, the Doc and Greta spoke softly to Jaffas. The unfamiliar sound of the siren penetrated the cabin. Greta jumped. 'Police!'

The Doc said, 'Time for us to leave. Go, now, Jaffas.'

The Doc hurried around to the passenger door of the troop carrier and opened it. Jaffas clambered over Greta. She did not speak; she sat and devoured his face with her eyes. Jaffas stood a moment, irresolute. He reached up and kissed the old lady's cheek, then kissed the other.

The Doc extended a hand to Jaffas. He looked at his own hand and withdrew it quickly. *Not a handshake, not this time.* He would not shake hands, he would not tell the child to be a man. The old storyteller squatted before the boy and wrapped his arms around him. He felt the body closeness of their morning stories. He held him for a moment, released him. 'Go. Go to Carrots.'

Jaffas walked uncertainly away.

He turned into his own street. He saw a cluster of people in the driveway of his house. An ambulance officer looked up and saw this second boy, like the first, but this one carrying a soccer ball and with a full head of red hair.

Sahara leapt at the boy, licking furiously. The boy did not react. He rested a steadying hand on the dog's head and walked together with her into the crowded driveway.

72. First Night

In the kingdom of confusion, police try to take statements from two red-headed boys who seem to be mute. Or stupid.

Forensic staff sample, bag, tag and seal bloody garden soil and dog saliva, and demarcate a suspected crime scene; ambulance officers retrieve a red-headed corpse; a small hurricane hound exchanges his menacing growl for brief monosyllables of yelp, as she whirls from one small boy to the other, sniffing, leaping, licking, charting a bewildering new world where one has become two.

A fire truck arrives and officers hose blood from the driveway; police intrude upon the jubilation of two parents and regret to intrude; they remove themselves, promising to return tomorrow, while colleagues tow away a small white car. An older policeman and his female fellow head for a nearby suburb where they will death-knock the door of the registered owner of a white car who, unsuspecting, has been expecting this knock daily, ever since the dark times when her boy first surfed away from her on a riptide of chemicals.

Driving with all prudent speed, an aged Toyota troop carrier with South Australian plates bears an odd-looking couple away from the kingdom of confusion; the thin upright frame of the passenger heaves silently, rhythmically; then subsides into stillness, into the old struggle to fossilise feeling. The driver mutters into his console, 'Geelong ... Great Ocean Road ... Warrnambool ...'

Aloud, the Doc says to Greta, 'Might just as well stop at the Warrnambool Aboriginal Co-op. If there's anything on the news about a white troopie, we can lie low there among the Gunditjmara. See if anyone looks like your family, Greta. Show old folks the photos of Samuel and Malachi as kids.'

Greta sits up straight. She stares at the Doc, shakes her head vigorously, stops and looks away.

II

Afternoon is soon evening.

An unfamiliar family meal that no one eats; a mother, frantic with joy, psalms on her lips, throws together everything from vegemite to *dulce de leche*, every comestible of celebration.

One boy, electric, anorectic, his scalp a red semi-desert, sneaks food to a dizzy dog beneath the table; his brother, his scalp crowned in luxuriant flame, estranged from unhunted viands, toys with the processed foods before him; a father, exultant, disregards all undercurrents, buries his face in the strong stream of family. He drinks deeply and is sated.

Evening becomes night. Sahara, confined now outside the house, submits and whimpers her confused cries. In their room together, the two brothers, alone now, search for each other.

They are strangers. They share memories of which they cannot speak, of a past time when they were one. In this strange present, they are lost.

The room holds two small beds, but the brothers never slept

apart. Carrots, skeletal in striped pyjamas, looks yearningly at his brother, who stands unclothed. Misreading Jaffas' nudity for invitation, Carrots responds. His hands begin their work. Surprised for a moment, Jaffas quickly remembers. But he remains passive, wordless. He knows that chapter has closed.

Carrots stops. He gazes at the brother who remains absent, chokes a cry, flings himself face downwards onto the bed. When he looks up, Jaffas has gone.

Carrots masturbates miserably. Ineffectually.

Quiet as a hunter at night, Jaffas prowls the house. He sees light under his parents' bedroom door. He hears soft sounds – gurgles, gasps, stifled laughing – the small noises he was wont to hear from the swag that Greta shared with the Doc.

Jaffas returns to the room he used to share with Carrots. The air is still, close. Quietly, he pulls open the window. He drags bedding from the second bed and fashions a rough swag. He lies down. But sleep, like a hillside in the Flinders, slopes ever away from him.

73. Among the Gunditjmara and Girai Wurrung

'Police investigating a death in Oakleigh are anxious to locate a white Land Rover seen parked near the scene. They believe the elderly driver and his companion might be able to assist them …' The Doc turns off his car radio. 'Thank heavens they got the make of car wrong. Greta, we'll go to the local Aboriginal Co-op. They might take in a sister – or an aunty.'

They pull up outside the Co-op. Greta goes inside while the Doc waits in the vehicle. Quickly, Greta returns. 'Good people – Gunditjmara. Said go hide out in Framlingham. Forest country. Aboriginal country. No whitefella police there.'

In Framlingham, the forest is young. Greta walks a distance between the trees, eventually standing still. The Doc knows that stillness. He recognises Greta's watching-waiting for *warraiti* behaviour.

The Doc speaks to a couple of older men who sit by a small fire. The youthfulness of the growth on land that he knows was long ceded to Aboriginal people puzzled him. He learns that the Ash Wednesday bush fires started here. Nine people died. Poorly maintained power lines were implicated. 'What happened to the people, the Gunditjmara, the Girai Wurrung?'

'Govement take whole mob out, away. Lot of 'em leave for good. Young ones. Never come back. Only old ones stay in town, come back forest after. Only old ones here now.'

The Doc hurries to the car, returning with photographs. The old men pass them around, one to another. One calls in a low growling voice. The Doc looks up and finds half a dozen new figures studying the images. A man – the Doc guesses he is in his fifties – waves the picture he holds and cries out a short sound. He calls it again and again. *Is it 'Mum'? Greta might know.*

The Doc rises. He hurries into the bush and returns with Greta.

74. Mismatch

Carrots doesn't know Jaffas anymore. Jaffas keeps slipping away from him, into silence, into separateness, into a place of long, slowly sloping grey-brown hills.

Carrots is in pain. Confused. He has wanted only one thing: that Jaffas come back to him. Now Jaffas is here but he is not. Jaffas does not fit in. He sleeps on the floor, refusing Carrots' bed.

Luisa speaks to Jaffas, but he does not reply; does he even notice his mother?

Back at school, his attention wanders.

At night, Carrots cannot sleep. He climbs to the top of the wardrobe and retrieves the letters he wrote to Jaffas. He sits on his bed and reads and re-reads them by torchlight. The light disturbs Jaffas. He watches his brother's tears gather to fullness and fall. Jaffas hears Carrots sob. He watches as Carrots' left hand prowls his scalp, seeking, pausing now at orange tufts. The thumb and forefinger secure a purchase and pull long and hard. A tuft comes away. Jaffas watches the red hairs move in a slow arc to his brother's mouth, as Carrots' eyes follow the words on the page.

Through narrowed lids, Jaffas looks upon the ruin of his twin. His eyes fill and he blinks. He tastes salt and emptiness. Jaffas watches Carrots climb the wardrobe and hide the letters again.

In the morning, Carrots walks Sahara. Jaffas, pleading tiredness, stays in the bedroom. He climbs and he reads. His eyes fill again; he understands. Return is not simple, it hurts.

Have I grown or has Carrots shrunk? Jaffas knows it is time. He takes the letter from his pocket, gives it to Carrots. Carrots reads, bemused.

My brother
I am alive, stolen.
I am in Egypt
Your brother
Joseph

Jaffas explains, 'I wanted to send it but I couldn't. If I sent it, you would not be safe.'

II

Jaffas needs Carrots to understand the important things. Things he learned from Greta. After dark, he takes Carrots outside and lies down on his back, looking up at the night sky. 'Carrots, lie down like me, next to me. I'll show you *warraiti*.'

Carrots lies down. Jaffas points to a darker patch of sky near the Southern Cross. 'That's the Coalsack, that dark stuff. There is *warraiti*'s head. That means the emu's head. And his body stretches away to the left of the head. You see that?'

Carrots shakes his head.

Jaffas says, 'Look, the head is there' – he points, his voice intense. 'When we can see *warraiti* like this we know it's the time when she is laying her eggs back there, on the ground.'

Carrots cannot see the head. He doesn't understand the connection between an emu in the sky and an emu laying eggs on earth. 'Don't the eggs break when they fall onto the ground from the sky?'

Jaffas says, exasperated, 'Too many lights here. Too many buildings, houses, too many shops. The sky is spoiled here. Not enough darkness. We can't see *warraiti* properly here.'

Back inside, Jaffas prefers to sleep on the floor. Sleep does not come quickly. He cries. He misses Abuelo and Abuela. Somehow he misses his brother.

Jaffas makes a decision: he will take Carrots to the Flinders, to the cabin on the track off the Arkaroola Road. To Greta and her stories. To the Doc and his many stories that are one great story.

In the morning, while Carrots walks Sahara, Jaffas writes a letter. The next morning Jaffas claims Sahara duties. He posts his secret letter.

75. Two Letters

Talcum Malcolm is the postie. When he sights a letter addressed to Greta in a child's hand, he is curious, concerned. He drives to her door and delivers it in person.

Malcolm waits discreetly in case Greta needs his help. The old lady tears open the envelope, her pale hands shaking. She reads, gives a little cry, waves the letter in the general direction of Malcolm, dances towards him, stops and reads the letter again. She sighs deeply.

'Everything okay, Greta?'

'Yes. Yes. Okay, yes.'

She dances back into the house.

In the evening, the Doc arrives and she shows him the letter. They read together:

Deer Abu and Abu,

We are coming to visit you. Carrots needs to know the stories you told me.

We will com soon as we can.

Yours Sincereley,

Jaffas and Carrots.

II

A courier delivered a letter addressed: To The Householder.

He handed the letter to Bernard. 'Sign here, mate.'

Bernard signed.

Curious, he studied the envelope with its official crest. When he opened it, he recognised the letterhead of the local Council with the words, 'Ranger's Office'. The letter was headed: 'Notice of Arrest and Destruction of an Animal (Domestic Animals Act, 1999)'.

Bernard rubbed his eyes. He read on:

> 'Notice is given herewith that the dog domiciled at this address, under Dog Licence No. PL496923/pj, is to be sur-rendered to the Office of the Ranger within three days of receipt of this letter.
>
> This Order is made under the relevant Act which stipulates that an animal involved in a fatal attack on a human is subject to arrest by the Ranger.
>
> If the Ranger determines that the dog is in fact the agent of human death, the dog is subject to subsequent humane destruction.
>
> This notice allows the licensee a compassionate period of three clear days.

The letter was signed: Patrick Crunden, Senior Ranger.

Bernard sat down, his face pale. Luisa came into the room, singing brightly, 'He maketh the barren woman to return home / A mother rejoicing with her children / Hallelujah!'

Bernard sighed wearily.

Luisa asked, 'Who was that at the door?'

Bernard handed her the letter. His head slumped. He covered his face with his hands and wept.

Luisa read the letter. After a while she said, 'The Ranger wants to take Sahara and kill him? Poor Sahara.'

'Poor Carrots, you mean!' Bernard roared at his wife, gasping, his words drowning in tears and phlegm. 'Don't you realise Sahara has been that boy's only living comfort for the entire sixty-seven days? None of us could reach him. Only that ugly mongrel – that bloody barking, snapping, growling, cowardly, aggressive, nipping, sniping, miserable fucking cur – only Sahara has been close to him.'

Bernard stopped and swallowed. He cleared his throat. 'Sahara's been all the family that Carrots could tolerate. And now, now Jaffas is back home, but Carrots is still pulling hair, still eating it. His head's a desert. He's lonelier than ever! They'll put that dog down and Carrots … Carrots will be lost. Carrots will become the son we have lost …' He could not continue.

Luisa, contrite, held Bernard's wet face against her belly for a long moment. Eventually she spoke. 'We'll do something. We'll think of something. We have to. The letter says we've got three days …'

Luisa looked up. Jaffas stood at the doorway, his face shining, ready to explode into utterance. How long had he been there? What was he bursting with?

Jaffas said, 'Me and Carrots need to go to the Adnyamathanha people.'

His mother blinked. '*Que?*'

'Me and Carrots, we need to be with Greta. And the Doc. Together. For a while.'

Bernard sat up straight. He looked at Luisa, pregnant now with inspiration of his own. Before he could speak, Jaffas went on: 'We can take Sahara. She'll be safe up there. From the Ranger, I mean … I heard you talking … about Sahara.'

II

They waited for nightfall the following day. Then the man and his twin sons and their dog left for the Flinders Ranges. The boys sat in the back. Jaffas spoke softly to Carrots, his voice intense. Bernard caught the odd word – *emu, Greta, warraiti, Lake Eyre,* Adnyamathanha, *cola drinks* …

On the third day, Luisa phoned the local council and left a message for the Ranger. She explained that she was unable to comply with the Order – unfortunately the dog in question had gone missing. The family was searching for Sahara and if she turned up, they would contact the Ranger's office promptly. But in the event that the Ranger might happen to find Sahara before the family did, would the Ranger be so kind as to call them so they could come and say their goodbyes?

76. Beware of the Dog

Sahara made herself at home in the Flinders Ranges. Those hills were one great dog park. Wherever people gathered, there were dogs without number. There were all sorts of dogs – ugly, breedless mongrels, clean-limbed dingoes, underfed bitches with litters at the teat, skinny hounds, arthritic old quadrupeds – all of them ranging free, all of them curious, most of them carrying some contagious infestation, generally hungry, some malicious.

Dog met dog. Being dogs, and curious dogs, they sniffed the newcomer's behind. Sahara being Sahara, she sidled around to the hindquarters as dictated by etiquette, sniffed conventionally, then bit down hard and suddenly on the new friend's anal glands. Once bitten, all the new friends proved very shy, avoiding Sahara and everything that bore her smell.

One by one, dogs deserted their homes and territory. Within a short time, Greta's shack was dog-free. The small towns of Iga Warta and Nepabunna soon followed, then Copley and Lyndhurst.

Sahara's yellow canine teeth had bitten off a powerful agent of ecological harm. With the dogs gone, game proliferated and hunting became more rewarding. More of the men, both old and young, brought home bush tucker. The grasses and the trees came back. Women found more quandong, they harvested wattle seed again, roasted and milled the protein-rich seeds and baked the old-time damper.

The Doc's hunter-and-gatherer patients were losing weight. Their diabetes improved. Infections were less common, people recovered more quickly.

Body sores were on the wane. Without their beloved camp dogs, the Adnyamathanha lost their living heat-bags, so they no longer itched, scratched and became infected. The fatal cycle of dog vector and human sufferer broke down. Fresh cases of rheumatic fever became a rarity.

One small, unattractive, dun-coloured, cowardly, sneaking, compulsively aggressive, thoroughly nasty bitch had turned back the page of history and health among the northern Rock People.

77. Obituary

'Albert Burns, 8 January 1946 – 13 September 2016.

Albert Burns, doctor, epidemiological researcher and eccentric, has died among his adopted people, the Adnyamathanha of the north Flinders Ranges. He died, after a short illness, of overwhelming septicaemia, the consequence of accidental injury by a needle contaminated by infected stool.

Well known for his unconventional research in the late decades of the last century, Dr Burns became a controversial figure in his field of interest, the spread and prevention of dysentery. While critics ridiculed his findings and ethics committees were outraged by his methods, Albert enjoyed the last laugh: the evidence of his success in preventing gastroenteritis among the Indigenous people of the Flinders was indisputable.

The Doc, as his Indigenous friends called him, is also credited with the recent dramatic rising trend of life expectancy in the north Flinders. Fresh cases of rheumatic heart disease and glomerulonephritis – both connected with streptococcal skin infections – are now rarely seen. Local authorities link the improvement with the disappearance of camp dogs from the area. While the Rock People were ambivalent about their lost dogs, their regard for 'the Doc' remains undiminished.

Around the start of this century, the Doc was linked by rumour to an unsolved case of industrial sabotage in the Flinders, in which parties unknown switched labels on cola drinks in Leigh Creek, something the Doc had long advocated. At the time, two boys, guests of the Doc, were questioned. No charges were laid.

Meanwhile, the Doc pointed out that no one missed the real thing. By this time, the coal seam had become sub-economic, the mine had closed and Leigh Creek was one more ghost of white men in the Flinders.

Following the closure of the mine, the Adnyamthanha took over the town and the store. On the Doc's advice, local elders banned all sugary drinks in favour of artificially sweetened drinks. New cases of diabetes became uncommon, obesity rarer and existing diabetics suffered fewer complications.

The eulogy at his burial was given by Luisa Wanklyn, mother of a kidnapped child whom Albert restored to his family some twelve years ago. In a chain of events that remain mysterious to this day, Dr Burns recovered the missing boy at a time when the regular police forces had been impotent. Coincidentally, the kidnapper died violently on the day the Wanklyn child returned home.

Luisa Wanklyn elegised the deceased:

How are the mighty fallen.

All the daughters of song are brought low; desire faileth: a man goeth to his long home. The mourners go about in the street and the dust returneth to the earth.

Dr Burns leaves a sister, Marguerite (well known as the *bête noir* of 'Big Milk' in West Africa), and his adoptive grandchildren, Noah and Jesse Wanklyn. He is survived also by his partner Greta and her once-stolen son Samuel, whom the Doc found and restored to her in the Victorian Aboriginal Community of Framlingham. The Doc also located the grave of Samuel's younger brother, Malachi, who died of an epidemic in an orphanage in Mount Gambier.

Albert's aged dog, Sahara, died a short time before his passing. At his request, Sahara's remains are interred with her master's. Their burial plots are on tribal land at a site chosen by the Adnyamthanha.

Man and dog lie alongside a legendary figure, Murti Johnny, the Indigenous identity who died some decades earlier, at the age of 114 years. He was believed to be Australia's longest-lived person. The local people chose this auspicious resting place for 'the Doc' in recognition of the added years of life that his work brought them. In the words of his long-term partner, Greta, 'Doc give us Adnyamathanha mob long, long life. Get old, like Murti Johnny.'

Chief among the mourners, Greta did not speak. She participates in the present 'sorry business' that will continue for an indeterminate period to mark the passing of the Doc.

The Adnyamathanha have placed a great stone of bleached rock to mark Dr Burns' resting place. Carved into the rock is the image of an emu, its wings spread in full flight.

A plaque reads simply:

THE DOC'

Acknowledgements

As always, I thank my beloved family and my friends for their help, their patience and their candour. I am grateful to Professor Joseph John Mann of Columbia University, who advised me on the lasting effects of PCP upon human behaviour. And I owe warmest thanks to the identical twins, Hella and Stephanie, who survived Mengele's attentions in Auschwitz, and who have trusted me with their experiences.

Further Reading

Bird, Carmel (ed.). *The Stolen Children: Their stories: including extracts from the Report of the National Inquiry into the separation of Aboriginal and Torres Strait Islander Children from their families*, Random House, Milsons Point, 1998.

Norris, Ray & Cilla. *Emu Dreaming: An introduction to Australian Aboriginal astronomy*, Emu Dreaming, Sydney, 2009.

Posner, Gerald L. and John Ware. *Mengele: The complete story*, Futura Publications, London, 1987.

Segal, Nancy L. *Indivisible by Two: Lives of extraordinary twins,* Harvard University Press, Cambridge, Mass., 2005.

Segal, Nancy L. *Entwined Lives: Twins and what they tell us about human behavior,* Plume, NY, 2000.

The Holy Bible. Gideons International (undated).

Tournier Michel, translated by Arthur Goldhammer. *The Wind Spirit: An autobiography*, Beacon Press, 1988, Boston.

Tunbridge, Dorothy (in association with the Nepabunna Aboriginal School and the Adnyamathanha people of the Flinders Ranges, South Australia). *Flinders Ranges Dreaming*, Aboriginal Studies Press for the Australian Institute of Aboriginal Studies, Canberra, 1988.

About the Author

Howard Goldenberg is a writer, a reader and a doctor. He is the author of the highly successful memoir, *My Father's Compass* (Hybrid, 2007) and *Raft*, an intimate and candid account of his work as a doctor in dozens of remote indigenous communities, over many years (Hybrid, 2009). *A Threefold Cord*, a novel in 67 chapters for shared reading by a person aged eight to twelve and an adult, will be published in 2014.

Howard's published works also include opinion pieces in broadsheet newspapers and innumerable essays and stories in various print and online media. He writes a regular blog at www.howardgoldenberg.com. In addition, Howard is the creator and sole practitioner of a distinctive literary genre, the rhyming medical referral letter.

He claims co-authorship of three children and a causal connection with seven grandchildren.

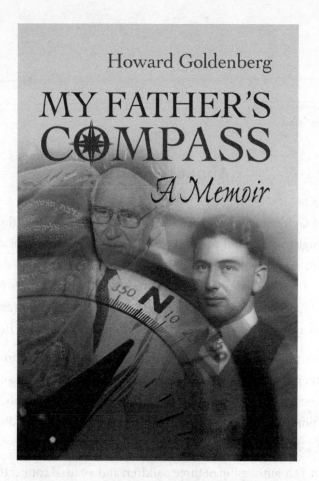

Howard Goldenberg

MY FATHER'S COMPASS

A Memoir

'Honest, funny, painful, shining with respect and love: a man's tribute to the severe beauty of his father's character.' – Helen Garner

Through the pages of this beautifully written book, Howard Goldenberg records and honours the deep faith, strength and vitality of his father, as well as giving the reader a glimpse into the soul of a tightly bonded family. From the naughty escapades of little boys to a tragic drowning, from the joys of sailing to the heartache of helping aging parents, Goldenberg's love, respect and intense loyalty shine through on every page.

HYBRID
PUBLISHERS

'A doctor in a yarmulka enters Aboriginal Australia ...
these are the clinical notes of a humble and compassionate man.'
Martin Flanagan

Howard Goldenberg

'Raft is a delicious, warm and endearing look at a side of Australian life known personally to very few of us.' – Alan Gold

Howard Goldenberg's second book, *Raft*, is a collection of unnerving true stories that reveal the author's experiences as a doctor in Aboriginal communities and inside an outback prison.

During a period of eighteen years, he made over fifty working visits as a relieving doctor for Aboriginal communities in outback Australia. On these visits he observed and recorded the lives of the people he met and treated.

**HYBRID
PUBLISHERS**

—